PRAISE FOR *When Universes Bleed*

"**A riveting fantasy** that does an especially good job of creating **powerful, engaging characters** that learn to interact not just with each other, but with the world… **a gripping atmosphere**…a fantasy that will be **a magnet for readers looking for action-packed scenes** and the interactive give-and-take between very different characters. **Highly recommended for young adults** looking for **well-crafted action and thought-provoking scenarios** of friendship and authority. It's a story that holds no simple or predictable plot, but goes the mile in creating **a satisfyingly complex dilemma** powered by characters who each walk out of the world and into their strengths."

— D. DONOVAN, SENIOR REVIEWER,
MIDWEST BOOK REVIEW

"**A fantastical romp** that utilizes Greek and Hindu mythology, this novel follows some young, misfit heroes as they attempt to save themselves—and presumably the planet—from an encroaching evil… The crew sets out to help Amaya on her quest, which turns out to be much more dangerous than any of the team members anticipated. **Featuring well-developed and endearing characters** as well as **brisk pacing and a satisfying amount of action and adventure**, the narrative by DJ Whipple and LA Whipple also contains a pleasing tone that blends myth and fantasy."

— KIRKUS REVIEWS

"**A rollicking magical realism adventure across time and space by a crew of teenagers charging towards adulthood** in a collision of cultures and philosophies, from contemporary Russians to traditional Japanese, to classical Greeks, to even more ancient Hindus. The central hero is Amaya Atlas who literally blasts into the story in a flash of lightning. As her Hero's Journey unfolds, she steadily gathers a team of skilled young allies, each equipped with exceptional abilities and knowledge, while their lethal enemies begin emerging around them. This first novel by father-and-daughter authors LA and DJ Whipple is **a joyful, suspenseful, intelligently challenging yarn**. It has **all the gripping plot zigs and zags of brilliant drama**…and feels like **the beginning of a bingeworthy series**."

— PETER SHANN FORD,
AUTHOR OF *GRAFFITI* AND *THE KEEPER OF DREAMS*

When Universes Bleed

DJ Whipple
and
LA Whipple

Piroska **Publishing**

For more information or to contact the authors, visit
https://www.facebook.com/theauthorswhipple/

Book cover design by ebooklaunch.com
Book interior design by Damonza
Proofreading by Ana Joldes

ISBN (paperback): 979-8-9863627-0-0
ISBN (ebook): 979-8-9863627-1-7

Printed in the United States of America

To the unsung creative endeavors of

unknown artists everywhere

AUTHORS' NOTE

Nothing in this novel is intended in any way to be an
accurate portrayal of any myth or religion.
Even quotes are inaccurate on purpose for effect.
The authors did not intend to offend, and hope that no one
is offended, by any liberties they have taken.

The asuras terrify us with their hideous shapes and foul disguises. In every place, around every grove, with evil thoughts these monsters rove. Fiends, they rejoice to slay and mar, grimmer than the blackest storm clouds of autumn they are.
— **The Ramayana, Book II, Canto CXVI**

Aided by thee, thunder-armed Indra, may we lift our weapons and conquer all our foes in war.
— **Rig Veda, Mandala I, Hymn VIII**

CHAPTER 1
REVERIE
AND RECOGNITION

(AMAYA)

Day 1 - Outside Redbird, Kentucky; Autumn 2033

HER UNREMARKABLE LIFE began remarkably enough—with a blazing bolt of lightning and a mighty clap of thunder.

She must have been *inside* the lightning. Because the blinding flash flashed and the deafening crack cracked all at a time. Then came a disorienting, tumbling, topsy-turviness. The next instant found her sitting dizzied in the middle of a perfect circle of downed corn with an electric sizzle and the smell of toasted husks hanging in the air. The aroma awakened a powerful hunger, like she hadn't eaten so much as a crumb since the beginning of time. She grabbed the nearest steaming ear and shucked it, her tiny hands struggling while bright yellow kernels burst from the cob. She took a bite. How sweet!

Farmer Bob Peetle and his wife Sam braked to a stop at the edge of the circle seconds later after sprinting down the rows together. They towered above her, lanky giants gazing down with warm, welcoming smiles that couldn't hide their concern and eyes as big and round as ladles, astonished to find a naked little brown-skinned girl in their field.

"Delicious!" She held up the ear of corn, waving it at them, oblivious that anything might be the matter.

Sam ran to her, kneeling to examine her. Bob tried to put her at ease (not that she wasn't), asking her name and how she came to be on their farm. She knew her name all right. Amaya Atlas. The only other thing she could remember was something about an orphanage she needed to find. The one they'd take her to later. The one she'd been raised in during the eleven years since and still lived in now.

Sam satisfied herself Amaya wasn't injured. Then she took Amaya by the hand, and they all marched single file through the high corn stalks to the old farmhouse. They passed big white wicker chairs that looked just the right size for giants, crossed a white covered porch as wide as a valley, and entered a bright, airy kitchen through the hall. Sam dressed Amaya in one of Sam's smallest tees, bunching the length into a bow at the bottom so Amaya wouldn't trip. She sat Amaya down at the dinner table, where Amaya plunged her spoon into the most delicious thing she'd ever eaten—still-warm, freshly-baked plum pie with a so-flaky crust and a scoop of vanilla ice cream on top. That day was one of the best of her life!

Amaya sighed a wistful sigh. She was all grown up now, lying in bed at the orphanage reminiscing. She couldn't chance going to sleep. Not that she'd be able if she wanted. She was too nervous and excited about leaving. She'd almost given up hope. Then she'd come across a clue after all these years that just might lead to the parents she never knew. She refused to believe they'd abandoned her. She was determined to find them and prove they hadn't. But was she ready to go out on her own to search for them, especially with Spike tagging along on what might end up being a dangerous mission?

Spike might be the most loyal and caring friend she could wish for. But he had two potentially problematic peculiarities regarding the assets one might need on a quest to find your best friend's long-lost parents. First, while he could be brave, he was physically frail. That could slow them down or put them in greater danger. On the other hand, Spike always did his best in his own enthusiastic way. The Jove sisters loved him for that, though they loved everyone. Even Mandy. Equanimity was the hallmark of the way they ran their orphanage. Amaya loved the Jove sisters for that.

Amaya loved Spike's enthusiasm too, though occasionally she lost her patience with him. Like the weekend before. They'd been watching the return landing of the first crewed mission to Mars.

Spike called it the first *wo*-manned mission; he was so proud of its historic all-female crew. He couldn't stop talking about President Patsis. How she'd commanded the dais at the Space Center in her smart Tiffany-blue pinpoint suit, holding hands and lifting arms with the returned astronauts. Amaya had gotten testy waiting for Spike to settle down enough to review the day's lessons. But she always regained her patience as quickly as she lost it. Spike's enthusiasm was disarming as well.

Amaya strained her eyes to check the wall clock again, probably for the seventh time in the past hour. Only a few minutes left. She'd always known it might come to this. She could scarcely believe they were about to run away.

Spike's second peculiarity, a trait the Jove sisters attributed to his "terrible, terrible childhood," was his refusal to grow up. It meant Amaya would need to be extra protective of him on the road. She didn't mind. Spike would eventually grow up on his own. Amaya didn't care how long that might take. He'd always be her best friend, no matter what. She'd known that the moment he first stepped through the front door nine years ago, tattered and malnourished, freshly rescued by the Jove sisters from an unspeakable foster-care horror he couldn't remember. *That* was an even bigger reason to love the Jove sisters.

Abandoning Spike to contend with Mandy on his own wasn't an option, no matter what issues he had. On the positive side, leaving the orphanage meant they'd finally be rid of her and her constant attacks. But Amaya would sorely miss the Jove sisters. And more than anything, the Peetles' Sunday visits. She pushed those thoughts aside. It would all be worth it—once she found her parents.

Amaya forced her eyes wider to watch the last seconds of the hour tick off to exactly two a.m. No sounds of stirring reached her ears, only Mandy's snoring, which was a fitting musical accompaniment to Amaya's departure. Amaya got out from under the covers, fully dressed, and tiptoed out the door to go wake Spike. He hadn't gone to sleep either. He was already standing outside the boys' dorm room, looking lost and a little frightened.

She put a finger to her lips and motioned for him to follow. They slipped down the stairs without making a peep. They crept along the dark hallway and sneaked out the back door, the cool night air sharp and sweet in Amaya's nostrils. Then they gathered the backpacks they'd hidden earlier in the woods and were on their way. Amaya wished she knew where to. Wherever it was, she would just have to trust they'd get there.

CHAPTER 2
AN IMMORTAL SUGGESTION

(GAIA)

Day 3

GAIA SCANNED THE woods on Earth, desperate to find
the right target. Amaya Atlas was approaching her first criti-
cal crossroads. She needed help, and Gaia's heart ached with
worry. Because the only help Gaia had to offer was small and
pitiful—a mere suggestion.

At least Gaia didn't need long to spot a near-perfect candi-
date—a bear about to cross the shallow creek not too far from
where the diversion would need to take place. Gaia made her
suggestion with little time to spare.

Turn north, she sent.

The animal plodded a few more steps west, then stopped
on the rocks of the creek bank. Gaia held her breath, waiting…

But the bear stayed put. It sat on its haunches and turned
its head back and forth, sniffing the air like it was carefully
weighing which direction carried the more inviting scent—
west, north, or south. Precious seconds ticked by, sending Gaia
into a panic.

How could she—mother of Titans, grandmother to Zeus—be forced to stand idly by, robbed of her powers with disaster about to strike?! All because of an indecisive bear?! She did the only thing left her. She screamed, willing the bear to move with a frightful shriek that was shriller than the wail of the worst storm Poseidon had ever summoned.

The scream ended. With echoes of that song of desperation still ringing in Gaia's ears, the bear dropped to all fours and headed upstream, her cubs right behind.

Gaia heaved a great sigh of relief.

CHAPTER 3

WHEN MINXIE MET YUNOSHO

(YUNOSHO)

TWIGS SNAPPED BENEATH Yunosho's feet, the crisp sound reverberating through the forest. Thrushes sang cheerful tunes high above his head. Sunlight winked down from the treetops. He'd been roaming for months, a happy wanderer rediscovering the outside world, the world he'd left behind to fulfill his father's dying wish. He'd completed that task, and now his future stretched shiny and new and full of promise before him.

He picked his way through brush and over dead, fallen trees. He stepped in and out of light and shadow, immersed in the pleasant, musty smell of rotting wood and decaying leaves as worms, bugs, and microbes turned them into soil. He breathed it in, his chest expanding with the always-present thankfulness: thankful for how things had changed so much for the better after his whole world had come crashing down six years ago and he arrived at Master Cee's doorstep, bewildered and terrified with nowhere else to go and no one else to turn to.

He'd been daydreaming in math class, gazing out the window at nothing in particular. He noticed a stranger pacing on the sidewalk outside the perimeter fence, casting anxious glances at the main entrance. The stranger wore a peaked cap, an eye patch, and a navy-blue pea coat. He limped along using a cane. Alarm bells clanged in Yunosho's head. His mother had taught him to stay alert for danger, its nature something she only vaguely understood. This could be his first encounter with it.

He sprang from his seat, registering the surprised look on the face of his math teacher as he spun toward the door. He tore down the empty halls, cut catty-corner across the gym to exit the back of the building, and sprinted home through the woods. He reached their cottage house in Tuckwater Springs. The door stood wide open. He was too late.

His mother lay over the threshold, shot through the heart—dead. Blood pooled beneath her, a look of innocent surprise frozen on her face.

He stared down at her pale body, his hands pulling at his hair, his head buffeted between disbelief and an irresistible urge to fall apart and sob. He couldn't. He'd promised. She'd drilled it into him—if anything were to happen to her, he had to take the blue packet under the floorboards in the closet and run as fast as he could to the dojo, to Mr. Oniki, his sensei and mentor for the past seven years.

Yunosho steeled himself. He swallowed his tears. He knelt beside his mother and pulled her eyes closed with his fingertips. His whole body shook with grief. Then he kissed her forehead and ripped himself away, terrified he'd never hear her tender voice or see her loving smile again.

He grabbed the packet and raced through town, looking straight ahead, taking no notice of his surroundings. His feet pounded the pavement; his head pounded with despair. He arrived breathless at the dojo. The training room was empty. He found Mr. Oniki in the back office and blurted out what had happened, stuttering, his mind groping for words to convey the horror of it.

But when Yunosho opened the packet, he was overcome with joy. It was a letter. From his father! He read it aloud.

My Dear Son,

If you're reading this, your mother is gone, and you're in tremendous pain. My heart aches with yours. But you must remain strong, as difficult as that may be. And you have to go—now! You're in danger.

There are coordinates on the overlay attached to the back of this letter. Go there. Mr. Oniki doesn't know where you're going. Don't tell him. When you arrive at your destination, wait—someone will find you.

You'll need nothing there, only to give up your will. Do everything you're told for as long as it takes.

I send forward in time the vast love I hold for you and your mother. It's there whenever you need it, in the tides of the universe.

Always honor the black tiger spirit in you. It will guide you well.

Your Loving Father,

Evgeny

PS: Watch out for that monkey.

"What monkey?" Yunosho asked, puzzled. He knew the black tiger story, but his mother had never mentioned a monkey.

Mr. Oniki apparently didn't know either. He shook his head, mumbled "No time, no time," and rushed Yunosho into the car, then drove to the train station like a madman, a state Yunosho had never witnessed him in before. He squealed to a stop at the drop-off point, causing a few pedestrians to jump with fright. Yunosho exited the vehicle. Mr. Oniki came around to the sidewalk and handed Yunosho a duffel he'd stuffed with clothes, snacks, and a sleeping bag.

Hurried people brushed past them. Yunosho clutched tightly to the duffel's strap as if it were a lifeline, not knowing what to say. Mr. Oniki cleared his throat. "I shall very much miss training the best student of a lifetime." He spoke in a monotone, his face blank. He bowed. But cracks had formed in his stoic demeanor when he came erect again—his eyes shone with sadness, and his lower lip trembled. "You must go," he said, his voice raspy and brusque, suddenly full of emotion.

Yunosho hesitated. Tears began pushing from the corners of his eyes. His nose was running. He wiped it on the back of his hand, sniffling. "Goodbye, sensei." He forced the words, returning the bow. Then he pulled himself away without risking another look at Mr. Oniki and merged into the moving crowd, passing into a new and alien world, one without his loving mother in it.

He changed clothes in the washroom to disguise himself. He purchased his ticket, avoiding camera recognition the way Mr. Oniki had shown him. Then he settled into his seat on the train, his thoughts jumping wildly. Why hadn't Mr. Oniki seemed surprised? Had he just been acting calm for Yunosho's benefit? His father had mentioned Mr. Oniki by name. How had they known one another? One thought kept up a loud, insistent pinging above the din in his brain—his mother *couldn't* be gone. It can't have happened. It was a nightmare. He just needed to wake up.

The train arrived at his stop. He disembarked to switch to the Knob Mountain Metro line and looked up at the vidwall. The newsfeed read: "Double-Murder Tragedy Strikes Small Town." He didn't understand at first. The vid showed their little cottage. Yunosho's chest shuddered from the unbearable memory of having left his dead mother there. Then the vid cut to Mr. Oniki's dojo. Yunosho froze. Yellow police tape crisscrossed the storefront's shattered glass. The caption said: "Local Karate Instructor Tortured / Slain."

Yunosho's eyes widened with terror. His duffel dropped to the floor with a thud. He'd lost everyone. He was on his own now, an eleven-year-old orphan. He'd never felt more frightened.

The peaked-capped man had murdered his mother and tortured Mr. Oniki, presumably trying to find where Yunosho had gone. Why? Had he wanted to murder Yunosho, too? Yunosho's father would know, but he was dead, killed in a fight with four Russian soldiers on Cape Soya the day after Yunosho's birth. The same day Yunosho and his mother sailed for America on a Chinese freighter out of Tokyo with new identities in hand, the ones his father had arranged before his death.

Yunosho pushed the painful memories aside. They struck too deeply. It felt like that peaked-capped stranger had put a hole through his heart too. One day he'd find him if he could ever figure out where to start looking.

Light glinted through the tangle of vines and brush up ahead. The welcome sound of rippling water reached Yunosho's ears. He arrived at the creekbank and scrambled down, struggling through the thorny thicket into the open water—and ran right into a bear! A big black one, about fifty feet downstream.

She snapped to attention, popping her jaws and huffing while two skittish cubs paced behind her, squealing with distress.

Yunosho stopped moving and let his shoulders sag the way Master Cee had taught. The momma bear stomped and snorted for another minute, then settled down and turned her attention back to the cubs, who calmed as well. Yunosho kept a wary eye on them while he dipped his bottle in the stream. He took a long drink, the water bright and pleasant on his parched throat. Then he refilled the bottle and waded the rest of the way across, tramping uphill through the dry meadow grass on the other side. He didn't mind the detour. It wasn't like he needed to be home in time for supper.

As he neared the top of the hill, he heard an odd buzzing drift down from it. He paused, cocking his head to listen, then picked up his pace, curious to see what lay up ahead.

He rounded the ridge.

And stopped dead in his tracks.

Across the field, a Hindu princess was repelling a thrumming swarm of giant flying insects! At least she looked like some kind of princess—white tunic blouse, wavy dark hair, light-brown skin.

How was she doing it?

He moved closer. Dragonflies! Mechanized ones and big— about six inches across, smooth-bodied, and battleship gray. Their wings beat a loud tremolo while the high-pitched whine of their motors pierced through the din of clacking metal.

But it only appeared the girl was repelling them from the magical way she danced through and around them, ducking and whirling with otherworldly gracefulness, her arms weaving and waving in a blur. And she had her eyes closed!

Move! his brain commanded. He'd wasted enough time being fascinated.

He dropped his backpack. He went down on one knee, slid his sword out, and unwrapped it. He almost hadn't brought it. He would've sworn until this moment he'd been carrying it for no good reason.

He grabbed the hilt, pulling the sword from its scabbard, and pushed off his knee, already running. By the third bound of his legs, he could see the clacking's source—powerful jaws snapping shut over and over, gleaming with nested layers of serrated metal teeth that looked as diabolical as teeth could get.

He bridged the distance before he could even think what those teeth might do to the girl. He dove into the swarm. His sword sliced high, then low, then up again, flashing in the sunlight, meeting the machines' precision with his own. He became the storm, and she, the eye of it, standing unbothered while all around her dragonflies popped apart with loud staccato bursts of steam.

Even with his Zen focus trained on the menace, his peripheral vision pieced together a portrait of the girl. A regal face, strongly framed, sensuously drawn. Almond-shaped eyes the color of emeralds. A black dot in the middle of her forehead.

He destroyed them all before he knew it, but for two that stayed high up out of range. One sped away. The other hovered, watching. A quick stroke of his sword sent a pebble rocketing up from the ground. The last dragonfly dropped from the air, dead.

CHAPTER 4

SPIKE'S LEAP

(SPIKE)

SPIKE HAD WAITED long enough.

He *never* should have let Minxie go off on her own. He left camp and crossed the woods, heading in the direction she'd taken. The woods emptied into a meadow. Spike froze at its edge, gasping with horror. A tall sword-wielding kid leaned over Minxie at the other end, peering down at her lifeless body lying crumpled in the grass.

Spike's hands flew to his temples, squeezing his forehead. His face contorted with grief. His best friend, his only friend— gone?! It couldn't be!

He wouldn't let this vile misdeed go unpunished. He gathered his courage. He wiped his sleeve across his face. He gritted his teeth and brought his hands down into fists, a huge scream of anger pressing against his skull. Then he took a deep breath and exploded into a run, launching himself into the air.

"NOOO!" he cried, screeching so loud he surprised himself with it. He landed on the swordsman's back, wrapped one arm around his neck, and started beating him on the head with the other.

The kid was strong. He dropped his sword, bent over, and reached behind to take Spike by the waist. He pulled Spike over his head. Now Spike was upside down, facing the swordsman at arm's length, throwing punches that weren't connecting and kicking at nothing but air.

"What the?" the swordsman spluttered. "Why are you attacking *me*?"

"You murdered my best friend, you rat-master!" Spike struggled to free himself, his lungs wheezing. He might be small and spindly, but that wouldn't stop him from avenging poor Minxie.

"First, I'm not a rat-master, whatever that is." The swordsman seemed totally unruffled, which frustrated Spike even more. He quit trying to mangle the swordsman's pleasant-looking nose and banged on his forearms instead, the only things within reach. "Second, I didn't murder anyone. Unless you count these dragonflies you might want to notice lying around." The swordsman gestured toward the ground with his eyes. "They were trying to tear this girl to pieces. Who's not dead, by the way. I think she just got overwhelmed."

Spike glanced at Minxie. Even from upside down, he could see her chest rising and falling. A swell of relief washed over him. He relaxed. The swordsman let go, and Spike, unprepared for it, dropped on his head and bleated. He rolled over, looked up, and glared.

"Sorry." The swordsman shrugged. "I thought you'd catch yourself." He pointed at an oak across the field with a black backpack lying at its base. "We need to get her in the shade. I've got fresh cold water in that pack too."

Spike jumped up, eager. The swordsman lifted Minxie by

the shoulders. Spike took her ankles. They carried her to the tree, settled her into the thick meadow grass, and sat down beside her. The swordsman grabbed a black bandanna from his pack, moistened it with water, and dabbed Minxie's forehead.

"What happened?" Spike asked. Minxie had warned they might encounter danger, but he could never have imagined robot dragonflies.

"I came up the hill over there"—the swordsman pointed toward the ridge with his commanding chin—"and saw this girl surrounded by a bunch of bugs trying to make lunch out of her. So I ran over and started swatting. I turned around when I finished, and she was lying there. Out cold."

"Stop calling her 'the girl.'" Spike punctuated his complaint with an angry snort. "Her name's Minxie. She's my best friend."

"I can tell." The swordsman nodded. "It was pretty brave of you to attack me, seeing how I was brandishing a deadly sword and all."

Spike's chest puffed. It was the first time anyone other than Minxie had called him brave. "Aw, that's nothing." He threw the swordsman a dismissive wave. "I'd go up against *three* of you if I had to." He meant it. He'd give his life to defend Minxie. "What are you doing out here with a sword of all things? You worried about running into evil Samurais or something?"

The swordsman chuckled. "No, but that sounds like fun." Spike didn't think it sounded fun at all. "It's kind of a long story." The swordsman dabbed Minxie's forehead again and stuffed the bandanna and water bottle into a pouch of his pack. "Let's just say I've been hiding out, so I brought the sword along for protection. What about you two?"

Minxie's eyes fluttered.

"Look!" Spike leaned over her, excited. "She's coming to!"

CHAPTER 5
THE BAND OF MURUGAN

(AMAYA)

AMAYA'S BRAIN WAS awash with confusion.

Was she reliving her last encounter with Mandy at the orphanage? How? Was this déjà vu? It seemed real.

There was Spike in the rec room, realizing he'd forgotten his study guide down in the cafeteria. There was Amaya, bounding down the stairs to retrieve it. She reached the third step from the bottom and her senses tingled with danger. Her enemy was afoot. Her consciousness reacted and took control. Her mind entangled with her surroundings. That familiar warm fuzziness, the thing she called all-rightness, engulfed her. She closed her eyes. She wouldn't need them.

She turned the corner and ducked. The book bag sailed over her head and smacked into the wall, heavy textbooks spilling from it. Amaya pivoted left. Mandy's fist slammed empty space, the puff of wind made by her punch tickling the tip of Amaya's nose.

Amaya pedaled backward to the opposite wall of the hallway before Mandy could swing again, waiting for Mandy's next move. Out of the blue, a frightening presence pricked the edge of Amaya's consciousness, rattling her with a head-to-toe shiver. A terrible, dark menace, faint, hard to discern, lurked far back in the background noise of the universe. A second, even stronger, shiver hit Amaya, sending surprise and exhilaration coursing through her veins—the Menace had recognized her! If it recognized her, it *might* have something to do with her parents.

She struggled to identify it, but it was gone before she could gather more than a vague location. She disengaged from her connection, frustrated. Then she opened her eyes and threw Mandy a wary glance, though she knew Mandy had already abandoned her attack. Mandy was like Tom to Amaya's Jerry, accustomed to losing these games of cat and mouse but never ceasing to try.

Mandy screwed her face up in a sneer. "I'll nail you one of these days, brownie." She was leaning against the other wall, her thick, strong arms folded across her chest and one canvas-shoed foot crossed casually over the other. She wore her hair in the same blonde pigtails she'd worn since Amaya had first met her. "I still don't get how you do it, witch."

"Super-hearing," Amaya fibbed. "I can hear hate squeezing your heart from miles away."

"Bitch!" Mandy's eyes flashed hatred, and Amaya immediately regretted making the insinuation. Neither of them would ever forget the episode with Mandy's heart. It had changed Mandy forever, and not in a way that made Amaya proud. "Just wait," Mandy spat, "next time, instead of hearing my hate, you'll be paralyzed with terror as it steals your life from you."

Amaya would never forget that threat. Mandy had meant it. That dragonfly formation seemed like the very kind of sneak attack Mandy would devise, though Mandy couldn't have been involved.

Wait! Dragonfly attack?! Of course! Amaya's memory rushed back to her. Mandy's figure began to swim, her face fading. Muffled murmurings and a familiar voice—Spike!—replaced Mandy's. The entire scene with Mandy at the orphanage receded with a whoosh and was gone. Amaya blinked open her eyes.

Spike's boyish face hovered above hers, out-of-focus, his brown curls dangling over his forehead. The sky above him seemed exceedingly bright. Then her vision cleared, and she glowered. A stranger!

"Who are *you*?" She sat up too fast, making herself dizzy. At least she knew where she was now. She'd been lying flat on her back in a field.

"Whoa." The stranger waved his open palms at her. "You need to take it easy."

Amaya scowled. She didn't like people telling her what she needed to do, especially strangers. Then she remembered him— the boy in the black cargo pants and the untucked jersey who'd come up the hill. His sharp eyes, sculpted nose, and determined mouth lent him a noble air. But the choppy, black hair made him look like a dark, brooding pop star more than anything. She wondered suspiciously what he was doing out here in the middle of nowhere with a sword.

She scooted back to give herself space and glanced around to get her bearings. They were sitting beneath an oak tree, about sixty feet from where the dragonflies had attacked. Amaya's forehead felt cool and moist. She noticed a wet bandanna and a green water bottle sticking from the pocket of a backpack.

"You blacked out. We don't want that happening again," the stranger continued. "As for me, I'm that guy who wanders forests all day looking to rescue girls from savage mechanical insect attacks, which, you know"—he rolled his eyes—"happens *all* the time."

"I was doing fine on my own," Amaya snapped. "For just being a girl.

The swordsman leaned back, exaggeratedly startled. "That's the second time today someone lectured me about calling you a girl." He gave Spike a knowing wink, which only peeved Amaya more.

Why this friendly winking? Had he become Spike's best friend in the space of what? Ten minutes at most? And why was Spike here? He must've gone looking for her despite her having *commanded* him to stay put no matter what.

"Are you sure you didn't get bit, Minxie?" Spike shot her his you-should-know-better look. "You're kind of acting like it."

Spike was right—she needed to calm herself. She took a deep breath and straightened up into lotus. "I'm sorry," she said, embarrassed by her lapse. "I should be grateful to this young gentleman." She pressed her palms together, doing her best to appear contrite despite how difficult that was for her. "I give you my deepest thanks, sir."

"No 'sir.'" Yunosho stood and bowed, sweeping his arm in front of him as if he were a Musketeer holding a big feathered hat. "Just plain Yunosho, milady."

"Minxie's my nickname," said Amaya. "My real name is Amaya. Amaya Atlas."

"And I'm Spike, Mr. Just-Plain-Yunosho." Spike pushed up from the ground and offered his hand. "Nice to meet you."

"Same here." Poor Spike winced when they shook. Yunosho's grip looked vice-like, which didn't surprise her given the chiseled muscles rippling beneath his shirt when he moved.

"Now we're properly introduced"—Yunosho sat back down without using his hands—"maybe *someone* can tell me what those dragonflies were all about?" Spike tried to imitate him but landed with a hard plop instead.

"I'm unsure," Amaya replied. "I happened upon some information about a dark disturbance in the area, so we came out to investigate." She kept the real reason to herself. Not even Spike knew her true quest was to find her parents so she could prove they hadn't abandoned her.

"From where?" Yunosho continued.

"We ran away," Spike interrupted.

"From what?"

"From the orphanage," Amaya replied.

"And she has these powers," Spike interjected again.

"What powers?"

"I do not have powers." Spike was giving up the very information she wished he wouldn't—and to a stranger!

Spike leaned forward and whispered. "Like super-sense or something."

"Spike, *please* do not exaggerate." Amaya shook her head. "I'm no superhero."

Yunosho raised a doubtful brow. "You used *something* to avoid those dragonflies, and it certainly wasn't your eyesight."

Her ability to evade the dragonflies with her eyes closed had not gone unnoticed. She'd need to provide an explanation. Explaining to Spike had been difficult enough. How would this odd swordsman react?

"Sometimes my surroundings meld with my consciousness, especially when I'm faced with danger," Amaya said. "It's how I sensed what the dragonflies were doing. It's also how I ended up in this field to begin with. My connection picked up danger here."

"I guess you found your dark disturbance all right," Yunosho said. The swordsman seemed to take her story in stride, making him even more unusual. "Those dragonflies were evil *and* annoying." He smirked and dragged the loose hair back from his forehead with his index finger. "*If* you catch my drift."

Amaya didn't understand. The dragonflies had been far more than annoying. She glanced at Spike for help.

"He means annoying—as in *disturbing*," Spike said.

Amaya shook her head, even more puzzled.

"As in dark disturbance. Get it? Evil annoyance? It's a pun."

"Not a very good one," she said with reproach. She didn't care much for puns—especially bad ones. She turned a disapproving eye on Yunosho. He pushed out his lower lip and shrugged, an act Amaya might otherwise have found comical if she weren't so irked by him at the moment. "The dragonflies were the danger," she continued matter-of-factly. "The disturbance is bigger—and fuzzier. I can't identify it."

"Let me see if I have this straight." Yunosho leaned in, his head cocked toward her. "First, *you* two are runaway orphans. Second, *Minxie* here"—he pointed his index finger at her—"has some kind of enhanced enlightenment ability—"

"Ha!" Spike interrupted again. "Enhanced Enlightenment would be like E-squared or mass-squared times the speed of light to the 4th power, which would be super-fast!"

"—that occasionally lets her operate in a state of oneness with her surroundings." Spike's interruptions hadn't bothered Yunosho at all. At least there was one good sign about his character, though it did nothing to quell Amaya's suspicions. "And this ability revealed some vague threat you decided you had to look into?"

"Correct." Amaya nodded.

"Well, whoever sent *them*"—Yunosho pointed his thumb sideways at the dragonfly pieces—"must've known about your ability. They seem specifically designed to overcome it."

Yunosho was right. The Menace had known somehow. "Then I need to find that dark disturbance." She was more certain than ever the Menace had recognized her, or at least something about her. "It's the most likely source."

"One thing's sure." Yunosho scratched his head. "If I'd heard your story *before* I saw the dragonflies, I'd be convinced the two of you were in desperate need of a shrink."

Amaya sniffed the air with scorn. "I fail to see how reducing our size could help anything."

Spike chuckled. "Don't mind Minxie." He shook his head, his eyes lit with fondness. "Sometimes she takes things, you know, literally? But you'll get used to how she talks."

Amaya's cheeks burned. "Shrink" was another idiom she'd failed to recognize. Why did she have such difficulty with them? Sometimes she believed English couldn't possibly have been her first language, even if she spoke it perfectly well.

"Speaking of which," Yunosho said to Amaya, "what's that accent, like that bit of *v* mixed in with the *w* when you say *what*?"

She folded her arms across her chest, her mouth turned down. Did this swordsman like even one thing about her? "I've always spoken this way."

"And guess what?" Spike added. "No one knows where she came from either."

"Well, if that doesn't add more weirdness to the already weird." Yunosho got up from the ground the same way he'd sat and looked from Spike to Amaya and back again, like he was in the process of making a momentous decision. Amaya had a sneaking suspicion what decision and wasn't sure how she felt about it.

"Listen," he finally said. "There's no place I need to be. And your investigation into this amorphous evil menace thing sounds kind of intriguing. So… I was thinking…" He trailed off, looking suddenly unsure of himself. "Maybe… um… we could…" He lifted his shoulders in a small, helpless shrug and squeaked, "Band together?"

Spike clapped. "That's a *great* idea! A band of soldiers fighting back the tides of darkness. We can call it the *Band of Murugan*!"

Yunosho appeared relieved by the interruption this time. Why had he been so nervous, to begin with? Then it dawned on her—she *might* intimidate him. She could only hope. She didn't want him getting any ideas despite his attractive physique.

Yunosho glanced at Amaya. "Who, or what is a Murugan?"

"Hindu god of war? Supreme commander of the armies of the gods?" Amaya answered the obvious.

Spike raised his finger in the air. "*And* he rides a peacock."

"How do you two know so much about this Murugan guy?"

"We receive an excellent education in mythology at the orphanage," Amaya replied. She stood and brushed debris from the back of her pants. Spike stood too.

"Chalk up yet another strange thing about you two." Yunosho grabbed his pack and swung the strap over his shoulder. "A peacock, huh? Seems out of place for a god of war. Wouldn't a dragon be more fitting?"

Amaya shook her head with disdain. This swordsman didn't understand the first thing about Hindu gods.

"I like peacocks." Spike was bouncing on his heels, either indicating how highly he regarded peacocks or, far more likely, excited about being part of a band, even if he'd only just invented it. "Let's make the peacock our band's symbol!"

Spike might be eager for Yunosho to join them. Amaya had to weigh the consequences. Letting a stranger join their quest seemed risky. She didn't want to admit it, but she also feared he could end up being an unwelcome distraction.

On the other hand, she could protect Spike from a mean-spirited bully like Mandy, but how would she protect him from something like evil dragonflies? Or worse? Her concern for Spike made the choice obvious—a capable swordsman would be a huge help. At least he hadn't exhibited any outward signs of mental illness—except for his poor taste in puns, that is.

"While joining forces to oppose evil *might* be a good idea"—she gave Spike a sharp nod to signal she was only agreeing to this whole Yunosho thing for him—"*I* wish to avoid violence. I would rather put things together than tear them apart."

"I see." Yunosho squinted at her. Then he pretended to unroll a scroll and announced in a British accent so ridiculously poor that Amaya cringed hearing it. "We hereby grant the entire realm of Putting-Things-Together to the peculiar pacifist with the odd manner of speech." Returning to his normal voice, he added, "The tearing up, beating up, et cetera stuff you can leave to Spike and me. Right, Spike?"

Yunosho winked at Spike, and Spike beamed with pride. Amaya liked the wink this time. Maybe this swordsman wouldn't be such a bad traveling companion after all.

CHAPTER 6
NOT VERY JOVIAL

(ELMO)

ELMO GRINDQUIST FELT the full brunt of the Meshterek's displeasure over his dragonfly debacle. But Elmo wasn't to blame.

He'd devised the perfect weapon: nimble, deadly, and far too numerous for the Atlas girl to handle. The vid from the dragonfly that returned to his abandoned wine-cave headquarters showed a sword-wielding Japanese boy coming to the Atlas girl's aid, ruining everything. But the surprising extent of the girl's ability to repel the attack on her own bothered Elmo even more.

The Meshterek wanted to know—*what went wrong?* Elmo sensed hunger burning behind their impatience, a gluttonous need.

The boy was unexpected, Elmo transmitted.

He reclined in his creaky chair, immersed in the fugue state he entered to communicate with them. He could feel the mildly unpleasant bursting of capillaries beneath his skin. His eyeballs pushed against his eyelids like they wanted to escape, and his arms, bent at the elbow, levitated at his sides instead of resting on the armrests of the chair.

There'd been no indication the girl had any help, he told them. Something more than the dragonfly failure was agitating them.

His arrival can't have been a mere coincidence, they sent.

Now Elmo understood. They were worried! They believed they'd obliterated their enemies out of existence. Then the Atlas girl showed up on their radar. And now this—a talented boy appearing out of nowhere.

We want her alive now, they sent.

They ordered Elmo to recruit a girl at the orphanage to help with the capture—Amanda Duggan. She'd have useful information, having grown up despising Amaya Atlas. Elmo wasn't sure how they knew this, but of all the things the Meshterek could do, one was long-distance observation.

And the Japanese boy?

Neutralize him. One way or the other.

The Meshterek showed Elmo the orphanage. A pebbled driveway led to a Victorian mansion with lavender wood siding. Next to its portico entrance and porch, a round turret with a conical roof climbed above the rest of the building.

He saw gray-haired twin sisters wearing pastel-colored shirt-dresses and disgustingly genuine smiles ushering children into classrooms. A large print of an elephant-headed four-armed man dressed in brightly colored silks took up the wall of one room. A white-robed woman with a quiver on her back raised her bow beside a giant wild boar on the wall of the other. Elmo recognized them, though he didn't know how—so much of his memory had gone missing: the Hindu Lord Ganesh and the Greek goddess Artemis. A sturdy, blonde, pigtailed girl sat at one of the desks, her lips pressed tightly into a frown. *That* was Amanda Duggan.

The Meshterek showed Elmo the dormitory on the second floor of the mansion where Amanda slept with the other girls and the wide wooden staircase covered with floral carpet runners leading up to it. The transmission stopped after a few more tidbits of information. Elmo opened his eyes. He grabbed a tissue and dabbed the drops of dark gelatinous blood leaking from his nostrils. His skin, which had become angry and blotchy as if thousands of tiny mouths were sucking on it, began returning to its normally ashen color.

Elmo had already decided on a plan of action. Talking Amanda Duggan into a vehicle was out of the question. There'd be no time to wait for that kind of opportunity. He'd need to snatch her. He wasn't disappointed about needing to do it at all. It wasn't often an assassin got to snatch someone.

He dressed all in black and put on a black baseball cap. He outfitted himself with a black-handled knife sheathed to his belt, a can of ether, and two syringes of fast-acting anesthetic. He clipped to his shirt pocket what looked like a pen but was actually a miniature laser metal-cutting tool built using Meshter-Tek—advanced technology the Meshterek had put at his disposal. Then he donned his skin-tight black leather gloves and left his underground base of operations, headed straight for the orphanage in Redbird, a faint echo of excitement bouncing off the walls of his deadened heart.

CHAPTER 7

ON THE ROAD AGAIN

(AMAYA)

AMAYA AGREED—AN EXAMINATION of the dragonflies was in order. They visited the scene of the attack one last time to gather pieces to bring with them. The area looked like a dragonfly parts junkyard, though Yunosho's sword work had been precise—he'd scattered the dragonfly debris in a near-perfect circle.

"Look"—she pointed at the ground next to Spike—"a head without a body. It's still moving!" The bullet-shaped head lay in the trampled grass, its crystal eyes glinting and its jaws still opening and closing in slow motion. The teeth reminded her of that terrible clacking, and she realized her head needed clearing. Confusion had settled over it like fog the moment she'd come face-to-face with these dragonfly remains.

"And look." Spike pointed a few feet in front of Amaya. "There's a body without a head, and *it's* still smoking!" Wisps of steam curled from the dragonfly's gray body. Water droplets sputtered from the hole where the head used to be.

"Be careful, Spike," warned Yunosho. "Don't touch anything that's still active."

"Maybe we can put one back together," Spike said.

Yunosho held half a wing in his hand, examining it. "Maybe. But I'm no engineer. One thing's sure: They're well made. Take these wings. Metal, the same as the bodies, but super-thin and veined like real ones. Whoever built these has access to pretty cool tech. We'll find out more once we deliver these parts to my engineer friend for a look-see."

The reason for Amaya's bewilderment became apparent as she tiptoed around the debris. She remembered the swarm of dragonflies rushing toward her in formation while she stood there, wide-eyed, arms hanging at her sides, paralyzed for a moment by the mere sight of them and the increasing racket they made as they approached. Her thinking mind dissipated the very next moment, like it had turned to dust and been blown away. She became one with everything, the oneness blanketing her in serenity, swaddling her in complete well-being—a feeling that everything was all right, no matter what. Even no matter the dragonflies.

Now she felt distraught and uncertain. Someone had gone to great lengths to harm her. Who would want to hurt her so badly? And *why*? And how was *any* of it connected to her parents?

Spike crouched down, making sure the pieces he wanted to pick up weren't moving. "Wish I'd seen these things in operation."

"They were as fast as real dragonflies and maybe nimbler," Yunosho said.

Spike looked up at Amaya, shaking his head in wonder. "I'm amazed you never got bit."

"That was my E^2 power, as you call it." Amaya decided she could call her ability a power for now. Like Yunosho said, it was *something*. And it had been improving, even surprising herself with how she avoided losing even a single piece of flesh to this horde of winged carnivores.

Spike handed a few more pieces to Yunosho, who stuffed them into a pocket of his backpack. "We should get moving." He stood and lifted his pack, slipping his arms into the straps. "It's a bit of a hike."

"To where?" Amaya wondered whether Yunosho's engineer friend would be capable enough. The dragonflies involved advanced technology. Yunosho didn't seem like someone who spent a lot of time socializing with scientists.

"Outside Westwardlee." Yunosho pointed in the direction. "One of the burbs along the Knob transit line. We should get there by tomorrow afternoon. We'll stay off the roads as much as possible and skirt any towns. We don't want to risk being spotted by any crazy dragonfly dispatchers."

Dispatchers. The term was apt. They'd tried to dispatch her from her life. She wondered what they'd try next time, certain there'd be one.

Yunosho followed Spike and Amaya to their camp. They packed up their belongings, leaving the site as undisturbed as possible. Then they trod southwest through fields of tall grasses and woods carpeted with twigs, branches, and leaves. Yunosho took the lead, steering them clear of houses and well back from barking dogs. Amaya kept pace, relieved not to have to make decisions for the time being. Spike lagged, not only because he was slower. He also couldn't resist inspecting the interesting plants and bugs he happened upon along the way.

They passed through a field along the edge of the forest, the late afternoon sun warm on Amaya's face. Clouds of gnats hung silent in the dry, sun-cleaned air, redolent with the smell of wild herbs and sweet mint. "I have to ask," Amaya said to Yunosho. She'd been thinking about it ever since she'd seen him racing toward her, his body determined, his legs pumping, his sword raised to strike. "How did you end up in that field?"

"It's funny." Yunosho rubbed his smooth, angular chin "Now that you mention it. I wouldn't have but for the bear."

"Which bear?"

"I went to fill my water bottle at the creek down the hill from where I saw you and ran into a mamma bear traveling with her cubs. I crossed to go around them, and that put me right in the middle of your little dragonfly dance." Her suspicion was confirmed. This time instead of sending the cat to jump in front of the car or the message to move the dresser that would have cracked her temple when Mandy pushed her, whoever always seemed to be helping her had sent a life-changing bear.

"I see. Luck was with me again. I *am* grateful you came to my aid."

Yunosho's forehead creased, and Amaya winced inside. Was something about her bothering him? She wanted people to like her. Most of the kids at the orphanage found her too serious. Amaya didn't want to be serious—she *had* to be. She'd needed to focus if she wanted to discover why she had these abilities, what, if anything, they had to do with her parents, and why her parents had dropped her into a cornfield for no apparent reason. In her childish, needy heart, which she'd never revealed to anyone—not even Spike—she was sure her parents could never have simply abandoned her. The encounter with the dark disturbance and the dragonfly attack meant she might be closing in on answers, but they also made her question the price she'd be willing to pay for them—she worried she was already putting Spike in terrible danger.

Yunosho looked at her askance. "I guess I like it."

An involuntary smile of relief crossed her lips. At least he liked something. "That I'm thanking you?"

"No." Yunosho laughed. "The singsongy thing in your voice."

"I'm glad you like it, but I can't explain it. I can only recall to the age of five. I believe I experienced a trauma that blocked memories earlier than that."

Yunosho shook his head. "I doubt it. Most people can't remember that far back. I mean, I don't remember much about my early childhood."

"My memories are quite vivid, especially my first memory—a kind farmer couple found me in their field."

"That qualifies as strange." Yunosho nodded. "I get the distinct impression strange might be the new normal with you. How'd you get there?"

"I don't know, and the Jove sisters could find no further information about me."

"The Jove sisters?"

"The twins who run the orphanage."

"Hey, guys!" Spike came running up from behind. "How much longer?" He was out of breath when he reached them. "I'm getting tired. And bored. And hungry. Aren't there some franks and beans in that backpack?"

"They had franks and beans at the school cafeteria, but I never tried them," Yunosho said. "Mom always packed a Bento box for me."

"You mean you never ate *franks and beans*?" Spike threw up his hands in exasperation. "They're these baked beans. They're sweet, with these pieces of hot dog in them. Those are the franks part. *You* know. Frankfurters?"

The sun was hanging low, the autumn light exaggeratedly

sharp and clear. Insects scraped and chirped in the early evening's calm. "I suppose we should set up camp before it gets too dark and warm something to eat," Amaya said.

"Sounds good to me, Minxie." Spike paused. His arms hung at his sides, and he'd tilted his head in a big grin. "As long as it's franks and beans!"

He laughed as he said it, and wonder caressed Amaya like a soft, warm breeze on a cool June evening, sending goosebumps up and down her arms. Spike's grin, the amusement in Yunosho's eyes, the magic of the autumn twilight—they all told her, even without her connection, that everything was all right in the world.

CHAPTER 8

SWEET AND SOUR CAMPFIRE

(YUNOSHO)

YUNOSHO HAD BEEN FORCED to leave his childhood friends behind when he'd escaped to Master Cee's mountain abode. But he'd made one new friend since coming down off the mountain, and he hoped—no, he believed—he was making two more today.

He found a suitable clearing for camp and began gathering wood to get the fire going while Amaya and Spike struggled to set up the pop-up tents. They made a well-balanced pair of friends. Spike's eagerness and enthusiasm contrasted happily with Amaya's serious, reserved nature.

They heated cans of baked beans and sauerkraut, opening them so they wouldn't explode. They ate in silence, warmed by the crackling fire, wood smoke billowing around them. Yunosho finished his plate, set it down beside him, and leaned back against a fallen log. "We'd call that sweet and sour." The beans and sauerkraut had run together on the plates.

Spike licked his plate. "Whatever *you* call it, *I* call it delicious." He licked his lips and wiped his mouth with his sleeve.

A wry smile crept over Yunosho's face watching him, then Yunosho turned his gaze to Amaya. She'd set her plate and spork down. She stared into the fire, lost in thought. The flames sparkled in her eyes, but firelight couldn't dim the intensity of their greenness. Fortunate destiny had put those bears in his path, launching him on an odyssey with this strange girl and her even stranger story. The second he'd spied her in the middle of that swarm of dragonflies, he'd felt the strongest prickling of curiosity.

He wanted to know everything about her, and he'd been wondering about that nickname all day. Amaya was a minx the same way he was a serial killer. He hoped it wasn't a touchy subject because he'd already decided to ask.

"So… Amaya." Yunosho gave her a wary glance, concerned she might chew off his head for asking. "Minxie's an unusual nickname. How'd you get it?"

"Ooh, let me tell that story." Spike rubbed his hands together, his eyes gleaming with excitement. "It's one of my favorites."

"Every story Spike tells is his favorite." There was amusement in Amaya's voice and a fond smile on her face as she gazed at Spike. "But he does tell them well."

"Then let's hear it." Yunosho put his hands behind his head and stretched out his legs. "What else are campfires for?"

CHAPTER 9

HOW MINXIE GOT HER NAME

(SPIKE)

EIGHT-YEAR-OLD MANDY TUGGED hard on one end of the blue-winged plastic pony. Amaya sat on the floor of the rec room, holding tightly onto the other. Spike already knew how this disagreement would end—the same as any disagreement with Mandy: badly.

"It's not *yours*," Mandy screamed.

Mandy pulled hard on the pony. Amaya's fingers slipped. Mandy stumbled backward.

BAM!

The back of her head cracked against the bare wooden floor. Spike would've cried after a knock to the head like that, but Mandy didn't. No one had ever seen Mandy Duggan cry. She sat up and smiled in triumph, rubbing her head with one hand and clutching the pony to her chest with the other. The kids all stopped playing to watch.

"You are correct, Mandy." Amaya remained sitting. "It belongs to everyone."

Mandy seethed. Spike imagined steam shooting from the top of her red-faced head like in the cartoons. It didn't matter *what* Amaya said. She could've told Mandy how beautiful her blonde hair looked today, and it only would've made Mandy madder.

"You… you… *minx!*" Mandy shouted. She leaped up and stomped around Amaya in a circle, one foot after the other, like an angry rain dance. She pumped the pony up and down, chanting, "*You minx! You minx!*" over and over. Spike didn't know what that word meant. He was pretty sure Mandy didn't either.

Everyone giggled, nervous because Mandy had worked herself into such a frenzy. Amaya ignored her. She closed her eyes, crossed her legs, and folded her hands in her lap, calm and relaxed. Mandy stopped behind Amaya and held the pony like a knife, cocking her arm above Amaya's head.

Spike *flew* at Mandy. He knocked her to the ground with all the force his small body could muster. The other kids hooted and hollered.

"Go, Spike!"

"That's it, Spike!"

Even Joe Trubly, the oldest boy who usually made sure the others behaved, encouraged him. "Get her, Spike!" he called out. But Mandy rolled Spike over, pinned his arms with her knees, and slapped his face back and forth with the palm of her hand. Spike turned his head halfway to let one cheek take the brunt of it, but it still hurt—a lot.

Joe stepped in. He grabbed Mandy's wrists. He had to lift her high into the air because she kept trying to kick Spike, then Joe too, as Joe pulled her away. Joe dropped her into the corner, while Amaya helped Spike off the floor and ushered him into the boys' dorm and onto one of the beds to inspect his face.

"Aw, I'm all right," he grumbled. Both of his cheeks stung, one worse than the other.

Amaya sat beside him and wiped the tears from his cheeks.

"Mandy is so dramatic." She shook a finger at Spike. "But I wish *you* would keep out of it."

"She could've killed you," Spike pouted.

"She could not. I knew what was coming. I only had to move my head to the side. I knew you were coming too."

"*How*?" Spike grimaced with incomprehension.

"Sometimes," Amaya used her patient, explaining voice, "I can connect to everything around me. While I'm connected, I can sense things without needing my eyes or ears."

"That sounds *crazy*, Amaya." Spike nursed the sorest cheek in one hand and stared at his feet hanging over the edge of the bed, swinging side to side. He didn't understand. How could Amaya see what was going on without looking? She might be the best friend anyone could ever wish for, but boy, she could be confusing sometimes.

"What was that 'minx' thing she kept yelling?" Spike asked.

Amaya pinched her lips and shook her head. "I don't know. But I *won't* let it bother me."

"You not getting bothered is what drives Mandy nuts." Amaya's lack of concern frustrated Spike. "You need to be *careful* about driving her nuts."

"I will not let name-calling upset me. In fact, you will call me Minx from now on."

"No!" Spike pleaded. "Every time someone calls you that Mandy's going to blow her top. It'll be like rubbing a dog's nose in its own poop."

"No matter." Amaya had that tone to her voice, the one

that meant there'd be no changing her mind. "You have to try. Right now."

"I won't." Spike had to protest. He wanted to protect Amaya from Mandy. This would only make that harder, maybe impossible.

"You *will*," Amaya replied firmly. Then her tone softened. "Because you're my best friend."

It was a bad idea, but Spike couldn't say no to this girl he loved so dearly with his seven-year-old's heart. He stared down at his feet again and, with great reluctance, mumbled, "Okay, Minxie."

It stuck.

CHAPTER 10
BEDTIME FOR KIDDO

(AMAYA)

"WHY DOES MANDY hate you so much?" Yunosho asked.

"She has her reasons, *I suppose*." Amaya shrugged, her cheeks flushing from the reminder of the incident with Mandy's heart again. "She's also the only child at the orphanage who's not actually an orphan." Amaya believed she herself wasn't an orphan either, though she refused to accept that her parents hadn't loved her. That would be too much to bear. That's why she had to find them—or what happened to them—and prove it.

"Yeah," Spike said. "Her mom's in prison."

"Prison?" The flames of the fire jumped, illuminating the surprise on Yunosho's face.

"She murdered someone." Growing up, Amaya had often thought having a mother in prison must be better than not knowing who your parents were at all. At least Mandy didn't have to live with uncertainty eating away at her.

"Murder?" Yunosho's brow went up again. "That's serious business. Who'd she murder?"

"A boyfriend. She claimed it was self-defense." Amaya remembered overhearing the Jove sisters call her "that poor woman," as if they'd thought Mandy's mother had been wrongly jailed. Did they believe it for Mandy's sake or did they have more facts about the murder, a suspicion not entirely without merit given how they were on such good terms with Chief Raynor? "Mandy had a very difficult childhood, which explains quite a bit. She's also the opposite of me in appearance—pale-skinned, blonde, and blue-eyed."

"I think her mom raised her to hate people who are different." Spike unsuccessfully stifled a yawn. "Amaya is definitely different." Spike's yawn gave Amaya the opportunity she'd been hoping for. She wanted to speak to Yunosho alone. Their conversation was going to be awkward enough without Spike's need to interrupt and ask questions.

Amaya sat up straighter as if making to go. "It seems Master Skopos needs to retire for the evening. Don't you agree, Mr. Yunosho?"

"I do." Yunosho's knowing grin meant he might be inferring the purpose behind her question. Or getting the wrong idea.

Spike waved them away, the shadows of his movement dancing like spirits on the tree trunks behind him. "You two treat me like a kid. I'm not. I'm fifteen."

The corners of Amaya's mouth lifted into a wry smile. "Exactly the age at which beauty sleep becomes paramount."

"Stop teasing, Minxie." Spike put his hand over his mouth and yawned again.

"There you have it," Yunosho said. "Undeniable confirmation of Spike's dire need for sleep, beauty or otherwise."

"Well, I am kind of tired," Spike said. "That was a long hike."

"Shall we?" Amaya rose and gestured toward the tents. Spike stood with her.

"Goodnight, Spike." Yunosho watched, leaning on one elbow as they made for the tent. "Sleep tight. Don't let the bedbugs bite."

Spike stopped abruptly. He shot Yunosho a look of horror. "Bedbugs?!"

Amaya wrinkled her nose at Yunosho. "Your new friend is only teasing, Spike. Bedbugs do not dwell in the woods."

"Whew…" Spike swiped the back of his hand across his forehead. "*That's* a relief. Goodnight, Yunosho."

Amaya returned to the campfire after getting Spike settled into the tent. Yunosho was adding more wood to the blaze. A chill had settled in. She sat in front of the fire with her back against the log and her arms around her knees. Yunosho remained standing, warming his hands in front of the flames, smoke swirling in waves around him.

"Spike says he's not a kid, but he sure acts like one. How come?"

"Spike had a difficult childhood too. He copes by refusing to grow up, a far better way of dealing with it than the one Mandy chose."

"Skopos. Greek?"

"We think so. Spike was the child of orphans who both perished in a factory fire. No one could find any relatives." Amaya lifted her chin at Yunosho. "What about you? Who are you, and from where do you come?"

"Isn't it a little late for another story?" Yunosho sat down beside her, fingers of shadow made by firelight caressing his face. Amaya recognized resistance in it as if there were things in his story he didn't want told.

"What else are campfires for?" Amaya only half-joked. Inside she hungered for information that could shed light on her parents. Knowing someone had probably sent Yunosho to her made him a piece of her puzzle, a piece she wanted to examine more closely. "I can tell Spike is thrilled to have you join us, but I have to be the responsible one."

"Come on…" Yunosho gave her a skeptical glance, shaking his head. "I'm no criminal."

"Of that, I'm sure. But I owe it to both Spike and myself to know more about the person with whom we could be heading into a potentially violent storm."

"Fair enough." Yunosho pushed the hair from his forehead and looked into her eyes. "Where would you like me to begin?"

Amaya gave him an encouraging smile. "From the beginning, of course."

She didn't expect the shame that grew in her breast as Yunosho told his story. The biggest challenge she'd faced growing up was wondering who her parents were and why they'd left her—and whether they were even still alive. Yunosho had lost his entire extended family. First, his dad, who'd been some kind of top-secret Japanese spy in Russia; then his mom, the most important person in his life; and then his sensei too, who'd trained him since he'd been three and had been the closest thing to a father he'd ever had. By the time Yunosho finished, he'd wrapped his arms around himself and his head hung low, his black hair glistening in the light of the campfire, hiding his face.

He looked so vulnerable. Amaya reached over to put her hand on his forearm to comfort him, then stopped herself. Tangling herself up with emotions wouldn't do them or her mission any good. She kept her hand back, but a big piece of her heart went out to him all the same.

"Thank you for telling me your story," she said in a respectful whisper. "I am honored to have heard it."

Yunosho rose and began absent-mindedly tending the fire, his back to her. "You're welcome."

Amaya stood too. "Your parents would be so proud of you," she said, certain it was true. What would her parents think of her if they were around or if she ever found them? Would they be proud as well? Would they even care?

She had more questions—it couldn't have been a coincidence that a trained swordsman like Yunosho had shown up out of the blue to help—but she didn't want to press him. He was probably as sleepy a storyteller as she was a listener. She took one last appreciative look at him, said goodnight, and went to her tent, hugging herself, feeling safe, as if Yunosho's fire were casting magical protection over the three young orphans with its warm, yellow glow.

CHAPTER 11
SLEEPING BEAUTY

(AMANDA)

Day 4 - 1:24 a.m.

MANDY AWOKE IN a panic. A wet cloth pressed down hard over her nose and mouth. She tried to scream but couldn't. A cold, sickly-sweet odor filled her nasal cavity. She struggled to escape, but something held her tightly in place. A horrid face loomed above hers, illuminated by the bluish moonlight from the windows—a compressed, crooked head, a long scar beneath a droopy eye, stringy hair sticking out the sides of a baseball cap.

Her muscles relaxed despite her fighting with all her mental strength against it. Her thoughts grew thick and syrupy.

A bee stung her.

Her ears buzzed. Her brain began turning numb. Her eyes widened with fright, and the face smiled in response—thin, purplish lips twisting in opposite directions, sliding across wildly uneven teeth. Then Mandy fell. Down and down into the deep blackness engulfing her. The last thing she saw, like looking through a pinhole, was that frightful face, pinched and laughing, a soft, rhythmic "cheh, cheh, cheh" coming from the back of its throat.

Like the sound of someone being strangled to death so far... far... away...

CHAPTER 12
ELMO THE KNIFE

(ELMO)

THE DUGGAN GIRL stopped struggling. Her eyes closed. She was out. To be certain of it, Elmo slowly withdrew the hand holding the ether-soaked cloth; then, he lifted the leg and arm he was using to pin her and raised himself noiselessly from the bed.

He'd entered the orphanage through a basement window and stolen to the second floor where he'd found her and the others fast asleep. Now he waited, perfectly motionless, listening for changes in the other girls' breathing, making sure no one had come awake. The small laugh that had escaped him had been unfortunate, but he hadn't been able to stifle it. The pitiful look on the girl's face had released a powerful memory into his half-dead blood. Something about killing a young woman in the most pleasant of ways, though Elmo couldn't remember exactly how or even who or why.

He heard nothing out of the ordinary, so he stuffed the can of ether and the emptied syringe into his jacket pockets. He went down on one knee, slid both arms under the girl, and lifted, whisking her up and over his shoulder in one swift motion. Then he turned and stepped into the dark hallway, careful to let their combined weight fall along the length of each foot as he did. Using one hand and the controlled push of his free shoulder, he nudged the door shut without making a sound.

He started down the stairs, faster now, the carpet runners muffling his footfalls. He reached the bottom. One of the twins, he couldn't tell which, stepped into the hallway, her head down, looking at papers she held in both hands. Light streamed across the hall from the open doorway. Elmo froze. The woman looked up. The papers fluttered to the floor.

"Oh my," she uttered like a hiccup, her face confused and worried, an expression instantly replaced with one of determination. "This simply won't do." She gave Elmo an abrupt shake of her head, spun around, and hurried back into the same doorway from which she'd come.

Elmo followed, the girl still on his shoulder. He reached the door. The twin, her back to him, was halfway to a desk, headed toward something there, purpose in her stride. She didn't speak to any kind of AI; either she didn't have one, or it wasn't active. Elmo didn't care. She wouldn't have time to talk.

He unsheathed his knife with one hand, and flipped it, catching the tip of the blade between his thumb and forefinger. Holding tightly to the girl with one arm, he cocked the other behind his ear and let fly.

The blade tumbled through the air and penetrated all the way to the hilt with a dull, satisfying thud. Her body jerked, once, twice, and she crumpled to the floor, sprawling forward, gasping for air.

Time to go, Elmo thought. He hefted the girl into a better position, bounded to the front door, and flipped both deadbolts open. He twisted and pulled on the door handle, and he was into the cool night air, rushing across the porch and down the stairs, certain of his getaway.

50

CHAPTER 13
SESSY'S PLIGHT

(JOE)

THE LOUD SNAPS of the front door unbolting downstairs woke Joe Trubly from his light sleep. He slid out of bed, sneaked out of the dorm room, and ran straight into Tessy Jove coming down the stairs from the twins' third-floor living quarters.

"Joseph, what are you doing up?" Tessy whispered.

"I heard noises."

"Me too. Let's go make sure everything's all right."

Joe padded downstairs with Tessy. They found the front door wide open. A cool breeze drifted in along with the sound of hurried footsteps crunching the pea stone gravel. They stepped onto the porch in time to see a dark squat figure carrying someone on its shoulder disappear around the edge of the property.

"What do you make of that, Joseph?"

Joe swallowed hard. "It can't be good." He started down the steps. A car motor whined to life. "I'm going after them." He stepped off the porch, determined to follow. A black vehicle tore through the intersection. Joe sucked in a breath and took off running.

"Joseph!" Tessy commanded. "You stay right here!"

He'd gone five strides before he stopped, watching the red tail lights disappear. Not because Tessy had stopped him; he'd simply remembered he couldn't outrun a car. He turned back, shaking his head, his lips pulled tight with disappointment.

She shook a bony finger at him. "Joseph, I can't have you chasing after dangerous people like that. What would the world think of how we take care of our children were something to happen to you?"

"I'm sorry, Miss Jove." He hadn't meant to give Tessy a scare. "I guess we better go check on everything."

"We certainly shall. And we need to call Chief Raynor right away. I *think* that miserable creature had one of our children on his shoulder." Tessy was putting on a good face for Joe's benefit. He was glad she did.

She closed the door once they were inside again and locked it. Joe examined the hallway. A slant of light streamed from the office doorway. Papers lay strewn about the floor.

"Look." Joe pointed.

"Sessy?" Tessy called out to her sister. "Is that you?" No one answered.

They went to the doorway and peered in. Sessy lay prone on the floor, unmoving, a black knife handle sticking out of her back with a red stain around it. Joe gasped. Tessy let out a terrible cry.

"Oh my goodness! Sess!" She rushed to her sister's side. Joe followed, kneeling beside Sessy, uncertain of what to do. He'd never been in a situation this dire before. Sessy was out. *Or worse*, Joe thought. Then her eyes blinked open, and Joe breathed a sigh of relief.

"Gone," Sessy gurgled, like she had water in her lungs. Her eyes were open, but they seemed dim.

"Stay still, Sess," Tessy said, her voice taut with panic. "I'm getting emergency services right now."

Tessy called the dispatcher. The phone trembled in her hand while she showed the dispatcher the knife's location. The woman instructed Tessy to carefully turn her sister onto her right side and keep her there. By no means should she try to remove the knife.

Tessy told the dispatcher to call Chief Raynor right away. One of the children might have been kidnapped. And they should fetch Bertha and Brea, the orphanage's staff.

"He'll know who they are," Tessy finished.

"Right. Bertha and Brea," the woman repeated. "I'll stay on the line in case you need me."

Joe felt better. They had instructions, something to follow. He helped Tessy roll Sessy onto her side, then supported her shoulder to keep her there.

"Okay, Sess…" Tessy took her sister's hand in both of hers, squeezing it rhythmically, like she was urging Sessy's heart to keep beating. "You need to tell me what happened."

"Ghoul took Amanda," Sessy said in a gasping whisper.

"A ghoul?" her sister asked.

"Looked like one," Sessy said. "Gray face. Black clothes. Amanda was out. Drugged, maybe."

Joe couldn't believe it—a kidnapper in their orphanage! Sessy's eyes closed again.

"Sess, you *have* to stay awake. Please!" Tessy blinked back tears.

"Trying," Sessy mumbled, a soft moan escaping her lips.

The sound of sirens in the distance reached Joe's ears. Hope flickered in Tessy's desperate eyes. "Joseph, go show those emergency folks right in." She took hold of her sister's shoulder.

"Yes, ma'am. Right away." Joe jumped up, eager. The one

thing Joe loved was to be useful. He dashed to the hallway, unbolted the front door, and opened it.

It seemed like an eternity, but he counted only twenty seconds before the ambulance pulled up in a blaze of flashing lights and a blare of jarring wailing. Three crew members hopped out. One rolled out the stretcher. The other two ran up the steps, carrying equipment.

"Follow me," Joe yelled, waving them in. Rubber boots clomped behind him. Inside the office, the techs began attending to Sessy, but Tessy refused to budge from her side.

"We'll take it from here, ma'am," one of the crew told Tessy.

Tessy patted the woman's arm. "I'm going with you, right?"

"Of course you are." A look of relief so deep came over Tessy's face that Joe almost cried seeing it. He didn't. He needed to stay strong for the others.

Tessy told Joe to round up all the children into the cafeteria and do a headcount after locking the door. "Don't let anyone in unless it's Bertha, Brea, or the police," she instructed.

"I'll take care of everything." Joe headed toward the hallway to gather the children but stopped at the doorway, glancing back to check on Sessy one last time. One of the techs had just given her a shot. Her eyes opened wider, and she seemed more alert.

"Don't you worry, my dear," he heard her tell Tessy, who stood beside the stretcher, still clutching Sessy's hand in both of hers. "I'm going to make it."

"Oh, I can't help but worry, sis." Tessy had tears in her eyes now, the ones Joe knew she'd been holding in since the moment they first looked into that office. "How could I possibly go on without you?"

CHAPTER 14

HOORAY FOR GEEKS

(SPIKE)

SPIKE GAZED UP at the complex of white concrete apartments that snaked along the Magneta River for what looked like an entire mile. Seeing buildings this big and tall in real life gave him the sensation of being dwarfed. It dizzied him. They'd risen early, eaten energy bars for breakfast, and made their way here where Yunosho's engineer friend lived in one of these thousands of apartment units.

"Before we go up," Yunosho said as they approached the outdoor elevators, "I want you to know my friend's a little different."

"What do you mean?" Amaya asked.

"Weird clothes, totally into tech, and super smart."

"A geek?" Spike asked.

"Spike, *please* don't call my friend that. You'll embarrass me." They stopped in front of the elevators. Yunosho pushed the up arrow.

"Yunosho is correct. You shouldn't label people." Amaya's

face had taken on that serious expression, which meant she was headed into one of her out-there lectures.

"This characteristic you call geekiness," she continued, "goes with scientific talent. The ability to solve complex problems involves qualities others term geeky. But 'geek' is merely a label. Each of us has unique qualities that make us uniquely geeky in our own way. For instance, I could label Spike a positivity geek or call myself a Hindu mythology geek. Tat Tvam Asi. We are all essentially one."

"Hold on, Minxie." Yunosho shook his open palms at Amaya. "I don't know what this tava missy thing is, but—"

Oh boy, Spike thought. *Here it comes.* Yunosho had mispronounced something sacred.

"Tat. Tvam. Asi." Amaya's jaw was taut, her chin punctuating each word with disdain. "'Thou art that' means we are each a *part* of the whole as well as the *entire* whole, all at the same time. It's an experiential as well as a—"

"Okay, okay," Yunosho pleaded, shaking his head. "This orphanage really did a number on you two. Look, I'm only saying. Don't walk in there and embarrass me by letting your mouths hang open when you meet my friend. Can you handle that?"

"No problem." Spike was impressed with how Yunosho cut Amaya's speech short, something Spike could never bring himself to do. "I like weird. That's why I like you two."

"And you?" Yunosho crossed his arms and gave Amaya an exaggeratedly stern glare.

"I assure you," she answered with a smirk and a sharp nod of the head, "I will be as indifferent as an English butler."

"Don't be too stiff." Yunosho rolled his eyes and spun around to greet the elevator doors as they opened, then muttered under his breath, "It's not like you're not stiff enough already."

The elevator whisked them to the thirtieth floor. They exited onto a narrow exterior balcony that traversed the entire length of the building. The view of the downtown with its magnificent buildings, some with spires jutting into the sky, called to mind castles and fairies and fair maidens needing rescuing from evil dragons. Spike couldn't take his eyes off the cityscape—until Yunosho knocked at No. B-3003.

The door sprang open as if it had been eagerly awaiting their arrival. An attractive girl with spike-cut, bright-red hair jumped out wearing a black-and-white checkered miniskirt, high-heeled motorcycle boots, and a banana-skin top.

"Yunosho!" She wrapped him in a hug, rocking back and forth.

Spike's brain began a strange tingling as soon as he saw her. Amaya went slack-jawed, and her forehead wrinkled in disapproval. Yunosho wagged his finger at her, probably because her detached butler imitation wasn't going too well. How could Yunosho have described *her*, this marvel, as a plain old geek?

"How are you?" She disengaged from Yunosho, her blue eyes blazing with excitement. "It's great to see you again!"

Spike saw Yunosho's mouth move in answer, but it sounded like unintelligible gibberish to Spike, who'd focused his entire attention on the magnificent creature in front of him. He felt a strange sensation, like he was bursting inside to hear what she said next, as if each word was permission to take another breath and keep living.

"Who are your friends?" She put her arms akimbo, looking Spike and Amaya over like an engineering project.

The question pulled Spike out of his awe. He suddenly *had* to speak to this divine being.

"We're not just friends," Spike blurted out, "we're a band— the Band of Murugan!"

Yunosho chuckled. "Gigi, please meet Amaya and Spike."

"It's so cool to meet Yunosho's friends." She cupped a hand to her mouth and whispered loudly, "Poor guy didn't have *any* until he met me."

Yunosho tapped his foot. "I'm standing right here."

Gigi ignored him. "Please come on in and tell me all about this crazy-wild band of yours."

They stepped into a narrow apartment packed with equipment. Vidwalls lined with worktops crowded with parts, tools, and papers took up most of the space. Spike had never seen the likes of it. The Jove sisters enforced strict orderliness around the orphanage.

"Data, freeze current project," Gigi said.

"Project is frozen." The AI used a voice Spike thought he recognized from an old sci-fi series.

"Don't want my research getting messed up while we talk." Gigi cleared books from her bed. They were all technical except one—an old, hardcover edition of *Twenty Thousand Leagues*. Spike *loved* Jules Verne. He and Minxie must have read that book together at least five times. "Find a place to sit, guys."

Spike squeezed in between Amaya and Yunosho on the bed. Gigi swiveled her desk chair to face them and plopped down in it. "I can tell you're here for something important," she said. "What's up?"

"I'm surprised you weren't more careful about security," Yunosho said.

"I have five nanocams hidden outside. They pop up on the vidwall as soon as they recognize human activity. I saw right away it was you, and these two seemed harmless enough. I mean, no one had a gun pointed to your head."

Spike found it hard to imagine anyone putting a gun to Yunosho's head.

"That's good to know. We need to be cautious." Yunosho pulled a handful of dragonfly pieces from his backpack and held them up. "Here's why. These could use a good dose of your research mojo."

"What are they?" Gigi grabbed an examination tray. Yunosho placed the pieces on it.

"Dragonflies," Spike whispered as if they were something magical.

"Mechanical ones," Amaya added. "They attacked me. While I was evading them, Mr. Emushi happened to come along and make excellent work of them with his sword."

"Emushi? Your family name?" Gigi asked.

"Sort of," Yunosho replied, "but that's not important right now."

"Uh-oh," Spike cautioned. "Don't say that. You'll only make it super important later."

"Only in the vids, Spike," Yunosho scoffed. "Or books." To Gigi, he said, "If anyone can figure out the origin of these things, it would be you. They blew out puffs of steam when my sword hit them, so I'm pretty sure they're steam-powered."

"We haven't seen major advances in steam technology in a while." Gigi eyed the pieces closer. "That makes me curious. Well, there's no time like now."

"Actually"—Amaya sat up taller—"now is the *only* time. Despite our misguided efforts to live elsewhere, we can only exist in this 'now,' a pregnant temporal present that holds not only all of the past but the entirety of all possible future moments as well."

Yunosho chuckled. "Pay no attention to the girl behind the white blouse. Apparently, some Hindu-crazed twins at the orphanage where she grew up brainwashed her."

"Hindu *and* Greek," Spike corrected. "The Jove twins. Tessy and Sessy. They run the orphanage. Sessy's a Hindu mythology expert, and Tessy's a Greek mythology expert, so we learn a lot about both."

"The orphanage sounds fascinating." Gigi swiveled back around to face the wall and rolled her chair to the only cleared desk space where tools were neatly arranged beside a few lab-type machines. She put the exam tray down there. "Maybe we can talk about that later. Right now I'm dying to dig into these dragonflies."

"Sure." Spike didn't mind at all. He found himself wanting to do everything Gigi told him. He struggled to think of the word for the way he felt. It came to him after a few seconds—enthralled. He would've *never* thought being enthralled could feel so *wonderful*. But he *had* started to babble. She was *way* too smart for a babbler.

"Data, new project called 'Nasty Dragonflies,'" she said.

"Your new project titled 'Nasty Dragonflies' is confirmed," replied her AI program.

Spike watched her every move and listened intently to her mumbled remarks.

"Never saw this before." "Wow, this is some crazy tech." Followed by, "Can't be from *this* Earth."

She pulled the dragonfly jaws apart and retrieved liquid from behind the teeth. Using a dropper, she applied drops of the liquid to a plate and covered them with another plate. She inserted the plates into a piece of equipment consisting of two parts connected by a white tube. The process intrigued Spike, but the magical pixie conducting it fascinated him even more.

The AI program informed Gigi the results were ready. She told it to correlate them with some info on the web. The AI mentioned a golden frog. Gigi whistled, then spun her chair back around to face everyone. "Boy, oh boy."

Spike leaned forward, hanging on her words.

"That doesn't sound good," Yunosho said.

"You guys are lucky to be alive," she said. "These things have poison injectors in their teeth. Highly fatal poison."

Spike's eyes went wide. Amaya shot Yunosho a knowing glance.

"It's a good thing the motors stopped working. If you had picked up pieces while the pumps were still functional? Well, I think you get the picture."

"Some of those pieces were still moving," Spike said, trying to ignore the large, painful lump in his throat.

"What else did you find?" Yunosho asked.

"No fingerprints. And they're made with earthly materials."

"We didn't think about anything extra-worldly," Yunosho said.

"There's a big but," Gigi continued. "It's likely the tech isn't from this world. Nano steam engines power these things, which seem to use cold muon-particle fusion. Unless someone has been undertaking serious efforts to hide the technology, it's only theoretically possible today. Also, the design mimics the old Victorian era, but the construction is even more exact and delicate. It's too perfect." She picked up one of the wings from the tray and held it out in her palm. "The filigree work on these wings and the thin-metal tech… well, it's amazing!"

"Are we talking about aliens?" Amaya seemed surprised by the possibility. It surprised Spike too, a lot. But nothing could detract from his intense interest in everything Gigi.

"Either that or a more highly developed parallel universe." Gigi laid the piece back on the tray. "It's the most unexpected thing I've ever encountered. Both are possibilities. I can't eliminate either one at this point."

Yunosho straightened up. "See, Amaya? We came to the right place. Thanks, Gigi, it's a great start."

Spike agreed wholeheartedly. This Gigi had forever shattered his image of geeks. Now he couldn't think of anything in the world better than a geek. His newfound enthusiasm for geeks swelled and swelled inside him until he couldn't contain it any longer. He threw his fist above his head.

"Hooray for geeks!" he yelled.

Yunosho buried his face in his palms, his head shaking back and forth.

"I'm so sorry," Amaya said. "Spike can get carried away."

Spike felt embarrassed too. But when he looked over at Gigi, she wasn't angry. She was grinning! "It's okay, Spike," she said. "I'll let you in on a secret. My real name isn't Gigi. That's a nickname I got in high school. It's two Gs together. They stand for Geek Girl."

Even better, Spike thought. He raised his fist again and shouted. "Hooray for Geek Girl!"

Amaya burst out laughing, something Spike had never seen her do before. "I second that." She waved her hand like she was asking to be called on in class.

Yunosho removed his face from his palms, looking relieved, but the remains of a cringe still cast a shadow over his face.

"So what's next?" Gigi asked.

"We seem to have a conglomeration of Victorianism, deadly tech, and aliens or other universes to deal with," Yunosho summed up, "all converging to put young Miss Atlas here in peril. Whatever we do has to take all that into account."

"Well, count me in." Gigi grinned. "I guess I'm joining your band."

Spike felt like he'd just won the super-mega-jackpot in the new-friends lottery. From the way his facial muscles were pulling in different directions, his face must be setting its own personal best beaming record. He only hoped he didn't look too foolish doing it.

CHAPTER 15

OFF TO CEE, THE WIZARD

(AMAYA)

GIGI'S ANALYSIS PUZZLED Amaya. Why would aliens or people from another universe want to kill her? How did they even exist? And what possible connection could they have to her parents?

She'd never expected the quest to find her parents to become quite this baffling. Indeed, before the Menace, she'd thought it would entail mostly just searching through old records once she figured out where to look. Though the Jove sisters had told her they wouldn't be able to release "what little" records they had to her until she turned eighteen.

"Let's recap what we know." Yunosho was taking charge, standing between the kitchen and the living area in Gigi's cramped apartment. Gigi was sitting backward in her chair, with Spike beside Amaya on Gigi's bed. Amaya decided to let Yunosho *think* he was in charge until the time came to disabuse him of that idea. "We know we're dealing with a disturbing force that sent some pretty nasty and potentially otherworldly tech to do away with our friend, Amaya."

Spike cringed. His exceptionally vivid imagination made his reactions to negative imagery more visceral—another reason Amaya worried how he'd fare against what might get thrown at them out here in the real world.

"We also know it's active somewhere in this general geographic area," she said. "But I'm uncertain whether I was drawn to the hill because I sensed the dark disturbance or merely the danger of the coming attack."

Gigi drew back in her chair a little, a combination of surprise and doubt on her face. "Are you saying you have the power to see the future?"

"No. It's not predictive." Amaya's voice was firm. She wanted Gigi to understand—she wasn't a fortune teller. "When I'm threatened, I can connect with my surroundings. I can discern existing threats when I'm in that connection. *Not* future ones."

"I'm not aware of any hard evidence that would support what you describe," Gigi said. "Almost all instances of paranormal phenomena have been disproven as hoaxes or the result of some scientifically explainable cause."

"Amaya isn't a hoax," Spike explained. "I grew up with her. I've seen it."

"I'm not saying she is," Gigi replied. "I'm only reserving judgment until I see more conclusive evidence."

"We definitely need help," Yunosho said. "I vote to go visit my sensei."

"Isn't Mr. Oniki dead?" Amaya pictured the poor man the way she imagined him—tortured, fingers missing, lying in a pool of his own blood on the floor of his dojo. She could scarcely call Yunosho's story a happy one.

"Not that sensei." There was a glimmer of pain in Yunosho's eyes. Amaya regretted mentioning it. "My mountain teacher."

"You never did tell me his name," Amaya said.

"Cledwyn?" Gigi asked.

"Yes," Yunosho answered. An unexpected twinge of jealousy hit Amaya—this attractive girl knew something about Yunosho Amaya didn't. Amaya wasn't accustomed to feeling jealous. She didn't want it to distract from her mission.

"Cledwyn?" She quashed the unwanted thoughts. "What sort of name is that?"

"He's Welsh. He grew up in Japan and Brooklyn, so he's got a strange accent that can be hard to understand." Yunosho glanced at Amaya and grinned. "Even harder than someone else's in this room."

Yunosho took obvious pleasure in teasing her for some reason. The best course of action was to ignore him. "Why go there?" Why should their next stop should be a martial arts training facility? They needed to go visit the space agency or a research university with a Parallel Universes Department.

"Master Cee has all the experience and resources we need. You'll see. He also happens to be the best trainer in the world. You need help figuring out what this E^2 business is and how to use it. All of you could benefit from a little training too."

"Ugh…" Gigi grimaced. "Training? Really?"

"Don't forget. We also need to find out who those dragonflies belonged to," Spike added.

"To *whom*," Amaya corrected.

"Jeez, Louise," Spike complained. "Let me talk normal."

"*Normally.*"

Spike folded his arms on his chest in a huff. "I'm shutting up now."

"Where is this Master Cee, and how do we get there?" Amaya asked.

"Look, his location is top secret. You can't reveal it to anyone, okay?" Amaya, Gigi, and Spike all nodded. Yunosho pointed out the back window at the mountain, its top partially hidden by a swirling mist. "It's right up Knob Mountain."

"It appears to be quite a distance and very high up." Amaya was thinking it might be difficult for Spike, who wasn't that strong and had never climbed more than a hill before. Though, as she thought more about it, neither had she.

"We can take the train to the last stop on the Knob line," Yunosho said. "After that, it's a hike followed by a fairly steep slog up the side of the mountain. Cee doesn't exactly have a doorbell. He could be out. It could be two or three days before he gets back."

Gigi slid off her chair and squeezed past Yunosho to open her small pantry. Amaya burned with jealousy again, seeing Gigi's ample curves brushing against Yunosho's hard body.

"I have tons of food tubes." Gigi pulled a few out of the cabinet. "I live on these things when I'm deep into research. Let's stock up."

Amaya helped Yunosho fill the water bottles and stuff food tubes into the empty spaces of their backpacks while Gigi went to change. When Gigi came out wearing tan pants and a loose-fitting blouse, the amount of tension that drained from Amaya surprised her—one more reason to be concerned about the negative effect of distractions on her mission. She was just going to have to put these feelings in their place—stowed away.

"How do you choose which equipment to bring?" Spike asked Gigi as she stuffed technical-looking devices into her pack.

"I try to anticipate what might come in handy," she replied. "Fortunately, almost everything's miniaturized these days. My goggs also do a lot on their own."

"Goggs?" Spike moved closer to see what she was packing.

"My LCEs. Lightweight computing eyewear." She pointed to a pair of round tortoise-shell glasses on her desk.

"I thought those were regular glasses." Spike picked them up for a closer look.

"Nope. See how the lenses are thicker? That's for creating viewing depths and screen-on-screen overlays. We call them goggs because back in the day, they were big unwieldy goggles that covered half your face. Not fun to wear. But the name stuck."

"Make sure nothing you're carrying is connected for now," Yunosho told Gigi.

"Already done." Gigi stowed the goggs in her backpack. "Data, show me the Knob Mountain transit line schedule."

The schedule popped up on the vidwall. "Schedule posted," said her AI.

"Enter secure lockdown mode after we're out the door," Gigi added.

"Secure lockdown confirmed," the AI replied.

"Let's get moving." Yunosho picked up his pack and slung it over his shoulder. "We can hike to the edge of the foothills, camp overnight, and climb in the morning. That should put us at Cee level around noon to tomorrow." Yunosho was grinning like a kid. "Get it, *Cee* level? Master Cee?"

Gigi glared at Yunosho and punched him in the arm. Apparently, Amaya wasn't the only one who hated bad puns.

CHAPTER 16

MAY THE GODS BE WITHIN YOU

(GAIA)

IT WAS ALL Gaia's fault.

The Greeks wouldn't be in this mess if she hadn't hob-nobbed with the Hindus and fallen in love with Indra, their Lord of the Skies. But blaming herself wouldn't get them anywhere. Amaya's abilities might be improving, but she still needed help. The more Gaia understood how they'd all blindly walked into this trap eleven years ago, the better she could use what little power she had left to influence things. Who knows? She might discover a way for Amaya to free them.

"Correct, Praj." Indra was recounting how it had all started—a visit to his good friend Prajapati, Lord of All Crea-tures. "I traveled up Mount Meru to Praj's magnificent summer palace, the one with those spectacular views. Towering lapis peaks. Enchanting Cosmic Ocean glistening down below." He sighed. "I'd give anything to see those sights in the flesh again."

"Do you remember what you said when you arrived?" A wry smile lifted the corners of Praj's mouth.

"About what?" asked Indra.

"About Gaia, my man!" replied Praj. Gaia's ears pricked. She couldn't help worrying that Indra might have said something unflattering about her. She hated how insecure she could feel around him. It would be a lot easier to trust him if he didn't suffer from such a dreadful reputation—drinker, womanizer, lost cause.

"Are you going to embarrass me again?" Indra asked. "I'm quite capable of doing that to myself, you know."

"I must!" Praj's eyes sparkled with merriment. "You see, Indra came into the courtyard, plopped down at the table, and poured himself a chalice of Soma, complaining about how Airavata, his querulous elephant steed, argued with him the entire trip. When I asked about the lovely Greek goddess Indra was rumored to be seeing, a frown came over his face as if I'd mentioned the awfullest of things. '*That* woman!' he exclaimed. 'She's maddening!'"

A painful snuffle clenched Gaia's heart. Did Indra hold her in such disdain?! Was she nothing more than a source of irritation to him?!

"I asked what he meant," continued Praj. "He looked at me like little-boy-lost, pulled at his hair with both hands, and said, 'She's maddeningly attractive and maddeningly captivating. I can't stop thinking about her, and that's maddening as well!'"

The hurt in Gaia's heart fled as quickly as it had appeared. She shouldn't have doubted it. Indra *did* love her! She only wished his dreadful reputation wouldn't keep getting in the way.

Indra coughed and lowered his eyes. "My dear Praj. I certainly didn't intend those comments to reach everyone's ears."

He lifted his eyes, a flash of annoyance in them, and indicated Gaia.

"You'll thank me for it later." Praj winked at Gaia.

"To get on with the *important* part of the story." Indra rolled his eyes. Gaia was sure the cheeks under his dark skin had turned bright red. "Praj asked the reason for my visit. I took off my crown, ran my hand through my hair, and told him my story. How I was sitting alone on my terrace the night before, drinking Soma, lamenting my loss of stature among the gods. I reached my usual conclusion, that it didn't matter because no one, not even I, can escape being one with the universe. Then a sudden premonition hit me like a hammer in the middle of the forehead. Really, more than a premonition. I simply *knew* it—the asuras were back."

"My first thought was 'impossible,'" said Praj. "Indra and Vishnu destroyed the asuras ages ago. The news terrified me all the same. If true, those demons would stop at nothing short of torturing and destroying the entirety of humanity. I told Indra we'd need to act; the situation was serious enough for an all-hands meeting. We could hold one at Vishnu's retreat."

"That's it!" Gaia cried out. "*That's* how they knew! The asuras listened in somehow. They'd been spying on Indra—which would explain his premonition as well. *But from where had they listened? And where are they now?*"

Nobody had a clue, though the answers to those questions were as important as getting out of the trap. Except for Indra's inklings, no one had seen the asuras coming. They couldn't afford to make that kind of mistake again.

CHAPTER 17

TWO TIMES TWO

(SPIKE)

SPIKE COULD SEE why they called it Knob Mountain. It took the shape of a knob higher up, with steep sides and a nearly flat top. According to Yunosho, they would hike halfway around the base and head straight up the far side without needing to undertake anything more than a mildly demanding climb for a novice.

They left the road for a narrow trail into the woods. Yunosho and Amaya took the lead, with Spike and Gigi bringing up the rear. Spike was excited to be hiking. He'd always looked forward to field trips into the woods with the Jove sisters. But he'd never experienced these kinds of butterflies before, from being with Gigi on his own. He found himself enjoying this new and pleasurable discomfort.

He walked side-by-side with her. Their shoulders brushed against one another as they pushed past branches and thorny bramble sticking into the trail. Spike began experiencing a strangely heightened sensitivity to Gigi's proximity, something like magnetism; he kept bumping into her despite his best efforts not to.

"Look." Spike pointed at the ground. "A blue-tailed skink." A metallic-blue tail disappeared under a rock beside the trail.

"Hey, Spikie." Gigi's eyes were beautiful with mischief and laughter. "Can I call you that?"

"Sure. Minxie calls me Spikie sometimes." Spike had to stifle a sudden overwhelming urge to grab Gigi's hand and hold it.

"Who's *Minxie*?"

"Oh. That's Amaya's nickname. Kind of a long story."

"Storytelling time isn't in scarce supply at the moment, Spikie."

He laughed at that. Then, for the second time in as many days, he told Minxie's nickname story.

"Mandy sounds mean," Gigi said after he finished. They slowed to a leisurely stroll. Gigi picked a fern leaf from the forest floor and began thoughtfully pulling its blades apart one by one, like petals on a daisy.

"She's super mean. She probably would've tortured me every day if Minxie hadn't watched over me. I'm not sure why Minxie did, but I'm glad."

"She cares about you. A lot. I think that's why. Amaya seems like the kind of friend who'd stand by you forever."

Minxie *was* that kind of friend. The day Spike arrived at the orphanage, the Jove sisters cleaned him up, sat him in a chair way too big for him in their office, and reassured him that things would be much better now they'd gotten him out of that awful foster-care situation. Afterward, they lined up all the other orphans in the hallway to introduce him. Right away, for no obvious reason, the blonde girl with the pigtails started making scornful sneers at him behind the Jove sisters' backs. Amaya noticed. She shoved her fists down at her sides, stormed straight over to Spike, and stood shoulder-to-shoulder beside him. Then she folded her arms across her chest and gave Mandy an "I dare you" glare. No one had ever done *anything* like that for Spike. He and Amaya had been best friends since.

"Mandy tried to hurt her a bunch of times," he continued. "Minxie never got mad about it, which made Mandy hate her even more. Then, one day, Minxie fell into one of her spells around Mandy. After that, Mandy turned into the meanest meanie ever."

"Spells?" Gigi's fern leaf dropped to the forest floor. "What do you mean by spells?"

"Sometimes, Minxie falls into this kind of trance for a minute or two. She usually comes out of it with an important piece of information or some lesson about life."

"Like what?"

"Oh…" Spike thought for a moment. "Like this one time, she came out all smiles and gave me a great big hug. It was weird because she almost never hugs anyone. She whispered 'everything is just so' in my ear like it was the most wonderful secret. I thought she meant the orphanage, but she didn't."

"The orphanage?" Gigi's nose wrinkled in puzzlement. "Why the orphanage?"

Spike laughed. "That's its name. The Just-So Orphanage."

Gigi's brow arched. "Really?" The path narrowed. They switched to walking single file. Spike let Gigi take the lead.

"Sure. In addition to being nuts about mythology and philosophy, the Jove sisters are fans of those old Kipling stories. But Minxie didn't mean the orphanage or those stories. She told me the entire universe, as it existed in that moment, was just so, just the way it should be." Spike shook his head in disbelief. "She wasn't even eight years old yet. The only reason

I remember is because of how completely crazy it sounded at the time. Not that Amaya didn't say plenty of crazy-sounding things."

Gigi pushed back a branch and held it for Spike to take so it didn't whip back at him when she released it. "I *guess* Amaya has some pretty special talents. I mean, look at the whole dragonfly thing."

Spike knew Gigi was dubious. But she was also the kind of person who eventually would prove to herself how real Amaya's abilities were. "She sure does."

"Which brings us back to the story you were about to tell me?"

"Oh yeah." They reached a small ravine that crossed the trail. Gigi made it up the other side first and held her hand out to Spike. He grabbed it, and a delightful current of warmth flooded his body. He couldn't help himself—he held on longer than he needed. He didn't know whether to hope she had or hadn't noticed when he finally let go. One thing was sure—the pleasure he felt during those extra couple of seconds far outweighed the guilt.

"Minxie found out she has this other kind of ability," he said. They started down the trail, side-by-side again, Spike doing his best to mask the tempest of confusion Gigi stirred up inside him. "We were all in the rec room. Minxie and I were on the floor in the corner, talking about Sessy's class. Minxie was helping me study. Mandy was in the middle of the room with her two friends."

"Were you Amaya's only friend?"

"Sort of." Spike focused his eyes on the ground. He hung his thumbs in his pockets and kicked a rock off the trail. True, Amaya kept her distance from everyone by being serious. But he didn't want to give Gigi the impression that Amaya was antisocial. "Minxie didn't get *real* close with anyone else except Farmer Bob and Sam."

"Who are they?"

"That's a whole different story. Do you want to hear it too?"

Gigi laughed. Her laughter tickled his eardrum in such an agreeable way he wanted to find ingenious ways of making Gigi laugh just to hear it again and again. "I think we can stick to this one for now."

"Sure, okay," Spike said, disappointed. He'd have to wait for more Gigi laughter. The rest of *this* story didn't have a single funny thing in it. "To start with, Minxie's nice to everyone, even Mandy and her friends."

"Hmm." Gigi gazed up. "I suppose if she's that in touch with the universe, she's more likely to be kind because she feels more connected to other people, right?"

"That's kind of where this story goes. Minxie didn't know about this other power. She regretted using it the way she did on Mandy." Spike stopped on the trail. This part of the story was important. He didn't want Gigi getting any wrong ideas about Amaya. Amaya might *seem* aloof, but she cared about people, even Mandy. "Minxie scared her," Spike almost whispered. "Bad. But she didn't mean to."

Gigi looked Spike in the eye, giving him her full attention. She nodded for him to continue.

"Mandy and her friends had their mirrors out, playing makeup. Not that they had real makeup. They weren't allowed. But they loved pretending. Mandy scowled at Minxie. Minxie just smiled at her. Mandy hated it when Minxie smiled at her. Honestly, you would've thought Minxie's smile was some kind of death ray shooting at Mandy the way she acted about it.

"Then Minxie fell into one of her trances. Her eyes closed, and her arms went all limp. Mandy took that as an insult.

Maybe she thought Minxie was saying, 'I'm not going to pay you any attention,' and Mandy needed attention. Even death-ray-smile attention was better than no attention to her.

"She jumped up, marched over, and started throwing a finger at Minxie, yelling about Minxie thinking she was better than everyone else, how she always had her nose in the air, and how Mandy was sick and tired of her." Spike's voice took on urgency. "I *told* Mandy to leave her alone, that Minxie was taking a nap. Mandy wouldn't listen. She was furious. She raised her hand and went to slap Minxie. Minxie snapped out of her trance and caught Mandy's wrist."

Spike's eyes grew wide. He moved his head slowly back and forth. Gigi watched him, absorbed in the story. "I've never seen anything like it. Mandy's face turned powder white. She pulled as hard as she could to get away from Minxie, like a terrifying ghost or death itself had taken hold of her. She ran to the dorm as soon as she got free and stayed in bed through supper and into the next morning. She told everyone she was sick."

Gigi raised a questioning brow. "But she wasn't?"

"She was, but not in the normal sense. On the inside. Minxie told me that when she grabbed Mandy, she saw this putrid, black jellyfish-looking thing clamped around Mandy's heart, pumping hate into it. Mandy saw it too, which is what scared her so badly. But she was meaner and tougher than ever the following day. Every time she looked at Minxie"—Spike pulled his whole face into a squint—"her eyes crinkled with hate. I mean the worst kind of hate, like the I-want-to-murder-you-to-death kind of hate."

"How did you and Amaya put up with it?"

"We didn't. Eventually, Minxie said it was time to leave. That's when we ran away."

"Why didn't the Jove sisters step in?"

"Minxie would never tell on Mandy. That's not the way Minxie operates. Mandy attacked Minxie three more times before we finally did leave. Minxie always stepped to the side or changed some little thing to avoid getting hurt, which drove Mandy nuts."

"I'm curious about this ability to show a person what's inside them. Has Amaya ever done it with you?"

Did Gigi worry there might be some horrible jellyfish thing in him too? He didn't think there was. If he found one, he'd kill it before he *ever* let Gigi see it. "Nope. She told me it was too dangerous. She felt awful about the way it happened with Mandy. Minxie says people need to open their eyes gradually to the darkness inside them, the same way your eyes need time to adjust when you come out of a dark cave into the light." Spike gave Gigi a sharp nod. "*That's* why we meditate. She says meditation shows me what's inside me and even changes it for the better. You know what? I think she's right."

"I'm glad to hear it, Spike." They started back down the trail. "You deserve it." She gave Spike's shoulder a little pat, sending warm fuzzies through him all over again.

"Thanks, Gigi. You're not so bad yourself." Spike wanted to pat Gigi's shoulder too. But he'd better not, given the whole handholding incident. He couldn't be sure what might come over him or how she might react. Instead, he pointed up ahead. Yunosho and Amaya were still visible, but they'd put some distance between them. "Let's catch up," he told Gigi.

"Sure." Gigi took off running without giving Spike a chance. "Last one there's a putrid ovum encased in calcium carbonate crystals," she shouted, her ticklish laughter trailing behind her. Spike followed as fast as he could, grinning like a Cheshire cat.

CHAPTER 18

SAME TIME, DIFFERENT PLACE

(ELMO)

ELMO LEFT THE still-unconscious Amanda tied to a cot in the office while he worked on a new plan for dealing with the three "Mouseketeers," the name he'd given that bothersome trio of Amaya Atlas and friends. He couldn't remember where he'd heard that name or what it meant.

Mouseketeers, he thought. *Because they're harmless as mice? But mice can chew cables and cause them to fail at the most crucial moment.*

"For want of a nail," he said aloud, the phrase floating up from his diluted memory. Something about for want of a nail the horse lost its shoe, and the king lost his kingdom? One small mistake could lead to disaster, as the Meshterek always warned. He needed to be much more vigilant this time.

Elmo reviewed the data on his adversaries, trying to make sure the Mouseketeer trap he devised would be infallible. He'd found no information on the Atlas girl before the age of five.

The Japanese boy disappeared off the grid right after his mother was murdered. *How nice it would be to meet her killer*, Elmo thought, smiling at the prospect of pursuing shared goals with a like-minded fellow.

As he worked, his mind kept harking back to the "leakage"—what Elmo called the images that flickered in the misty background of his fogged-up brain during his communications with the Meshterek.

This last time he'd seen a planet inhabited by blue-skinned chimp-like creatures. They traveled using large hand-like feet to bounce through the air in the low-gravity world they lived on. Families smiled and waved at one another mid-air, bouncing their way to picnics in the park or to see a show or get a treat. Elmo liked these creatures despite his deadened feelings and disdain for anything pleasant. They led a contented, untroubled existence—until the Meshterek showed up.

The Meshterek used conscripts like Elmo to disrupt the food system. They destroyed the water supply. They turned the planet into a desert and poisoned whatever food remained. The creatures couldn't figure out what had put them into their predicament. They couldn't find a way out either with their minds deranged by all the tainted food they'd been eating. Elmo suspected the Meshterek could've fixed things with Meshter-Tek, but why would they? They wanted to create havoc, not resolve it. Suffering sustained them.

Things fell apart. Chaos took hold and spread like a virus, worming its way into every aspect of the creatures' lives, pitting creature against creature to fight for incessantly dwindling resources. All that remained in the end were heaps of white skeletons bleached by the sun. Piles of gnawed bones sitting next to dead bonfires. Dried, leathery corpses hanging from beams like grisly ornaments decorating the tall, airy hallways of their empty cities.

The Meshterek orchestrated a mass extinction, greedily devouring every morsel of pain and suffering they caused. When it was all over? They moved on.

Elmo wondered what plans the Meshterek had for his world. He *tried* to care. But each time he examined his hollowed-out feelings, he couldn't find even the smallest crumb of concern.

CHAPTER 19

A BLACK DAY INDEED

(GAIA)

GAIA KNEW HOW the asuras had tricked them. Now she wanted to find their hiding place. She had a pretty good idea where to start. Indra had experienced a sudden terror in the split second before the asuras sprang their trap. He couldn't recall what had sparked it, but *something* had. She decided to refresh everyone's memories to see if anything useful might bubble up.

"Do you remember when Herakles arrived with Atlas?" Gaia asked Zeus. Gaia had been chatting with Zeus at the time on the sea-cliff terrace of her Aegean villa, waiting for Atlas, Herakles, and Indra to arrive. They'd all agreed to travel to the all-hands meeting together. Vishnu's retreat sat on a fast-moving asteroid that followed an unpredictable course at the outer edges of the Milky Way. They'd miss the destination unless they transported the moment the retreat sent its coordinates. "You asked Herakles about the odd yet strangely appealing outfit he was wearing."

Zeus chuckled. "I do indeed remember. The little

smart-ass whined, 'It's a suit, father. They've only been around for centuries.'"

Gaia laughed too, but she felt a twinge of anger. Herakles might joke about Zeus being so out of touch after holing up in that cave of his, always out of reach. But Gaia still harbored remnants of resentment about Zeus having abandoned her, leaving her to take care of the increasingly decrepit Greek-god populace on her own. Because *he* couldn't deal with it—because *he* couldn't accept how the lack of human adoration destroyed them little by little, year after year. Only those who still held a firm place in the human heart escaped the devastating mental and physical decay. She envied the Hindus and how they managed to stay relevant.

"Then Indra showed up," Gaia said drily. "And everything promptly fell to pieces." She laughed. She was teasing of course. She'd been dying to see him. She adored that dark hair and his devious mustache and the delicious way he could make her feel like a teen goddess again, something she hadn't felt in millennia.

"The way things always do when *I* get involved." Indra's grin dripped with self-deprecation. "I'll never forget how positively stunning *you* looked that day, my love."

She recalled him striding up to her, wrapping his arms around her and kissing her deeply. She'd blushed, feeling awkward in front of her grandsons, untangling herself from Indra's embrace and fussing with her hair as if he'd mussed it, though he hadn't.

"Remember, Indra?" she asked. "It happened the exact moment the coordinates arrived." She'd put her arm into his, gazing into those dark eyes. Instead of the tender love she'd expected, his face formed an expression of complete and utter alarm, shocking her. But it was too late. The black hole sucked them all in—viciously.

The hole pulled the first to arrive into it. Then it plugged up when an entire mass of powerful beings hit it all at once. Now it held them there, crushed and flattened, an unhappy pancake of useless immortal flesh. The danger had been far greater than they'd realized.

"A black day indeed," said Indra. "Those cunning asuras hijacked the coordinates. I *still* can't say what alarmed me. I could *feel* something was wrong, the same way I felt the asuras' presence."

Gaia's mind had been digging into her memory during the conversation, searching her own experience of that moment. She heard a mental clank, like a shovel hitting a buried treasure chest. "I remember!" she cried out, excited. "I remember what I noticed. There was a disturbance in the gravitational field right before we transported. I was too shocked to realize it at the time. It *must* be what Indra felt too!"

"By Krishna!" Indra exclaimed. "You're right! That's exactly what I sensed."

The clue didn't give them the asuras' location, but it was something to work with. It also reminded her of the one thing she'd *never* forget about that moment—the miraculous melding of her and Indra's minds the instant before the black hole sapped nearly all their powers.

CHAPTER 20

DARKNESS TAKING HOLD

(AMANDA)

"GET ME OUT of this!"

Mandy had awakened tied to a creaky metal bed in a dark room. A slant of light streamed in from a door that was ajar. She began bouncing up and down, frightened and disoriented, trying to break free.

"Let me up!" she screamed. The zip ties were rubbing her wrists and ankles raw. She kept tugging anyway.

That hideous face appeared in the doorway. It hadn't been a nightmare after all. Mandy screamed again.

"Stay away from me!"

Mandy remembered what to do with her panic. Her mother had trained her for it when she punished little Mandy by sending her to the dank, dusty crawlspace beneath the house for hours at a time with no light, food, or drink, keeping company with all the creepy crawlies she could hear and feel but not see. Mandy focused on her breathing, listening to it, feeling it. She'd calmed herself by the time the man reached her.

He set a grimy plate of chocolate mini-doughnuts and a

clear plastic cup of dirty-looking water on the bedside table. He pulled up a rusty metal folding chair and sat down on it, leaning forward.

"I'm not going to hurt you." His voice was flat, emotionless.

"I don't *care*. Let me go."

"Why would I, after I went to all the trouble of bringing you here?"

"What trouble? How did I get here?" The last thing Mandy remembered was the face's frightful laugh.

"I kidnapped you from that awful orphanage. I may have snuffed out one of those twins in the process. Here." The man gestured at the table. "I brought you some food and some water to drink in case you're hungry or thirsty."

The orphanage wasn't *awful*. It was a decent enough place compared to life with her whore of a mother. Still, she hated the twins and their fake kindness even if she never outright showed it. That one of them might be dead didn't bother Mandy at all. None of those stupid do-gooders *actually* cared about her.

She'd show this man she didn't scare easily.

"I want to know who you are and why you kidnapped me," she demanded, trying to look as tough as she could, a difficult task in her tied-up condition.

"I am simply a means. A means to achieve certain things, one of which happens to be the elimination of your best friend, the Atlas girl."

Mandy *almost* gasped but stifled it. So—this was no ordinary child-snatching. *Good.* She squinted an eye at the man, raising a brow.

"Well, well," she sneered. "It seems I'm not the only one who hates that little cow-kisser?"

"I was counting on that reaction, Miss Duggan. I believe you might be able to assist me." The man leaned back in his chair and folded his hands on his lap. "You grew up with Miss Atlas. I assume you have information about her that could be useful to me."

"Oh, I know quite a bit about that witch." Mandy felt her confidence growing. This man needed her. "Why do *you* want to get rid of her?"

"My reasons will be revealed in good time."

"I need to know. I won't help unless I'm in on it."

"What do you mean?"

"I mean, we work together. Partners. I'm not just going to play the snitch."

"Perfect." A sinister smile of crooked, yellow teeth twisted across the man's gray face, the same smile from the dorm.

This man might be a creep, but if he was going after Amaya, he could count Mandy in. Every time she tried to hurt that brown-skinned, brown-nosing butt-kisser, she avoided it. Every time Amaya avoided it, Mandy hated her even more. Then *That Day* came—the day Amaya grabbed Mandy's wrist. Mandy always suspected little Miss-Goody-Two-Shoes-On-The-Outside was pure evil on the inside. That moment proved it. Amaya used some kind of sorcery on her. Mandy decided that very night there could be only one way to break the spell. The chance may have just fallen into her lap.

But why did someone else want Amaya Atlas dead? Why would anyone care about a useless Indian girl at an orphanage in the middle of nowhere? It didn't add up. She better not trust this little troll. She better not trust anyone. "I still want to know why *you* want to get rid of her."

"Later, Miss Duggan." The man rose from his chair and began cutting the zip ties with a fillet knife he produced from a sheath attached to his belt. "Keep in mind there's only one way out of this cavern, and it's locked up tight."

"I'm pretty sure I won't be escaping *if* you're telling the truth. I'm also not about to drink the brown crap in that filthy cup or eat from that disgusting plate. You better get me a Coke and something tastier to eat, like a burger or a steak, if you want me to stick around."

"I can arrange that." The man finished untying her. "There's a change of clothes on the desk over there." He turned and walked away.

Mandy sat on the edge of the bed, rubbing her wrists. "What's your name, by the way?" she called out before he reached the doorway.

"Elmo. Elmo Grindquist," he said, his back still to her.

Most people would think Elmo Grindquist was choking or clearing his throat when he continued out the door. Not Mandy. She might even learn to like that laugh.

CHAPTER 21
PITMASTERS

(Yunosho)

SPIKE AND AMAYA got the tents ready with help from Gigi. Yunosho cleared debris from the rock-ringed fire pit—six massive boulders chiseled into throne-like chairs circling a ring of rocks for lighting a good-sized fire. A group of hunters had built the pit over a century ago. It was Yunosho's favorite spot for camping with Master Cee.

Twilight dwindled into darkness. They heated food over the fire, then sat in their boulder chairs, eating. For a pleasant moment, as he'd done on campouts with Master Cee, Yunosho imagined himself king of the forest, supping on his throne.

"Amaya." Gigi leaned back into her giant rock chair and pulled her feet up like she was lounging on a comfortable sofa instead of hard stone. "If you don't mind me asking something nosy, how'd you end up at the orphanage?"

Yunosho was glad Gigi asked that. He'd been wondering the same thing ever since Amaya hinted at the unusual circumstances under which they'd found her.

"I don't mind at all," replied Amaya.

"Let me tell that story." Spike's grin looked comically macabre in the shadowy firelight. "It's a doozy."

"The farmer who found me, Bob Peetle, loved telling it when we were little." Amaya looked like a prim and proper princess, sitting with her hands folded neatly on her lap. Yunosho couldn't stop glancing at her. Propriety might not be such a bad character trait after all. "He always told us it was the most fantastic thing that ever happened to them."

"As our resident master narrator"—Yunosho gestured with both hands at Spike—"I beg you, O Great Teller of Tales. Tell away."

Spike described how Farmer Bob and his wife Sam had been finishing up dessert on the porch of their old farmhouse when a lone lightning bolt cracked down from clear, blue skies into the cornfield, booming loud enough to shake the house. They ran into the field and found Amaya sitting there naked, eating corn cooked by lightning. The story was definitely a difficult-to-believe "doozy."

"No one tried to figure out how you got there?" Gigi asked Amaya.

Gigi's disbelief didn't surprise Yunosho. He barely believed the story himself—except Amaya had already convinced him she was extraordinary. It was one of the reasons he found her fascinating—but not the only one. Yunosho hadn't had friends for a while, not to mention girlfriends. He felt protective of all his new friends. But he felt *most* protective of Amaya. He'd joined the band because Spike and Amaya and their circumstances intrigued him. Then the boundaries of what he'd do for Amaya had disappeared pretty rapidly. He was falling for her. It was a scary. But Yunosho didn't scare easily.

"Not really," Amaya replied. "Farmer Bob and Sam aren't the kind of people to ask those sorts of questions. The twins treated me like I belonged at the orphanage. The police ran a missing-person search, but I wasn't a missing child. As for me, where would I even begin to look with the limited resources available at the orphanage?"

Yunosho suspected Amaya only feigned disinterest in her parentage. There had to be more to it. He'd read in his psychology course how even kids with parents could feel abandoned. He could only imagine how Amaya must feel. Yunosho had been fortunate compared to her and Spike. He'd had eleven precious years with his mother. After that, Cledwyn had provided him a warm place he could always call home, though Cledwyn had been a firm taskmaster and rightly so when it came to training.

"It was a fascinating story." Yunosho got up from his kingly rock throne. "We're looking at a strenuous hike in the morning. Time to get some shut-eye."

The girls agreed. They said goodnight and retired to their tent. Yunosho added more wood to the fire before joining Spike in the other tent.

Yunosho whispered to Spike, "What do you think of Gigi?" He'd noticed how Spike had been paying her an unusual amount of attention.

"Oh, she's swell. I like her."

"That's all? You *like* her?"

"Sure. I like her. Why?"

"Forget about it." Yunosho waved Spike off. Spike seemed to be succumbing to Gigi's attractiveness, smarts, and confidence. He probably didn't fully understand what was going on. Yunosho hoped for Spike's sake Gigi might feel the same.

CHAPTER 22

WHEN IS FOOD NOT REALLY FOOD?

(LAUER)

Day 5

BRETT LAUER WAS giving a tour of the public parts of the newest Mesh Industries food production facility in Ogallala, Nebraska, to Tom Faizwell, the Undersecretary of Agriculture, and Congressperson Burrai, head of the House Agricultural Technology Committee.

Faizwell had arrived at the tour gushing with enthusiasm for all things high-tech in agriculture. Mesh Industries was more high-tech than he might ever want to know. The Congressperson wanted none of it. Her district in neighboring Kansas had lots of farms, and the farmers were up in arms about the manufacturing plant. Lauer didn't give a hoot about farmers—they wouldn't be around much longer.

Three years ago, Lauer had been managing the local laundromat. Now he ran the largest food processing facility in America. He still found it disconcerting how he couldn't remember being involved with laundromats at all. He couldn't even remember doing laundry at one.

He gazed out with his guests from a second-story metal walkway into a giant, steamy production room where machines baked perfect loaves of bread that robots boxed up and robot pallet lifts loaded onto a track. The bread rolled out of impeccably clean stainless-steel ovens, cooling as it moved down the conveyors to the slicers. The slicers cut it, sprayed it with a mist, and slipped it into its plastic packaging. Lauer fed visitors who inquired about the mist the same lie he fed the FDA—flavor enhancers.

"I can't believe you make food using only water and raw materials." Faizwell wiped beads of sweat from his wide forehead with the back of his small, chubby hand.

"That's exactly what we do." Lauer purposefully didn't mention how they'd built the factory on top of the country's largest water aquifer. His factory used up water—lots of it. All the Mesh factories did. They'd built the earliest ones in the poorer parts of the world to earn a good name. Then they'd entered the more highly-regulated developed-country markets like the US. "We've eliminated animals and plants from the food production equation, factoring out weather, insects, disease, genetics, and anything else that plagues the living."

"Amazing." The Undersecretary gushed again. "To think you've already got over five hundred of these plants worldwide."

The Congressperson sneered. She obviously didn't care much for her traveling companion. "You're putting farmers out of business is what you're doing," she said, her face pinched with disdain.

Lauer wondered how much more upset she'd be if he showed her the most secret part of the factory, though he knew the Meshterek would never permit it. She'd find mixers the size of houses mixing Mesh Industries' manufactured protein with artificial fat made from mineral oil and inorganic sugar made from formaldehyde. The sugar gave the artificial meat that nice, caramelized look when you seared it.

She'd walk past an array of four aluminum vats, six stories high. A dump truck pulls up and spills its contents onto a large lift—flattened small-animal corpses, deer half-eaten by scavengers, chickens with fat, green pustules where feathers should be, bloated cows with purple-veined tumors, the flesh of their forelegs eaten away from standing in excrement all day, and young piglet carcasses covered in greasy brown lesions. The lift empties into the vat closest to the truck entrance, spraying the pile with enzymes and bacteria along the way.

Mosquito netting covers the second vat. Waves of white maggots float beneath clouds of black flies that push the netting to and fro like a dark, evil wind. Without the air scrubbers hard at work, the odor of fermented animal flesh would be overpowering. Decaying bones stick out from a bubbling green, oily goo in the third vat. And the last vat holds a fully-decomposed brown sludge, ready for processing into freeze-dried meat-flavoring crystals.

The meat mixture tastes like Elmer's glue on its own, a malady the flavoring remedies. But the meat's addictive quality comes from microdoses of a dopamine receptor—a psychotropic drug with the added benefit of driving people mad over time.

The mixer finishes. A high-pressure cannon vacuums up the fake meat and shoots it at high velocity into the stainless-steel wall of a collecting chamber, permanently binding the fat and protein molecules. Robot scrapers scrape the meat off the chamber's walls and floor and deliver it to the sculpting machine, which, with mechanical artistry unmatched anywhere on Earth, stains and forms the meat into perfect replicas of boneless aged sirloins. A conveyor moves the "steaks" into a cold room, packaging them two to a pack and labeling them in red lettering—*Hillbilly Slim's Perfectly Aged Beef Top Sirloin*. Beneath the text, a barefoot, stubble-chinned, gap-toothed hillbilly dressed in too-short coveralls holds a jug of moonshine in one hand and raises his straw hat in the other.

Lauer thought Slim looked like he was about to keel over from liver disease. That wouldn't stop masses of people from buying and eating this inexpensive, well-crafted, highly addictive meat.

CHAPTER 23

WHAT CEE SAW

(Yunosho)

YUNOSHO STOPPED AND turned to address his companions. "Almost there."

They'd started up the side of the mountain over four hours ago with Spike, the weakest, behind Yunosho, and Gigi, the strongest, at the rear, so the pace would be easier to set. "We're coming up to the plateau where Master Cee's bat cave sits. Like I said, we might need to wait until he notices we're here." The lock mechanism would recognize Yunosho and open the door if needed. But Yunosho didn't want to bring his friends into the cave without Cledwyn's permission.

"Will we have to camp another night?" Gigi was leaning on a branch she'd turned into a walking stick, worrying her lip. She'd confessed the night before she was afraid of bears after Yunosho had mentioned his run-in with them.

"Could be. Maybe even a few," Yunosho replied. "But don't worry, Jeej," he grinned, "I'll take care of any bears."

They came over the ledge onto the plateau. Gigi needn't have worried. There was Cledwyn, waiting for them, his legs planted on the ground like tree limbs in camo shorts. Deep black eyes twinkled from his big round face. The inch-long black hair that stood straight up from his head always made Yunosho imagine Cledwyn sticking his finger in an electrical socket every morning to get it that way.

"Master Cledwyn!" Yunosho ran up to hug him but caught himself and made a proper bow. Cledwyn returned the bow, then grabbed Yunosho in a bear hug and slapped him hard on the back.

"I heard yer comin' fer miles!" He held Yunosho by the shoulders. "Did yer fergets hows to be quiet, boy?"

"Sorry." Yunosho looked down at the ground and shuffled, feigning embarrassment. "I wanted to make sure you'd hear us. Wouldn't want you to think a sneak attack was headed your way."

"I sees," Cledwyn said with a chuckle. "And wid whom yer be travlin'?"

"Please allow me to introduce my friends—"

"—friends have yer *already*?"

"Yes, Master. I regret to report your years-long project to build a socially inept teenage misfit failed. Please meet my friends. First Amaya, the princess with the black birthmark on her forehead and some very special abilities."

Amaya lowered her eyes and dipped her head. "A pleasure, Master Cledwyn."

"Next, Gigi, our super-intelligent engineering prodigy." Gigi performed a dainty curtsy that looked both endearing and weirdly out of place in the woods.

"Last but not least, Spike. Amaya's best friend and stalwart protector." Spike stuck his hands in his pockets and gave Cledwyn his best "aw-shucks" look.

Cledwyn bowed, then gestured at the cave opening. "Inside

wid yer den. I'm guessin' yer'll be wantin' sometin' udder den beans ta eats."

"How'd you know about the beans?" Spike sounded mystified.

"Easy." Cledwyn's grin swallowed half his face. "Yer new pal tooted when I squeezed 'im."

Yunosho's cheeks burned with real embarrassment this time. He made an about-face and shot toward the cave's entrance. Giggles followed him, making matters worse.

They entered Cledwyn's mountain retreat through a four-inch-thick stainless-steel vault door covered in rock to hide it. It geared shut behind them with a quiet rumble. The open living area inside followed the shape of the main part of the cave, a scalene triangle.

"I'll show you your room." Yunosho was eager to share this part of his past with his new friends. "It's where I grew up." Returning to the cave after his first real absence reminded Yunosho that he hadn't grown up there by choice. Cledwyn might be the best uncle ever, but Yunosho had never stopped missing his mother. He still occasionally resented giving up his old life to hide. But resentment was the kind of feeling Yunosho was good at letting go of. Cledwyn's training dealt with physical *and* emotional limitations.

Yunosho led the girls down the hallway to the last door on the left. It opened into a spartan room with a bunk bed, desk, and chair. Four shelves stuffed edge-to-edge with real books traversed the entire wall above the desk.

"Nice book collection, Yu." Gigi ran her finger across the spines.

"I was homeschooled. I spent a lot of time at that desk pulling my hair out." The real issue hadn't been homeschooling. The lack of friends and social interaction had made life on the mountain difficult. He felt awkward around his new friends but did his best not to show it. He wasn't always confident about making decisions on his own since going off without Cledwyn as his sounding board. But under these dangerous circumstances, with inexperienced friends, it seemed best to exude confidence. Expressing self-doubt could sow seeds of discord that might sprout later at an inopportune time. He'd just have to live with it if his decisions screwed things up.

"Well, it doesn't look any worse for the wear," Gigi joked. "Your hair, I mean."

"I haven't seen any training facilities." Amaya sounded disappointed. "You told us you spent most of your time training?"

"The training room is out back in a converted part of the cavern. I'll show you later."

"Cledwyn's kind of cute." Gigi tilted her head. "Right, Amaya?"

"Yes," Amaya replied, "though I find him difficult to understand with that accent."

"Ha!" Yunosho laughed. "Look who's talking!"

शांति

They retired to the living area after supper, taking turns explaining the events of the past few days to Cledwyn. Yunosho had expected him to take everything in stride, but it surprised him that Cledwyn didn't show even a hint of disbelief, almost as if he dealt with unusual happenings on a regular basis. Maybe Yunosho didn't know as much about Cledwyn as he thought.

"That brings us to you, Master," Yunosho summed up. "We're pretty sure the dragonflies were meant to create a danger that would draw Amaya to them. I'm guessing our adversary will try to manufacture another dangerous situation."

Yunosho recognized the look on Cledwyn's face. He'd already made his decision. He grasped his thighs with his thick hands, leaned forward, and gazed directly at Yunosho, cueing him like in the old days.

Yunosho took up the cue. "Which means… we train, plan, research… and wait?"

"Exactly." Cledwyn smiled. Yunosho felt proud to be thinking like his Master. He'd already begun to think ahead. Waiting might be their only option, but they could use the downtime to figure out what the enemy might do next.

"Spike!" It was Gigi. He'd fallen asleep, and his head had dropped onto her chest. He awoke with a start, his face turning beet red.

"*Dat* means nighty-night, kiddos." Cledwyn smiled and pushed his substantial frame up from his chair. He told them to be up bright and early in the morning for training, then bowed and headed to his room. Spike whispered "sorry" to Gigi as they got up from their seats.

"No problem, Spikie," she said. "It was a tough trek. We're all tired."

"I believe I will have a superb night's sleep in a real bed for the first time in days." Amaya looked radiant. Yunosho wondered how she managed it after a long, arduous day.

"The bunks are comfortable enough," Yunosho said. "A definite improvement over cold, hard ground." Comfortable enough could be the theme of Yunosho's existence with Cledwyn. Cledwyn never let things get too easy. Yunosho's mother had raised him with a similar philosophy. They'd led a simple but comfortable life when she was alive. But with her, too, work always needed done.

"Goodnight." Amaya turned to go, tossing back her long, black hair. It glistened in the dim lamplight. Yunosho's heart skipped a beat.

Gigi followed Amaya down the hallway, imitating her by flipping back her spiked, pixie-cut hair with a quick wave of her hand. "Goodnight, boys," she said, turning her head sharply, a sly grin on her face.

Yunosho laughed. Spike didn't. He just stood there, mesmerized. Something was definitely up with that kid.

CHAPTER 24
ON THE CASE

(AMAYA)

Day 6

AMAYA TOOK ANOTHER bite of the polenta with maple syrup Cledwyn had made for breakfast. She sneaked another glance at Gigi, who was by herself in the living area, preoccupied with something on her goggs. *Why is Gigi being antisocial?* Everyone else was eating breakfast at the kitchen counter while Cledwyn cleaned up after himself at the sink.

"Guys, you need to see this." Gigi sounded urgent. She linked to Cledwyn's vidwall and pulled up a newsfeed. They spun around in their seats to watch. "It's the orphanage. I searched out of curiosity and found this from two days ago."

The footage showed the front of the mansion. The reporter announced that an intruder had stabbed Sessy Jove in the early morning hours and kidnapped one of the orphanage's young female charges.

Amaya's chest constricted. The cave dimmed. Black dots swam before her eyes. She forced a deep breath to stave off the dizziness. And that happy feeling about everything being right with the world? It fled from her like dust from a hard, dry wind, crumbling and blowing away.

The footage switched to Chief Raynor standing outside the emergency entrance to Redbird Hospital. He reassured the public the police were on the case. He described the intruder and warned everyone to be on the lookout for anything suspicious. The perpetrator had used an unusual high-tech metal-cutting device to break into the orphanage. It had sliced through the security bars like a red-hot knife through butter. The head of surgery standing beside the Chief reported that Sessy Jove remained in a coma despite the operation having gone well.

A photograph of Mandy flashed on the screen, a portrait taken last year by the school photographer, her blonde hair in the usual pigtails.

The kidnapped girl's name is Amanda Duggan. She answers to the name Mandy. Police are looking for any information that might lead to her whereabouts.

"Mandy! Someone kidnapped Mandy!" Spike cried out. It didn't surprise Amaya at all.

Nor apparently Yunosho. He glanced at her with a grim face. "She grew up with you, *and* she's your enemy."

"I know." The awful sinking feeling in the pit of Amaya's stomach unleashed a frantic round of second-guessing. Was she putting everyone she cared about in danger? Sessy's plight was surely her fault—Mandy's kidnapping wouldn't have happened if Amaya hadn't gone off in search of her parents. Maybe she should have ignored the dark disturbance. Maybe she never should have left the orphanage. Maybe she should forget about finding her parents. Maybe she wasn't cut out for her abilities. Maybe, maybe, maybe.

"The bad guys are getting ready for something," Yunosho warned. Cledwyn came out from behind the counter, nodding.

"There's no update on Sessy's condition." Gigi was still surfing. "Which means she's probably not out of the coma yet."

Amaya wiped the tears from the corners of her eyes. The panic began to subside—she *knew* what to do. She needed to improve her powers and figure out her connection to all of this before they hurt someone else she loved. A primal instinct, deep down, told her something dark and terrible had been set in motion. It was picking up steam and might not be stoppable for much longer.

"We need to get a message to the Jove sisters." The last thing Amaya wanted was for Tessy and Sessy to worry about her and Spike. Sessy would be thinking more about her missing children than herself when she came out of her coma—and Amaya believed with all her heart she would. The least they could do was tell her and Tessy they were all right.

"How about flowers?" Gigi sat up and removed her goggs. "I can order them untraceably. Have them delivered to the hospital with a card."

"That could work." Amaya appreciated Gig's helping hand. "No doubt Tessy is camped out at the hospital."

"Being Tessy, she'll read every card," Spike said, "over and over."

"We need to tell them we're fine, and we'll be looking for Mandy, without saying any of that and without revealing our names." Chief Raynor was always nice when he visited, but Amaya didn't want the authorities involved. Things were bad enough. Besides, how would they even begin to explain?

Gigi thought for a second. "The card could say, 'We're on the case.'"

"With a peacock underneath," Spike added. "Then Tessy will know for sure it's from us."

CHAPTER 25

WHAT SAYS THE VIXEN

(AMANDA)

AMANDA SLOUCHED IN the beat-up, wooden armchair, resting her feet on an overturned black-plastic wastebasket. She was bored.

They'd gone shopping for disguises. Precautions were in order now the media had broadcast pictures of her and a description of Elmo. Along with changing her appearance, she took the opportunity to reclaim her name as well. She never liked Mandy, that nickname her useless, never-satisfied wreck of a mother had called her. A name like Mandy would never command the degree of respect she deserved. Amanda was much more fitting for the sleek, smart woman she'd become.

She'd chosen a peppermint halter top with canary-yellow shorts that matched the four-inch yellow-vinyl sandal pumps she'd purchased. They dyed her hair jet black at the salon and cut it into a tapered pageboy, short in the back and long in the front. Dressing and looking this way gave her a newfound sense of confidence.

Elmo had suited up in Victorian clothing. Amanda didn't

understand his penchant for it. It looked way too old-fashioned, though anything was an improvement over how he'd been dressing.

He wore aviator goggles, khaki jodhpurs buttoned tight around the calves, and a dark-green double-breasted vest with brass buttons over a crisp white shirt. He topped it off with a brown bowler hat onto which he'd built brass gear-work around the crown's bottom. Apparently, the hat could spew a great cloud of thick, impenetrable smoke at the touch of a button on the brim, though she wondered when they might *ever* have use for such a contraption.

Elmo tinkered with the complicated gear-and-piston innards of what looked like a larger-than-human bot with eight legs and a semicircle head perched atop a disc-shaped body.

"Why are you wasting your time getting ready for Jap boy?" She examined her glossy black fingernails for flaws that weren't there. It thrilled her to be wearing *real* makeup and nail polish. "Amaya is our target."

"The boy won't have a chance against these."

"What are those going to be?" He'd lined six up on the assembly line. Amanda lifted her nose in the air. "They look like what you'd get if a spider had sex with an octopus. A Spidiepus?"

"Hmm…" Elmo gazed up at the arched ceiling. "Spidiepus. I like it."

"Why don't we just load these bots up with guns, sit back, and enjoy the show?" Amanda didn't like complications.

"I don't work with guns."

"What about that little Derringer you bought today?"

Elmo shot her an annoyed look. "A collector's purchase."

"Are six enough?" Amaya's ability to avoid danger worried Amanda. She wanted certain doom for Amaya, not maybe doom.

"Two will do the trick. The other four are the guarantee. But you, my dear, are avoiding the subject." Elmo snapped his fingers at her. "We need that weakness."

"I *told* you." Being pushed irritated Amanda. She worked at her own pace. "She evaded every one of my attacks."

"You need to get past the past." Elmo struggled with a connection on one of the machines. "There are all kinds of weaknesses. Maybe she has a germ phobia and needs to wash her hands all the time. I don't know how we'd exploit that particular weakness, but the point is to think outside the bun."

"You mean outside the box," Amanda corrected. "That's an old, old vid-ad. You're showing your age, Grindquist."

"Your job is to find a weakness in Miss Atlas, not to criticize me. As I said, there are other types of weaknesses. The Skopos boy, for instance. But we can't get to him as long as he's with her."

"Right." Amanda put her index finger to her chin. Her mind had started to engage with the problem despite her resistance to Elmo's prodding. "Maybe we could separate them?"

"You told me they're inseparable. We need a more reliable inroad."

"Maybe the Jove sisters. Amaya likes them a lot, though you've already put one in the hospital." A lightbulb came on in Amanda's head. She rocketed upright in her seat. "The Peetles! That's it! The Peetles!"

"What an exquisitely mundane name. Who are they?"

"The disgustingly nice farmer idiots who brought Amaya to the orphanage." Pure spite swelled in Amanda just talking about them. "Farmer Bob and Sam. Amaya loves those two like long-lost parents. Those dummies even wanted to adopt her."

"Why didn't they? That could be important."

"I don't know. Does it matter? Amaya will do anything if we threaten the Peetles. I bet she'd even die for them."

"Sounds promising." Elmo ran current through a Spidiepus leg. It stiffened.

The legs were a series of stacked stainless-steel pyramids, all connected by super-thin rope woven from nanofibers. According to Elmo, the rope segment could stiffen or flex depending on the charge provided to the pyramids, allowing the legs to move flexibly for fighting, stiffly for walking, or both for rolling. But Amanda hadn't cared one wit about the technical details.

"And where might we find this yawn-inducing farmer couple?" Elmo asked.

"In the countryside, not far from the orphanage. I was there once. For a field trip. It's very isolated."

"Sounding better and better." Elmo removed his hat, laid it on the assembly table, and scratched his greasy head. "We threaten the Peetles. The Atlas girl comes running, her two sidekicks in tow. One fell swoop."

Amanda was starting to like this Grindquist character. She found herself tuning right into the coldhearted strategizing like she'd been born to it.

"Isn't forewarning them a bad thing?" Amanda believed the only way to get to Amaya was by using the element of surprise. Elmo said he'd already tried that.

Elmo gestured with both hands toward the partially-built Spidiepuses. "Well, my dear, that's *exactly* what these are for."

CHAPTER 26
GIRLS' NIGHT IN

(AMAYA)

GUILT HAD PLAGUED Amaya since she'd learned of the attack on Sessy. Sessy's injury was her fault. She'd endangered Spike just by bringing him along. She was probably risking the lives of her new friends too. If the kidnapper wanted to harm others at the orphanage? How could she prevent it? She lay in the bottom bunk, unable to sleep, overwhelmed by the dreadful weight of unanticipated responsibility.

Time for the Random World, she thought. No matter what kind of day she was having, a visit to her Random World ended in a warm cocoon of deep slumber unmarred by the outside world's troubles. She recalled the day she'd first discovered it, one of the best days of her life. She'd been waiting for the Peetles to show up for their usual Sunday visit.

"They'll be here shortly, Amaya," Sessy sang out as she flitted past the doorway on her way to set up for lunch.

Not long after she arrived at the orphanage, Amaya started begging the Jove sisters for Farmer-Bob food, telling them at every supper how delicious it tasted. More than anything, she wanted to see Farmer Bob and Sam again. She'd felt enveloped in their love during the brief time she'd spent with them, and that was a big deal to little Amaya—she'd already begun to worry her real parents hadn't loved her at all.

The twins finally relented after a whole week of begging. They called Farmer Bob. He and Sam brought samples, overjoyed to see Amaya again. Tessy and Sessy fell in love with the things they grew, and Farmer Bob and Sam began delivering farm produce to the orphanage every Sunday. Amaya would wait for them on the back-porch steps, the same way she waited now.

The driveway gravel crunched. The old red truck with the wooden sideboards turned the corner, pulling around to the rear porch. Amaya ran to Sam and Bob and jumped into their arms, hugging them tightly, her heart full of love. They hugged her back just as hard.

"How's my little peach?" Bob rubbed the top of Amaya's head. "Or should I say plum since that's the fruit you love most?"

"Honey, it's so great to see you." Sam's eyes shone with happiness.

"We brought you a treat." Bob gave Amaya an exaggerated wink and grabbed a large, white bakery box from the truck's cab. He handed it to Sam. She brought it to one of the picnic tables where Amaya opened it, her eyes growing big at the sight of *four* of Sam's famous plum pies stacked in pie tins.

Amaya gasped. "My goodness! The children will be *thrilled.*" She'd make sure everyone got a taste of Sam's hard work. Sam looked at Amaya with pride, put her arm around Amaya, and hugged her again.

Amaya helped unload, carrying what her little muscles permitted. The Peetles brought food the children had grown to love—tomatoes of all shapes, colors, and sizes, tasty small white cucumbers with the thinnest skins, the biggest, sweetest, horn-shaped red and yellow peppers, the best potatoes for the fluffiest mash ever, and, of course, those yummy eggs with the pumpkin yolks.

The Peetles would sit for a spell after lunch on the front porch with Amaya, the Jove sisters, Spike, and a few of the other children, drinking sweet iced tea made with loads of lemon, the way the Peetles liked it. They talked about the orphanage, the farm, the weather, and whatever else tickled their fancy until the Peetles reluctantly pulled themselves away to get back to their chores.

Amaya always felt a pang of separation when they left. She knew it was only because of how happy she felt when they were there. To Amaya, happiness and sadness went together like the head and tail of a cat. If you saw the head coming, you knew the tail wouldn't be far behind.

Amaya settled into bed that evening, thinking how nice it would be to have more than memories, a way to retrieve your best moments as if you'd never left them behind in the past. She sometimes had trouble falling asleep. Remembering the good moments helped.

A voice whispered in her head. "Think about them," the voice said, "your best memories."

The whisperer sounded friendly enough, so Amaya did what it asked. She wandered the fields of her mind gathering her fondest memories the way a shepherd might gather tufts of wool. She focused on the memories the way the whisperer suggested. The memory wool wove itself into a tapestry of a calm sea. The whisperer told her to dive in. She did, and she fell into the tapestry's blue water, surfacing onto a sandy beach in a new world, a world the whisperer told her was her own blank canvas. She could paint memories on it any way she wanted just by imagining them, then they'd be filled with the living moments she gave them.

That night she painted purple plums with a lemon-pattern on their skins piled up high in a pie tin on a table made of lush, green, perfectly mown grass. Two high-backed white wicker armchairs sat side-by-side like the ones on the porch at the farm—but Sam and Bob were woven into the wicker of these chairs. Amaya bit into one of the plums and tasted the absolute best plum pie followed by that lemony iced tea. Bob-chair said, "Goodnight, little one," Sam-chair said, "Sleep tight, my dearest." And little Amaya fell out of her new world into a snug, delicious sleep.

"You asleep yet?"

Gigi's head popped upside down from the upper bunk, jolting Amaya out of her reverie.

"No," Amaya replied. "I wouldn't be now if I had been."

Gigi laughed. Amaya liked her laugh. It sounded so natural and unforced. Gigi grabbed the upper sideboard and swung down to the floor in one motion. "Wow! This training really works. Do you mind if I sit with you for a minute? I can't sleep."

"Of course you may." Amaya scooched up to the head of the bed with her knees up, wrapping her arms around them. "Is something bothering you?"

Gigi took up the same position at the opposite end of the bunk. She had something on her mind. "Umm… not really, but I *have* been thinking…" Gigi struggled to find her words. "Umm… you like Yunosho, right?" she asked.

"Of course." Where was Gigi heading with this? Maybe she wanted Amaya to keep her distance from Yunosho. "He's brave and helpful, though he's too informal and thoughtless sometimes. And he has that terrible bad pun habit. I'm also not sure why he teases me so much."

"You know," Gigi warned, "he only teases people he cares about. But I'm not talking about that kind of liking. I'm talking about, like, you know…" Gigi lifted her shoulders and gave Amaya a questioning glance. "In the girlfriend-boyfriend kind of way?"

Amaya blushed, praying that Gigi couldn't see it in the dim nightlight. Amaya rarely discussed personal matters with anyone. Especially *never* the whole boy-girl thing. But her instincts had been right and her jealousy justified. Gigi definitely was—or wanted to be—Yunosho's girlfriend.

Amaya crossed her legs into half-lotus and rested her hands in her lap. She wanted to establish for Gigi's sake that Amaya Atlas was in *complete* control of her emotions. "We have far more important matters than boys to think about," Amaya replied, realizing that instead of answering, she'd deflected. She was suddenly unsure what her true answer was.

Amaya had never given boys a second thought until Yunosho came along. On top of figuring out why she had powers, who her parents were, and finding them to prove they loved her, she'd also had to protect Spike from Mandy and make sure he did well in class. Besides, everyone at the orphanage felt more like siblings. Even Mandy, though she was probably the worst black sheep a family could wish for. But Amaya *had* been jealous of Gigi. She'd found the experience unpleasant, so she dismissed her new feelings. They confused her. They distracted from her mission. If Gigi wanted Yunosho to herself, it was for the best.

"It's just that… well…" Gigi hugged her knees tighter. "I don't want anything to stand between us. Yu's a good friend, but that's as far as it goes. I can tell he likes you. I'm just saying, don't get jealous of me. It'd be for no good reason if you did."

A wave of relief hit Amaya, startling her. Maybe she felt more for Yunosho than she'd realized. "I feel no disharmony with you, though I *do* envy how you handle that sensor suit in the training cave." Amaya was a prude when it came to body image, so it was a difficult admission to make. But if Gigi wanted to open up, the least she could do was return the favor in some small way.

"I can thank bullying for that." Gigi relaxed, letting go of her knees. She leaned back against the bed frame, crossing her legs in front of her. "Before I enrolled early in college, a clique of popular girls at high school used to give me a hard time about the way I dressed. They said pretty mean things about me for the longest time. Eventually, I got tired of feeling bad about myself. I decided never to let those girls *or* their nasty comments bother me again. I started dressing the way I wanted. Now I don't care what others think. As for you, I think you're just modest. It's kind of cute."

"Cute?" Amaya gave Gigi a hopeful glance. No one had ever told Amaya she was cute before other than Sam, who was more like her mother and didn't count. She liked being called that. It made her feel more like a regular female rather than some fanatic on a desperate mission.

"It's one of the things I like about you."

"I'm glad, but that doesn't make it any less embarrassing."

"You'll manage. You seem to be managing a lot these days." Gigi grabbed her toes and pulled herself forward, her expression serious again. "There is one other thing."

"What's that?" Amaya leaned forward too, her curiosity piqued. Amaya had never engaged in a girl-girl talk like this before. She was enjoying it. It felt like a kind of séance of sisterhood. But they were conjuring friendship instead of spirits.

"I don't want to step on any toes where Spike's concerned. I see how close you two are."

Spike?! Why was Gigi worried about Spike? "I would do anything to protect Spike." Amaya wanted Gigi to understand how important Spike was to her.

"That's another thing I like about you. I'm totally glad he has you by his side. He cares about you. He looks up to you too. I like Spike." Gigi grew earnest. "But I don't want you to think I'm butting in."

Amaya didn't understand Gigi's concern. Spike needed more friends. "I'm glad you care about Spike. I can't think of anything better for him than a new friend like you." She hoped that would put Gigi's concern to rest, whatever it was.

Gigi grinned, brushing her palms together. "All righty. Glad we got that out of the way. I *really* thought this was going to be an awkward conversation. It wasn't bad at all. Thanks, Amaya."

Gigi offered her hand. Amaya regarded it for a moment, puzzled, before she realized Gigi wanted to shake.

"We are… friends?" Amaya asked as they shook hands, still not completely certain what they'd talked about but very glad they had.

"For sure, Amaya. I'll be able to sleep now. Good night." Gigi grabbed the sideboard and somersaulted back up into the upper bunk. "I love this training," she whispered. She climbed beneath the covers. Her breathing deepened not a minute later, and she was out.

Amaya lay there, trying to sort through her thoughts. She liked Yunosho. But not that way. Or did she? Amaya couldn't say for sure now that Gigi had questioned her about it.

She'd been jealous of Gigi at first. Yet she felt a lot closer to her after this conversation. She remembered how much attention Spike had been paying Gigi and how he acted differently around her. Perhaps he was beginning to grow up. Wasn't that a good thing?

Amaya needed to put her thoughts aside. It was way past bedtime. *Time for the Random World*, she thought for the second time tonight. She closed her eyes and dove into the water. She'd already decided to add a new memory by the time she came up onto the shore—a Viking warrior princess. She gave the princess cobalt-blue armor that matched the color of her eyes. The princess raised a long broad sword in one hand. In the other, she held a silver shield bearing the image of a magnificent peacock. Her blue helmet had an open face. Her bright-red hair spiked out from the top of it like a Mohawk. Amaya put black motorcycle boots on her feet—and laughed.

That Gigi is something, Amaya thought.

Then she, too, fell into a deep, peaceful sleep.

CHAPTER 27

IT'S ORACULOUS

(JOE)

Day 7

JOE TRUBLY'S FAVORITE thing was to make himself useful. When Bertha asked him to find the teacher's editions of the mythology textbooks, Joe headed straight to the twins' sitting room on the third floor, the most likely place to find them. Sure enough, there they were, on the antique reading tables next to the overstuffed armchairs that faced the big picture window.

Joe snatched up the books. "Ha! Got you." He turned to go, but the pull-cord hanging from the ceiling caught his eye. He set the books back down and gazed up at the cord, itching with curiosity. Joe had often stared at the small, round attic window at the top of the tower while playing outside during recess as a young boy. He'd imagined pirate treasure or maybe the golden fleece hidden up there.

The cord was too high to reach, even for him. There had to be a tool. He glanced around the room and saw a long, hooked metal rod with a polished brass handle that had a medusa on each side of the grip.

Joe grabbed the rod and reached for the cord.

Stop! His arm froze halfway there. *You can't go up there without permission.* But something urged him on, despite knowing it was wrong. *I'm only going to peek*, he told himself. *No harm in that.*

He reached the rest of the way, hooked the cord, and pulled, bringing down a set of stairs that opened accordion-like to the floor. He climbed the wobbly stairs, peering up as he went, trying to glimpse what might lie in wait in the dimly lit attic.

He got to the top, poked his head in, and gasped. A small, wizened oak tree rose from the middle of the floor, its roots grown into the floorboards. Silver, gold, and colorful glass chimes hung everywhere in its barren branches. Joe popped through the opening into the attic, certain he'd found something more wondrous than pirate treasure—though he would've been more surprised to find only mundane things, like empty luggage and storage boxes. Joe had harbored suspicions for a while that things at the orphanage were not quite what they seemed.

An ancient-looking circular white marble bench surrounded the tree's trunk, each of its six legs carved into an Atlas holding up the bench instead of the heavens. The tree, leafless and nearly twice as tall as Joe, seemed to beckon. Joe reverently removed the blue chimney sweep cap he always wore, then stepped up to the bench and sat down on it, keeping his eye on the tree the entire time. He was pretty sure he knew what it was. He'd learned about it in Tessy's class. The oracle at Dodona in Greece had been an oak tree.

He gazed in awe at the chimes, still shocked by the tree's existence. Then his ears pricked, and he froze. He thought for sure he'd heard a tinkle, though there wasn't a hint of wind in the attic. He stilled himself, breathing quietly, listening so hard he thought he could feel the hair bundles in his ears standing at attention. Just when he thought he couldn't listen any harder, the chimes roared to life. They jumped and twisted in a fury, banging against one another so violently he would've sworn a hurricane had come raging through the attic. Joe clapped his hands over his ears, and the chimes stopped dead as suddenly as they'd started. The oracle spoke.

Not with words. With images.

Joe saw Mandy sitting in a chair in a yellow-brick cavern, talking to a ghoulish character who matched the silhouette that had rounded the corner of the orphanage the other night. Mandy looked different—she wore stylish black hair and fancy clothes.

The kidnapper was building something at a long work table. Mandy's lips formed the name "Amaya." Joe understood the message all right—Amaya was in danger!

The image disappeared. A real wind tore through the attic so hard it blew Joe off the bench.

He understood the wind's message too—*Urgent!*

He scrambled off the floor, got to the accordion steps, and slid down the rails using his hands. He pushed the steps back into the attic, then flew down both flights of stairs, almost tackling Bertha as he came hurtling around the corner on the ground floor. He stopped, breathing hard, his arms akimbo, looking down at the shorter and stouter Bertha.

"Did you find the books?" she asked.

"I sure did." Joe forced himself to remain calm. "I need you to take me to the hospital."

"The hospital? Did you hurt yourself?"

"No. I need to speak with Tessy. Right away."

"What could be so important you'd bother our dear Tessy, who's got bother enough right now?"

"I can tell you on the way, but please, hurry," Joe pleaded, recalling the oracle's butt-banging message of urgency.

"You'll have to do better than that," Bertha harrumphed.

"Amaya's in danger! We have to help her!"

Joe never shouted, so it startled Bertha as much as it did him. She sprang into action, grabbed her purse, and yelled after herself on the way out the door to Brea, who stood down the hall watching them with a bewildered look on her face. "Take over. We'll be back."

CHAPTER 28

THAT HELPLESS FEELING ALL OVER AGAIN

(JOE)

JOE RUSHED WITH Bertha up to the intensive care lobby. The nurse surprised them with excellent news: They'd moved Sessy to the general ward. She'd awakened from her coma.

"Oh, goodness gracious me." Bertha's round face lit up with a wide horse-toothed smile.

They took the stairs down a floor, then tiptoed down the hall. They found the room and peeked in to see Tessy sitting at the side of Sessy's bed, speaking in a low voice and holding onto one of those small floral greeting cards that come with flowers. Bertha rapped on the door jamb. Sessy glanced over, a smile spreading across her face as soon as she saw who it was. Tessy frowned.

"Bertha and Joe," she scolded. "What are *both* of you doing here? Brea can't possibly manage the orphanage on her own."

"Now, now, sis." Sessy's voice was raspy and out of breath. "I'm sure they've good reason."

"You're right, Sess. But *you* need to give your lungs a rest. Bertha and Joe, come sit and tell us what could be so important you'd leave the orphanage in Brea's hands."

Joe and Bertha sat in the chairs along the wall. He hadn't expected a warm welcome. He knew Tessy would be more concerned about Sessy's recuperation than anything else. But there was no getting around the fact—they needed to hear the message.

"I'm thrilled to see you up, Miss Sessy." Bertha clutched her purse on her lap. She couldn't stop beaming. "There isn't any better news in the whole wide world."

Joe felt the same way. Even more so. Bertha hadn't experienced the terror of seeing Sessy lying motionless with a knife sticking out of her back. To have her sitting up and talking like this again gave Joe hope for them all, Amaya included.

"Thank you, dear," Sessy whispered.

"Sess, *please* stop talking," Tessy demanded. "Why don't you mouth the words instead? We'll understand." Sessy gave her a thumbs-up.

"Go ahead, Joseph." Bertha patted his knee. "He made me bring him here, going on about Amaya being in danger and how he needs to speak with you straight away."

"Amaya?" Tessy asked. The sisters glanced at one another, a discrete communication seeming to pass between them. "We were just talking about her. What about Amaya?"

"You're going to be angry with me." Joe had betrayed their trust by going up into the attic without permission. He was prepared to accept the punishment for it.

"Don't you worry about that right now." Tessy looked tired and thinner, and she had dark circles under her eyes. "Go ahead and tell us."

"Yes, ma'am." Joe described how the attic drew him in.

How he guessed it was the oracle of Dodona when he saw the tree, and how it gave him the message. Tessy was so delighted he recognized the real oracle that Joe thought for a moment she was going to come over and stick a shiny gold star on his forehead. He didn't dare ask how the Jove sisters came to have an ancient Greek oracle in their attic, even if that was what he wanted to know most. He was still dizzy from all that had happened. The oracle's existence only added to the already disjointed feeling of stepping into some fanciful alternate unreality.

"Joseph, there's no call to be ashamed," Tessy said. "No doubt the oracle chose you. It wanted to give *you* that message for a reason."

"Still…" Joe knew, whatever the reason, it had been wrong to go up there.

Tessy shushed him again. "The oracle wants us to help Amaya, to warn her somehow."

Joe didn't have any idea where Mandy and the "ghoul" were. It seemed clear they were hatching some kind of dangerous scheme together.

No one knew how to find Amaya and get a warning to her. The twins also feared Mandy's kidnapper would exert a terrible influence on an already troubled child.

Tessy sighed. "I feel helpless for the second time in a week. What are we to do?"

"I have an idea." Joe had been thinking it through on the way to the hospital.

Hope grew in Tessy's eyes. "What is it?"

"I don't know of a way to warn Amaya, but I could research the cave. There can't be too many yellow-brick caverns around."

"Go on." Tessy seemed eager to hear more. "I can tell that's not all."

"I thought maybe I could sit at the oracle every day at the same time for an hour or so. The message felt incomplete. The oracle might tell us more."

"Joseph Trubly." Tessy clapped her hands. "What a *wonderful* plan. I feel much better."

"Me too," Sessy mouthed, pointing at herself and grinning from ear to ear.

CHAPTER 29

A PAT ON THE BACK

(AMANDA)

"YOU OKAY?" AMANDA asked.

Not that she cared, but Elmo's behavior worried her. She had to work with the man after all.

He reclined in his creaky, wooden chair. His eyeballs rolled around under closed eyelids. His gray skin had turned purple and blotchy, and his arms had lifted off the chair's armrests. Amanda sat on a desk, swinging her legs side to side, watching with morbid fascination. Either he couldn't hear, or he was ignoring her. The man might be disgusting, but she couldn't stop looking.

That creepy smile spread across his face a minute later. He opened his eyes. "Sometimes you feel like a nut. Sometimes you don't."

"What crap are you spouting now?" These gross spasms of his convinced Amanda he was way more than freaky. "You might not feel like a nut, but you sure act like one."

Elmo sat up and wiped drops of maroon blood from his nostrils with his kerchief. "I'm communicating with the lords."

"Lords?" This was the first she'd heard of anyone else being involved in their plot. Who were they? How was he communicating with them? By simply sitting in a chair?

"The Meshterek, the ones who commanded me to undertake this Atlas-girl project. They're pleased with our progress."

"I didn't see *or* hear anyone. Where are they?" The same eerie feeling came over Amanda again, like when the police took her away the night they'd arrested her mother—something momentous and life-changing was taking place.

"I don't exactly know. But they're powerful beings. They might eventually let you commune with them too. If you're a good little girl."

Powerful beings?! It took Amanda's breath away. Those ditzy Jove sisters always insisted their stupid gods were real. Amanda had attributed their insistence to age-related derangement. Now here was independent verification—greater forces might be at work. Amanda would need to be extra careful until she figured out who these Meshterek were and how they fit into the picture. The Meshterek were obviously using her and Elmo, which called for a healthy dose of caution.

"What did you mean with that little ditty about being nuts?"

Elmo sighed. "Only a memory. I don't have many. They're one of the few things that give me real pleasure when they pop into my head."

She gave him a sullen look. "You're weird, Grindquist. What's next?"

"We're leaving. It's time for our little drama to play out." Elmo walked over to the long table over which he'd draped a black cloth to conceal the final stages of his work. "Our Spidiepuses will deal with Japanese boy once and for all." He pulled the cloth away.

Amanda may have found his whole Spidiepus idea dumb,

but the finished product was impressive—six robots with disc bodies clad in scale-like Samurai armor, each suit a different color. Their semicircle heads wore color-coordinated Samurai helmets decorated with brass horns sticking out like large eyebrows. Their copper goggles glowed purple inside, giving them an eerie, diabolical look.

"My, my." Amanda hopped off the desk and sashayed along the work table, looking them over. "You've made Samurai Spidiepuses."

"Yes, indeed. They can roll, jump, walk, crawl, push, punch, slice, stab, and parry. I've armed them with Victorian infantry swords with fish skin grips, long Indian katar punching daggers decorated with elephant heads, and seven-inch, razor-sharp, rotary saws. Our young Japanese friend will be quite unpleasantly surprised."

Amanda remained outwardly cool and calm despite the whitewater rapids of adrenaline streaming through her veins. Her mind had seized on a plan.

"I can't wait," she said through gritted teeth.

CHAPTER 30

A PICNIC DOWN MEMORY LANE

(AMAYA)

Day 8

CLEDWYN ANNOUNCED A day off. Amaya secretly breathed a sigh of relief. She could use one. The training's intensity had begun to wear on her.

Gigi and Spike decided to stay in to search for Mandy and her kidnapper. Yunosho convinced Amaya to go on a picnic. She knew he wanted to discuss something. She only hoped the conversation wouldn't be as confusing as the one with Gigi. Amaya needed to clear up confusion in her life right now, not add to it.

She left Cledwyn's cave with Yunosho in the afternoon. The day was sunny with a cloudless, blue sky overhead. They hiked to a mountain meadow, where they laid out the picnic blanket Cledwyn had given them to use. Yunosho unpacked the basket. Amaya closed her eyes and tilted her head toward the warmth of the sun, losing herself in the buzz and whir of insects and the scent of wild meadowsweet in the air.

"A good day for the Random World," she whispered to herself.

"What's a Random World?"

Amaya blinked open her eyes, startled to hear another voice. She'd lost herself so much she'd forgotten she wasn't alone.

"Um… yes… the Random World." She stammered and looked down, picking imaginary lint from her jeans. She hadn't intended to bring up a subject as private as the Random World. Or had she? "It's a place I visit that's filled with memories."

"Like a dream world?"

"No. It's real, but only part of me goes there. A kind of avatar."

"How can you have a real place filled with memories?"

Amaya shrugged. "I don't know. I think it was a gift."

"A gift? A gift from who?"

"A gift from *whom*," Amaya corrected, noting to herself that Yunosho and Spike would make equally poor grammarians.

Yunosho chuckled. "I guess you can't help it. Okay, from *whom*?"

"One night, when I was little, I lay in bed reminiscing about an especially good day, and a voice in my head guided me there."

"You do realize how hard that'd be to swallow coming from anyone other than you." Yunosho gazed up, like he was trying to picture the Random World in his head. "So it's a place where you can walk around and *see* all of your best memories?"

Yunosho was eager to understand. And she wanted him to, despite her earlier misgivings. Here was a chance to open up instead of obsessing about her mission. She liked Yunosho. Why not let him into her personal space for an afternoon?

"Not only see them. I can form mementos in the Random World. When I interact with the memento, it recreates the original experience but anew."

"A kind of memory time machine?"

"That's a good way to describe it. But it's more than that. It's a living, breathing world where memories take on lives of their own. Maybe it would help if I told you about creating one of my favorites during a shopping trip."

शांति

The bus pulled up to the curb in downtown Redbird. A babble of excited talk rose from the young passengers as they disembarked and formed groups. Amaya joined Spike and the other bookworms in the bookstore group, feeling a big *Yes!* of relief when Mandy and her friends headed in the completely opposite direction toward the department store. Amaya had been looking forward to a day without them.

Amaya's group buzzed with book chatter on the way to the store. They bustled through the double doors together, eager to explore the shelves and see the new displays. Amaya dragged Spike to a cartoon-like poster with "RiRii" emblazoned across the top in bold blue letters. A thin girl in a blue jumpsuit sat at the counter of a small, cozy diner, happily slurping up noodles with chopsticks from a porcelain bowl. She had her honey-brown tied in a high ponytail. She wore a tan leather headband stamped with a golden symbol that looked like a "Z" tottering on an upside-down "V." Her fingernails looked like clouds.

"What's this, Minxie?" Spike was antsy. She knew he wanted to get to the sci-fi section. He'd made her swear to go there with him.

"I overheard some girls call this anime on our last trip. They seemed quite enthusiastic about it."

Spike shuffled his feet and muttered under his breath. "I guess it can wait."

A gum-chewing clerk in a ruffled, black tutu was busy arranging shelves in the middle of the aisle.

"Excuse me, Miss," Amaya interrupted her. "Do you know much about RiRii?"

"Sure." The girl popped a bubble. "It's a reissue of an older manga and anime series. It's hugely popular again."

"What's manga?" Spike asked.

"Manga is a kind of comic book from Japan," replied the girl.

"What's anime?" Spike asked.

"Anime is the vid version of manga," she replied.

"What does RiRii mean?"

"RiRii is the name of the girl on the poster."

"Why's she eating noodles?"

"Those are udon. A kind of Japanese noodle. RiRii is *crazy* about udon."

"Spike, *please*." If Amaya didn't stop him, he'd pester the poor clerk to death with his endless questions. "I want to hear RiRii's story, not just about the poster."

"Sorry." Spike gave her a sheepish look. "You know how much I like comic books."

"I could tell you one of the stories if you want," the clerk offered. "I'm pretty familiar."

"We would love that," Amaya said. The clerk's eyes lit up. She had to be a fan.

The clerk began. "RiRii's mother was a world-renowned Hungarian scientist who worked alongside RiRii's Japanese scientist father at a particle accelerator lab outside of Tokyo. An evil, anti-science, ninja anarchist group known as Lupae assassinated her parents when RiRii was still a small child. It was part of their global campaign to create chaos in the scientific community. RiRii ends up in the care of a kindly old benefactor named Sal, who trains her in the martial arts from an early age."

Spike had fallen completely silent, listening with rapt attention. He not only enjoyed telling a good story—he loved hearing one as well.

"Sal discovers the particle accelerator had genetically mutated RiRii's mother. The mutation amplified itself in RiRii, giving her the power to manipulate the most basic form of energy in the universe—" The clerk paused for effect. Then she said, "Rudimentum," in a mysterious voice. "The only external manifestation of RiRii's power is that she has what appear to be clouds for fingernails. You'd have to look closely to see they're not just painted on.

"Sal helps RiRii learn to control and use her power. She struggles with it. But circumstances force her to make real-world use of her power. One day, five Lupae ninjas attack during a walk with Sal in the woods on his estate. They try to kidnap her. Sal and RiRii fight back. One of the ninjas stabs Sal, wounding him." The clerk imitated someone stabbing her abdomen.

"Sal falls to the ground, clutching his side. RiRii *leaps* in front of him to protect him." The clerk threw out her open palms. "All five ninjas come at her like a human wall. The threat of further harm to Sal causes her power to surge.

"RiRii looks at her fingers." The clerk gazed down at her own fingers, wriggling them. "The clouds on her nails grow long. They merge with one another. Bolts of electricity crackle from her fingertips. She presses her palms together. A shimmering ball of energy forms, floating in front of her. She *snaps* her palms apart, and the ball hurtles toward the ninjas.

"*Boom*!" The clerk threw her hands up.

"The ninjas explode, disintegrating into millions of colorful particles. The particles spin into a tall, thin vortex that reaches up high into the sky, sucking all sound out of the air. The vortex suspends for a moment, hanging in the dead silence. Then *whoosh*!" The clerk threw her hands at the floor. "The particles crash to the ground and dissolve, bubbling into the earth. The forest feels cleansed. The air smells sweet. The birds take up singing as if spring has just sprung. RiRii rushes to Sal's side. But it's too late. He tells her it's up to her now. She must find and destroy the evil Lupae. Then he dies in her arms."

"Very dramatic." Amaya meant the story as well as the clerk's energetic storytelling. "I like that story. Thank you for telling it to us."

"Me too," Spike interjected. "I mean, me too, I liked the story and me too, thank you."

They thanked the clerk one more time, then wandered off to the sci-fi section, talking about pooling their allowances to buy the first few RiRii manga on the next trip. One of Amaya's admirers, six-year-old Claire, ran up to them.

"Minxie! Look what Miss Sessy bought me. Do you think we could play checkers? Please?"

Claire held a beautiful, antique, black-and-white chessboard in her small hands. Sessy had surely purchased the board for everyone's use. Amaya smiled at Claire and said, "Of course. I would love to."

Amaya and Claire played checkers during the ride back to the orphanage, the board on the seat between them. Spike peered over the seatback, giving a play-by-play analysis as if he were a sports announcer. Claire giggled a lot. She kept telling

Spike, "You're funny." And he was. They laughed so hard and had so much fun, Amaya didn't want the trip to end.

Under the covers later that night, Amaya thought about the wonderful day she'd had, especially because Mandy hadn't figured into it at all. Amaya closed her eyes and dove into her Random World, the same way she did every night, good day or bad.

This time she added RiRii to the Random World, but her RiRii wore a black-and-white checked jumpsuit and had checked sneakers on her feet. She had her own brand-new, bright and airy udon shop too. Checkerboard RiRii leaned over from behind the shop's counter, about to tell Amaya something *very* important. The last thing Amaya heard as she drifted off to sleep was, "Isn't udon the *Best. Thing. Ever*?!"

"I re-experience that day with Spike and Claire but anew when I visit Checkerboard RiRii in the Random World," Amaya said. "The same feelings but always fresh, as if for the first time again."

"It sounds totally unbelievable, like so many other things about you. But I have a much better sense of what you mean. How do you get into this world?"

"I quiet my mind and go there, like a mini-meditation."

Amaya suddenly had an idea, more than likely a bad one. She blurted it out before she could stop herself. "I *might* be able to bring you with me. You could see for yourself."

She felt like she was freefalling after stepping off a cliff. The idea of visiting the Random World with Yunosho exhilarated her. Maybe she hadn't wanted to stop herself.

"How?" Yunosho sounded eager.

"You could try tuning into my wavelength while we meditate. With all the training I've been doing, we might be able to connect in a way that lets you follow me in."

"Do you really think so?"

"We can try. Let me see." Amaya thought for a moment. "We'll need to sit back-to-back in lotus position. That way, you'll be in contact with my aura, and we can synchronize our breathing."

"You would know better than me."

"Better than *I*," Amaya corrected.

Yunosho laughed. "That's how I'll *always* be able to tell real-Amaya from evil-clone-Amaya. I'll use incorrect grammar."

Amaya wrinkled her nose at Yunosho's joke. He teased her a lot. As bad as his jokes were, they did help put her at ease. Maybe she shouldn't be so hard on him. She moved into lotus position in the middle of the picnic blanket.

"This is going to be fun." Yunosho slid into position behind her.

"You need to take this seriously and focus. We can't afford any excitement if we want this to work."

"I'll manage."

Amaya closed her eyes. "When you see an ocean, dive in."

She didn't need Cledwyn's lab equipment this time. She could see the tendrils of her aura form and coil even with her eyes closed. They reached out like thin vines and wrapped around Yunosho, a far more physical experience than she'd expected. She emptied her mind.

Light came out of the emptiness, a wide beam cutting through the dark, rushing toward them. It slid under them and whisked them forward. They rode the light like two shimmering surfers, the beam traveling faster and faster. Amaya's consciousness blurred. Speed, light, and emptiness folded into one another again and again until, with a tremendous flash, space and time collapsed. She tumbled with Yunosho weightless into a deep black space hanging above an expanse of bright blue ocean. Amaya dove in. She surfaced, Yunosho right behind her, out of gently lapping waves into the early evening cloudiness of a warm summer rain.

They were in!

Yunosho threw up his hands, a big grin on his face. "You did it! I shouldn't be surprised, given what you showed us back in the lab. This place is amazing! Look at that sky!" He spun around, his neck craned, gazing up at a collage of skies. A sunny, cloudless, azure-blue sky. A rapidly darkening sky where powerful charcoal-gray clouds flashed long, jagged lines of lightning. An inky-black sky stuffed full of stars as if someone had taken a pointillist paintbrush dipped in starlight to a black canvas.

"When you step under a sky, you experience the memory that goes with it," Amaya explained.

"Memories are what I felt when we arrived? It was you, your feeling? It felt like my own feeling. The joy of warm rain falling on me in the twilight."

"It is your own. The Random World regenerates the past inside you. It's the same feeling experienced anew in this time and this place. That rain is a memory from two summers ago when a sudden downpour caught me in the yard."

Yunosho's head bobbed up and down. "Okay. I *definitely* get it."

They walked past the Peetle chairs. Bob-chair said, "How's my little plum?" Sam-chair said, "It's so good to see you, honey." Amaya knew Yunosho was tasting plum pie and lemony iced tea and feeling the Peetles' love and affection.

"It's the Peetles! But they're chairs!"

"My mind builds the Random World randomly. The memory takes the form it has at the time I create the memento. Many of these memories are from when I was much younger, and since I am usually falling asleep, the memories tend to jumble together, like in dreams."

Amaya purposefully steered Yunosho away from the newest addition to the Random World. Instead, she led him to a sitting room where two laughing tulips played cards across a flat piece of white quartz. Their upside-down flowers, one pink and one yellow, looked like dresses. Heads with identical faces and bubble-cut silver-gray hair topped the stems.

"The Jove sisters would play cards most Friday evenings. Sometimes they let me stay up late to watch."

"How'd you figure out you could create these living memories?"

Amaya looked around as if seeing it for the first time too. Each memento took up its own distinct space, moving galactic-like around the others—turning, spinning, and revolving yet always grounded by the observer's point of view. There was the popcorn field shooting rainbow-colored popcorn into the air and a brightly lit merry-go-round where all the horses had happy children's faces. To the left, a bowling ball Spike hit a strike against ten blond-haired, pigtailed pins. Across the way, children slid on taffy sleds down the slopes of an ice-cream-cone-mountain covered in sprinkles and chocolate-fudge stripes.

"Whoever made this world included the ability to create these mementos. I already knew how to do it when I first arrived."

They stepped under a jack-o'-lantern moon into chilled air, clouds of moist, warm breath, and the excited anticipation of candy-filled pumpkins. Yunosho's eyes met Amaya's. It sent a warm current through her every nerve, making her hand want to reach out, to touch his cheek, caress his skin. He looked away before she could, and she felt oddly relieved. Had her own desire frightened her?

"What's that door?" Yunosho pointed at a small oval door standing on its own, suspended in space. A delicate wreath of forest ferns carved into the teakwood encircled five silver lightning bolts that struck out from a silver skeleton key. A powerful feminine arm thrust forward from the key's heart-shaped bow, ending in a key bit shaped like a fist.

"I don't know. It's the only thing that's been here since the beginning, other than the ocean and the beach. I've never succeeded in removing the key from the wood to open it."

"What do you suppose is in there?"

"I believe something I might have need of later. Otherwise, why would someone go to the trouble of putting it here yet not permit me to open it?"

"Very mysterious." Yunosho stepped up to the door and ran his fingers over the wreath, looking intently at the door's construction. "The wood and the silver appear to be fused together, almost as if the wood *grew* the silver."

"That's why I believe the key is not a real key but a message."

"You mean the key is inside this door? A key piece of information?"

Amaya grew guarded talking about the door. She believed the Random World and her parents were connected, especially that door. No one, not even Spike, knew how desperately Amaya wished to find them. She hadn't wanted to reveal quite this much of herself to Yunosho.

At the same time, a frightening thought occurred to her—her real body was sitting outside in an open field. Could it still sense danger out there? If Yunosho could get into the Random World, what about the forces that wanted to destroy her?

"It's time we returned," Amaya said abruptly. She'd already retreated into herself.

"Well, I did want to talk to you about something, and it is a little distracting in here." The sudden change in Amaya's attitude must have thrown Yunosho off balance. Amaya ignored it. She dismissed her earlier feelings for him. This trip to the Random World had convinced her—they would only get in the way.

"I normally wake up, and I'm in the real world again," Amaya said, "I think I'll need to break the bond we created to get us back now."

Amaya closed her eyes. She drew all the tendrils of her aura back into herself until only a slight glow remained. She took three quick steps away from Yunosho, felt a light snap, and opened her eyes to find herself still sitting back-to-back with Yunosho in the meadow.

They turned to face one another. "Minxie, that was incredible!" Yunosho was eager to talk. Amaya just wanted to get the conversation over with. She'd ridden enough of an emotional rollercoaster for the day.

"About what did you wish to speak?" she asked flatly.

Hurt flickered behind Yunosho's eyes. "You don't beat around the bush, do you?"

"Hunters beat around the bush to flush out prey. I seem to be the prey right now."

"Exactly why I wanted to talk to you. You're in danger."

"I'm aware of that." It occurred to Amaya that Yunosho had brought her out here to offer his help, not discuss difficult personal matters. She was being too hard on him again. She felt terrible about it. The whole situation with Yunosho was so frustrating—and confusing. Nothing she did around him seemed to come out right. "I think about it all the time."

"You have too much on your shoulders."

"I've put all of you in danger. Poor Sessy. And Spike—I should have left the orphanage without him." The regret she felt about dragging Spike along nagged at her constantly.

"Spike's like your little brother. He's highly protective. He never would've let you leave without him."

Yunosho was right. Spike would've followed her no matter what. She could never have left him alone with Mandy. Sending him back wasn't an option, either. He'd never go. But she couldn't protect him alone, not out here with someone trying to kill her. She'd known she was going to need help, dedicated help, ever since the attack. That's why she'd agreed to let Yunosho join them in the first place. Now the time had come, the time to ask the most difficult thing. Gigi said Yunosho might have feelings for her, and it seemed he was eager to protect everyone. Why else would he have joined them if he didn't think he could help and if he hadn't liked her and Spike? But this would be a big step. She didn't know how he'd react.

She put all the gravity she could muster into her voice. "Yunosho, I need you to promise something."

"About Spike?" Yunosho seemed to know what was coming.

"Yes. I worry about Spike getting hurt. Or worse. I want you to promise to keep him safe, whatever it takes." Amaya's breath caught, afraid of his reaction.

Yunosho answered without hesitating. "I'll keep both of you safe, Amaya."

"No." Amaya banged her fist on her knee. "If it comes down to it, you must save Spike. I need you to promise."

This time, Yunosho did hesitate. He thought for a moment, his face more solemn than she'd ever seen it. Then his expression changed. He'd decided. His eyes locked with Amaya's. "I promise. I will give my life if I must."

"Thank you." Her voice cracked, and she looked down, grateful and embarrassed for having asked.

He changed the subject right away, probably to spare her the awkwardness of the moment. She was grateful for that as well. "Listen, I've been thinking about this since we first got here. About what could be coming down the pike for you. This kidnapper took Mandy hoping to discover your vulnerabilities. He has to be aware of your E^2 powers because he designed the dragonfly attack to exploit a potential weakness. Send enough dragonflies, and you wouldn't be able to keep up."

Amaya tossed a defiant look at Yunosho. "Except he was wrong." She'd be ready for the kidnapper this time. They'd find him. They'd stop him before he hurt anyone else.

"He was. And he wasn't. You needed more energy than you had at the time to thwart the attack. Your system couldn't keep up. It's why we're training."

"I'm stronger now."

Yunosho nodded. "I think the kidnapper is looking for weaknesses that have nothing to do with your power. He'll try to create a situation where you won't be able to use it. Let's start with the standard vulnerabilities. The biggest would be the people you care about."

"The people I care about," Amaya repeated. She thought about Yunosho's mother and Mr. Oniki and how hard it must have been for him to lose them. She didn't know how she'd ever cope with a loss that devastating. The mere possibility of losing Sessy had sent her into a tailspin.

"Let's go through the list. The Jove sisters, the Peetles, maybe other children at the orphanage?"

"The four of you, but we're all together." An electrical jolt hit Amaya between the temples. She *knew*.

"It's the Peetles!" She sprang up, wild with terror.

Yunosho pushed to his feet, his brow knitted. "Wait. Slow down. How can you be so sure?"

"I sensed it. We have to go. Now!"

CHAPTER 31
A PELL-MELL RUSH

(SPIKE)

AMAYA BURST INTO the living area. "We need to go!"

Spike jumped up, startled. Amaya hurried to her room. Yunosho came through the door after her, blowing past Spike and Gigi without saying a word. It felt like a wave of panic had come crashing through the cavern.

Gigi and Spike followed Amaya to the guest room. She was hastily stuffing her belongings into her backpack.

"Hurry!" she said.

"Minxie, *what is it*?" Spike asked.

Amaya glanced up, glaring at them as if to say, *Why are you two just standing there?* The second her eyes met Spike's, the anger drained from her face. She broke down into sobs. Spike rushed to her side with Gigi. They hugged Amaya. Then Gigi took her by the shoulders and looked her in the eye.

"Tell us." Gigi gave Amaya a comforting nod.

Amaya brushed the tears away. She'd already started pulling herself together, the way Spike knew she would, the way she always did.

"The Peetles are in danger. They're going to threaten them to get to *me*."

The news didn't surprise Spike. If anyone wanted to get to Amaya, the Peetles would be the place to start. He wanted to tell Amaya everything would be okay, that they'd stay by her side and protect the Peetles. Yunosho appeared with Master Cledwyn at the doorway before he could.

"Master Cledwyn and I think all of you should wait here while we go make sure the Peetles are safe."

"I will *not* wait here." Amaya's voice trembled with defiance. "My power could help save them. Besides, the kidnapper wants *me*. If I'm not there—"

"We're going too," Spike declared. "We're the Band of Murugan. We're sticking together."

"I dunnot like it." Master Cledwyn cast a doubtful eye toward them. "But time's a' wastin'. Five minutes. Out front."

Master Cledwyn returned to the training cave. Spike and Gigi packed their belongings and went outside with Amaya to wait.

Yunosho followed a minute later, carrying his backpack with two swords strapped to it. "We're as ready as we can be. Did you sense anything else useful?"

"No, only urgency." Amaya's voice was clear and firm now. Spike didn't think she was going to allow herself to lose control again.

"You realize we're walking into a trap?" Yunosho said.

"I understand. I'm prepared to die if it can save the Peetles."

Yunosho's jaw stiffened. "We're not going to let *that* happen."

"That's right, Minxie," Spike agreed. "No way." He'd do everything in his power to keep Amaya safe. He already owed her his life at least ten times over.

Master Cledwyn came out carrying a black aluminum case

and his broadsword. He handed each of them a small flashlight and motioned for them to follow. They descended at a good clip. By late night, they'd reached the beginning of the trail. A black, off-road vehicle waited. They crammed their stuff into the back and raced off. It felt like they were driving into a dark void with the dangerous and unknown threatening from all directions.

The time had come for Spike to grow up. He wasn't sure he was ready.

CHAPTER 32

ENDURING FLEETING THINGS

(AMAYA)

Day 9

APPREHENSION GRIPPED AMAYA'S heart. "We're too late." Her senses had picked up a vision of the Peetles in their barn, their wrists bound behind their backs and their ankles zip-tied to the legs of their chairs.

The band of friends was only a few miles from the farm. She'd struggled to connect during the drive, trying to see what was happening there. She'd made progress with her power, but she'd never been able to slip into the entanglement at will, not even under Cledwyn's laboratory conditions. So the sudden glimpse of the barn had taken her by surprise.

Yunosho turned in his seat, his forehead creased. "What do you mean?"

"They have the Peetles tied to chairs in the middle of their barn. The man who took Mandy sits in front of them. He's dressed in Victorian clothing. Mandy sits off to the side on a bale of straw, keeping watch on the driveway. She has black hair now, and she's wearing loud clothes. She and the Victorian man are working together. They both have knives. They're waiting for me."

Yunosho squinted at her. "That's not good news."

"What should we do?" Spike sounded lost.

"They'll be expecting me," Yunosho said. "The dragonfly that escaped had a cam. They'll be expecting you too, Spike. Mandy will have told Victorian man you're with Amaya. But they won't know about Master Cledwyn or Gigi. They could sneak up the other side of the barn."

Cledwyn nodded.

Amaya didn't like what she was hearing. She'd known what needed done the moment she'd seen the Peetles tied to those chairs. "We're here to save the Peetles. I will give myself up."

Yunosho glared at her. "We can't let you do that."

Amaya harrumphed and pushed back into her seat. She wasn't going to argue. She was going to give that little man what he wanted. Whatever the reason, he wanted her.

"Drones up ahead," Gigi reported. She'd been monitoring electronic activity, linking her goggs to Cledwyn's vehicle systems.

"How many?" Cledwyn asked.

"Two."

"How close?"

"Over the farm."

Cledwyn slowed the vehicle. "Kin yer hack 'em?"

Gigi's fingers pecked rapidly at the air in front of her, typing like mad. "I need a minute. Finding my way in."

"You need to prevent them from seeing Master Cledwyn and you," Yunosho said.

"Understood," Gigi replied. "The tracking function runs

remotely. I can't disable it without giving myself away. The drone at the farm gate is a sentry. It'll only track this vehicle, so I can leave it alone. I'll disable the other drone's movement alarm, delay its vid, and install a cloning function to erase us before the vid leaves the drone. The drone will still track us but only show field and woods."

"Make it so," said Cledwyn.

"Star Trek," Gigi whispered. "Cool."

Amaya wondered what a difficult journey through the stars had to do with anything.

ॐ (Yunosho)

Cledwyn pulled off the road behind the cover of trees and bushes. They had a little over a mile to go. The dismal grayness fit the grim mood Yunosho couldn't seem to shake. They exited the vehicle and sat on the ground together, staring at the topographical and aerial hologram Gigi had pulled up using Cledwyn's sci-phone, which kept track of the drones' positions as well.

"The farm is over that knoll." Amaya pointed across the road. "The barn sits on top of the next rise, parallel to the road. Unless someone is watching, they won't see anyone coming from behind. The Victorian man sits not six feet from Sam and Bob. He literally could be at their throats in a second."

"Can we take him out?" Yunosho asked Cledwyn.

"Da barn be too high."

The setup bothered Yunosho too. "It's too chancy. There's Mandy to consider as well. Do you think she might go after the Peetles if we take out Victorian guy?"

"Mandy is capable of anything." Amaya's message came

through loud and clear: *Don't discount Mandy.* "She detests the Peetles."

"Well, we have a few surprises for them," Yunosho said. "Gigi, Master Cledwyn, and whatever's in the case."

Cledwyn patted the case. "Piercer n' Snipe."

Yunosho nodded. Snipe was Cledwyn's carbon-fiber, breakdown rifle. Piercer, a wide-barreled pistol, could take out hard targets with explosive, armor-piercing rounds. But hitting human bone could detonate the explosives too, injuring or possibly killing anyone nearby.

"We will *not* put the Peetles in further danger." Amaya was adamant. "I will give myself up."

Yunosho tried reasoning with her. "Look, Amaya, Victorian guy probably plans to kill you and them as well. Probably all of us."

"We will make the exchange." Amaya crossed her arms, glaring at him. "*Your* job is to get the Peetles out of harm's way."

"The exchange won't work." Their adversary, no matter the pretense, ultimately had only one thing in mind. He'd designed those dragonflies to kill, not injure. "That creep has seen you and me in action. He'll have something up his sleeve, something better than dragonflies."

"Things shall pass as they may." Amaya wasn't going to budge despite knowing the risks.

It frustrated Yunosho. But he couldn't fault her for it. He remembered her intense love for the Peetles in the Random World. Talking her out of the exchange might be hopeless, but at least he could steer things in a safer direction. "Okay. If we're doing it your way, we need to do it right. Master Cledwyn and Gigi will be the surprise element at the other end of the barn. Amaya, Spike, and I will show up at the driveway end of the barn and demand the exchange. Spike will stay off to the left in case Gigi and Master Cledwyn need help." Yunosho wanted Spike as far from the danger zone as possible. The promise Yunosho had made to Amaya weighed on him. This was a discrete way to keep it. "I'll move as close to the Peetles as I can. Gigi will cause a commotion as soon as we make the exchange. I'll use the distraction to get the Peetles to safety while Master Cledwyn comes from behind and rescues Amaya."

"You must let me make the exchange without interference." Amaya's stubborn streak reappeared. "I cannot ask any of you to risk your lives."

"You didn't, Minxie," Spike chimed in. "We volunteered. You're forgetting—we're the Band of Murugan." Spike continued to impress Yunosho with how brave a scrawny kid like him could be. Spike was also right. Whatever they did, they needed to do it as a team.

Yunosho threw a questioning glance at Master Cledwyn. "Master, what say you?"

Cledwyn scrubbed his chin. His experience had to be telling him an exchange was a bad idea, that the best course of action from a probability perspective was to turn around and leave. But Cledwyn looked up, and his face held the answer Yunosho had known was the right one all along. "We gots no choice."

With that, Yunosho's heart accepted the answer too. Amaya was right. Whatever will be will be.

They all rose.

"We'll give you a thirty-minute head start," Yunosho told Cledwyn. "I'll signal when it's time to make our move."

"Don't do anything rash. I couldn't bear it if anything happened to *any* of you." Amaya seemed concerned about everyone but herself, but Yunosho wasn't about to put his own life before anyone else's today.

"Don't worry, kiddo." Gigi wrapped an arm around Amaya and squeezed. "We'll be fine. This mountain will look out for me." Gigi gave Cledwyn a playful punch in the arm. He grinned and winked at Amaya. Yunosho couldn't help but love how goofy the big guy looked doing it.

He walked Gigi and Cledwyn to the other side of the road. They stopped beneath a sycamore. Cledwyn took Yunosho by the shoulders and looked him in the eye. "All tings be fleetin' in dis world, and we gots ta endure it." He leaned forward and whispered in Yunosho's ear. "But of all da fleetin' tings I seen, yer da one I loves most."

Yunosho's throat tightened. He forced back the beginnings of tears. "Master, I… I…"

Cledwyn bear-hugged Yunosho, clapped him on the back, and stepped aside, grinning. Gigi embraced Yunosho, her face worried.

"You be careful." She disentangled herself, shaking a finger at him.

Yunosho chuckled. "I will. You need to be careful too. Master, do you have a weapon for this girl genius?"

Cledwyn laid the case in the grass and took out an ebony-handled Bowie knife in a leather sheath. He handed the knife to Gigi. She slid it onto her belt.

Yunosho looked her up and down, whistling. "All it takes is a knife, and Gigi becomes the poster child for dangerous engineers everywhere."

They all laughed. It was a difficult moment for Yunosho. There'd been enough loss in his life. He didn't want to face more. He thought about his mother and how he'd been too late to save her. He told himself to be good enough, and brave enough, and fast enough this time to make sure they all came out of this with their lives and limbs intact.

Gigi curled her lips into a sad smile and turned her hand in a stiff little wave. Cledwyn gave Yunosho a sharp salute. Then Cledwyn and Gigi headed across the field toward the barn—and whatever fate awaited.

Yunosho returned to the vehicle. Amaya and Spike sat inside, waiting for him—Spike in the back seat, his elbows on his knees, his chin resting on the thumbs of his clasped hands, one of his knees shaking; Amaya in the front passenger seat, her brow knitted and her face drained of color.

Yunosho crawled into the driver's seat. "Amaya, are you okay?" He'd never seen her more on edge. She needed to be ready. They all needed to be ready.

"I can't connect!" The desperation in her voice made him want to take her in his arms, hold her tight, tell her everything would be okay. But now was not the time for that. There might never be a time for that.

"You should stop trying," he said. "We need our energy for what lies ahead in that barn. We're going to need every bit of our combined strength."

Spike sat up straighter, smiling. "The best way to stop trying would be to meditate. Amaya makes *me* meditate when I'm stressed."

Amaya forced a weak laugh. "I suppose if I make Spike do it, he can make me."

"Great idea, Spike," Yunosho said.

They leaned back in their seats. Yunosho closed his eyes and let himself detach. Within a few minutes, the grimness began to fade. By the time he opened his eyes again, Amaya's color had returned, and Spike had slipped back into his usual upbeat joviality.

"Attention, attention." Spike imitated a race track announcer. "The Band of Murugan is *ready for action.*"

"Just what Dr. Spike ordered," said Yunosho.

Amaya glanced back at Spike, flashing him a smile. "Whatever happens, I'm proud to call you both my friends."

"Me too." Spike squeaked.

"Me three." Yunosho grabbed the wheel with both hands, determination thumping in his heart. "Well, if we're the Band of Murugan, then this vehicle must be our peacock."

"Right." Amaya pointed down the road and shook her head, imitating wind blowing through her hair. "Then I command you. Fly, peacock, fly."

शांति (Amanda)

"Amaya won't give herself up."

Bob Peetle spoke up—*again*. Amanda wished he'd shut up. That stupid farmer thought he could reason with Elmo. No way that was going to work.

"She will," Elmo replied. "The Japanese boy is another story. But I'm prepared for him."

"What Japanese boy?" Bob asked.

"The unfortunate young man who saved the Atlas girl from my last attack. Only this time—"

"Why haven't you gagged these two?" Listening to their back-and-forth irked Amanda. Plus, she was bored. She wanted to get to the exciting part, the part where Amaya was standing right in front of her.

"I want them to be able to speak," Elmo retorted.

Sam stuck out her chin. "Mister, you're sorely mistaken if you think we'll let *our* little Amaya give herself up to the likes of *you*."

Amanda sneered at Sam's feeble show of strength. Sam Peetle was going to learn a lesson today. They all would.

"You may try to dissuade her all you wish." Elmo seemed much too unconcerned about this point, though the farmer dummies probably couldn't talk Amaya out of anything. That witch could be stubborn. "The substance of what you say won't matter. The important thing is that she hears your voices."

Amanda leaned back against the wall. "Like I said, I would gag them. I hated their stupid visits and cutesy little chats on the porch drinking their dumb iced tea. Why don't you just kill everyone when they get here? Except maybe Japanesey boy. He sounds dreamy."

"We stick with the plan." Elmo's plan was to make the Japanese boy stand down while Amaya gave herself up. The Samurai Spidiepuses would turn everyone else into minced meat once Elmo had Amaya. That was Elmo's plan. Amanda had something else in mind—something that didn't involve silly spider-robot-octopus thingies.

"You should be ashamed of yourself, Amanda Duggan," Sam scolded. Amanda stuck out her tongue and rolled her eyes at Sam. Let her talk. It wouldn't make a bit of difference.

Bob turned his head toward his wife, his expression nauseatingly earnest. "We agree, right? We'll do everything we can."

"We sure will, Bob." Sam had the most exasperating look of adoration on her face. "I never thought I could love you more. Then this day comes along to prove me wrong. You're a good man, Bob Peetle."

"Gosh darn, golly gee." Amanda spat at the ground, bile rising in her throat. "You two are disgusting. A couple of regular Norman Rockwells. Instead of us gagging them, *they're gagging me*." She stuck her finger in her mouth and mimed throwing up. "I'd kill them just for saying such stupid crap!"

"Calm yourself, Miss Duggan," Elmo said. That weird thing happened again. He gazed up at the ceiling. His eyes rolled up into his head. In a deep, gravelly voice, he said, "We will sell no wine before its time."

"Again?" It unnerved Amanda when he did that. She needed to keep her nerve right now. "If I cared at all, which I don't, by the way, I'd be worried about you."

Elmo's pocket buzzed. "They're here."

ॐ (Amaya)

Amaya exited the vehicle, making as much noise as she could without sounding too conspicuous, just as Yunosho had instructed. The noise would help cover the covert arrival of Gigi and Cledwyn at the other end of the barn.

Yunosho came around from the driver's side. He looked like Mr. Dark and Dangerous, his chest, thighs, and calves protected with the black, lightweight armor he'd put on before they'd turned into the farm. He sheathed both swords across his back, the hilts' mother-of-pearl inlays and crisscrossing copper wire shining through the gloom of the overcast morning. His head hung slightly, like he was brooding. Amaya knew from the training room it was focus. That only amplified the gravity of it all.

Spike had gone silent the moment they entered the farm gate. This whole ordeal might be proving too much for him. She hoped Yunosho would keep his promise if things took a bad turn. There'd be no turning back for anyone now.

They marched up to the wide, open doorway, Amaya and Yunosho together, with Spike staying to the left as planned.

"Far enough," the short, creepy man said after they'd

advanced to within forty feet of Sam and Bob. Mandy had moved into position right beside Sam, her dagger at the ready. The man stood next to Bob, a fillet knife in one hand and something in the other that must have been hidden earlier—a small, nickel-finish, double-barreled pistol trained right at Amaya. She had to stop herself from flinching.

"Ah…" the man breathed out. The bowler hat and aviator sunglasses obscured much of his face. He looked dapper in his Victorian clothing despite the sickly gray skin tone and the angry scar traveling across his left cheek. "The wonderful Miss Atlas. A pleasure to meet you in the flesh."

"I'm afraid I can't return the sentiment." Amaya stood straight, her arms at her sides and her chin up, not showing even a hint of weakness.

Mandy pointed her dagger at Amaya. "Hiya, brownie."

"Hello, Mandy." Amaya kept her voice steady. She couldn't let Mandy get to her. Not now.

"It's Amanda," Mandy hissed. "I ditched that wimpy nickname."

Amaya ignored her. She'd never give Mandy the satisfaction of calling her Amanda. Certainly not now.

"I see you've brought our young Japanese hero along." The man's crooked, yellow-toothed grin transformed him into a hideous Mr. Hyde, revealing a man capable of terrible things. It sent a shiver of revulsion along Amaya's spine. "Welcome, Mr. Emushi. Your name was easy to discover, given the news surrounding the deaths in your hometown. I would love to meet the perpetrator."

"I bet you would," growled Yunosho, his glare angry and hurt. "Who might you be?"

"For me to know and you to find out." The man tried to

laugh, but it sounded more like coughing or choking. "And young Skopos, the sidekick."

"Hi, Spike. How about we get those cheeks burning again?" It always worked when Mandy goaded Spike. Not this time. He took the jab without saying a word. Amaya had never seen him so unflappably quiet. Maybe he wasn't as nervous as she'd thought.

"Such a *nice* gathering," the little man gushed facetiously.

"Have they hurt you?" Amaya asked Sam and Bob.

"Don't you worry about us," Sam said.

"You shouldn't be here," Bob complained. "You know darn well Sam and I can take care of ourselves."

"Disgusting!" Mandy's voice oozed with contempt, reminding Amaya of how jealous Mandy would get when the Peetles visited. That jealousy seemed kind compared to the seething hatred coming from Mandy now. Amaya needed to get the Peetles out of there—fast.

Yunosho stomped his foot. "Let's do it. I take it we're exchanging Amaya for the Peetles?"

"Hmm." The little man tapped the gun's barrel against his thin, purple lips. "Exchange. Interesting concept. I hadn't considered that. I thought you would give me the Atlas girl, and I would simply promise not to kill these two."

Yunosho scoffed. "No way you're getting Amaya without releasing the Peetles."

"Don't you dare do it, Amaya," Bob pleaded. "You turn yourself around right this second and leave, little girl. Sam and I will be just fine."

"Please, Amaya." Sam's voice caught in her throat. "You have to go. Please! You *know* how much we love you."

Hope flickered in Yunosho's face, but Amaya wasn't having

any of it. She knew how far the Peetles would go for her. She wasn't about to let them.

"Sam and Bob." Amaya sounded more resolute than ever. "Trust us. Everything will work out." Then she scowled at the little man, putting steel into her voice. "If you harm them, you *will* regret it."

"Now, now. Come, come." The man's voice was toneless again. "This is a simple business transaction. As for regret, I'm sure I don't know how that feels." He gave Amaya a toady smile and made that choking sound again. It wasn't merely his creepy appearance that was unusual—something else felt off about him, something she couldn't put her finger on.

"What exactly do you want with Amaya?" Yunosho asked.

"I'll say it again. For me to know and for *you* to find out." The man couldn't have been righter. Amaya needed to figure out how all this related to her powers and her parents. This man held answers. Maybe she'd extract some from him—*if* she survived.

"Let's get this over with before I lose my patience and kill them all," Mandy snarled. Something besides the contempt in her voice bothered Amaya. "Except maybe for him." Mandy flirtatiously waved her dagger at Yunosho. "You're cute."

"Please refrain from interrupting, Miss Duggan." The little man seemed concerned about Mandy too. Maybe he'd also noticed the odd tone in her voice.

"You bring the Peetles forward," Yunosho instructed. "I'll bring Amaya. We'll exchange in the middle."

"Ho, ho." The man sounded like a twisted Santa. "I've seen you in action. I'm not getting anywhere near you. Miss Duggan will bring the Peetles forward. Miss Atlas will meet them in the middle. Alone."

"Not without me." Yunosho planted his feet and narrowed his eyes.

Amaya would make the exchange whatever way this little troll wanted—she needed Yunosho to accept that. "Yes. Alone."

The helpless expression on Yunosho's face told Amaya how much he cared. It tugged at her heart, but she quashed it. This was no time for those kinds of feelings. Maybe there'd never be a time for those kinds of feelings.

"Up, you two." Mandy kicked at the Peetles' chairs after cutting the bindings at their feet.

Sam and Bob rose. Yunosho leaned in and whispered to Amaya.

"Walk slowly. We need all the time we can get."

Amaya wanted Yunosho to be clear about one thing. "You save the Peetles," she whispered back. "Do you hear me?"

Yunosho nodded. Amaya wasn't sure he'd follow her orders. There was nothing she could do about it. She needed to move. She needed to get the Peetles away from Victorian man and, more importantly, from Mandy. She began walking step-by-step, putting one foot forward, moving the other to meet it.

"A procession." The little man smiled his repulsive smile, his eyes struggling to express something. Amusement? Disdain? Amaya had difficulty reading his face as if he didn't know what emotions were. Another not-quite-right thing about him. "How quaint. Please do likewise with the Peetles, Miss Duggan." He pointed the gun at Bob. "Remember, my young Emushi, I'll have this Derringer aimed right at Mr. Farmer's head."

Amaya moved slowly, but it worsened the terrifying feeling that time was running out. She wanted to be able to stop it, to freeze time and whisk the Peetles away. If only she could tap into her power. In training, the key to connecting was detachment. Right now detachment seemed desperately out of reach.

Amaya focused on Mandy's face as they neared one another, hoping to catch at least an inkling as to why Mandy's voice had sounded strange. Nothing showed. Mandy prodded Sam and Bob forward, her face calm and blank, her dagger tight against Sam's throat. Only a few steps remained before the Peetles would be safely out of Mandy's reach.

"We love you, honey." Sam's voice caught again, releasing an involuntary hiccup of sadness from Amaya's chest.

"My little plum pie," Bob said, like they were all back at the orphanage sitting on the porch, sipping that lemony iced tea, getting ready to dig their forks into that pie's buttery crust.

The love from Sam and that bit of normalcy from Bob did it. Amaya began to slip into the massive entanglement. Mandy's eyes twinkled with glee.

She slit Sam's throat.

Sam staggered. Blood squirted and bubbled from her neck, the dark stain of it spreading across her blouse. She slumped. Bob tried to support her with his shoulder, his hands still tied behind his back. A shot rang out. They both fell to the ground. The troll cried out, "Spidiepuses attack." Bedlam ensued.

Amaya leaned backward. Hard. Mandy's dagger sliced the air where Amaya's neck had been a second earlier, sending flecks of Sam's blood into the air, splattering Amaya's face.

Mandy's arm reached its full extension. She put one foot forward, leaning in, setting up, her arm reversing direction. Amaya couldn't move out of the way. Her mind had connected to Sam and Bob, and it was paralyzing her with grief.

Sam gazed at Bob, aching to hold him, the light fading from her eyes. *Oh, honey*, Bob thought, his heart wrenched by the sight. But Sam was already gone. Bob wasn't far behind. He pictured early this morning, before this had all begun, standing with her at the kitchen sink. He'd drawn her close and kissed her, telling her he loved her without saying a word. A quiet serenity fell over Bob. He let go too.

Amaya *screamed* but only in her head. She dropped into a crouch. Mandy's blade sliced the space above Amaya's head, cutting a lock of her hair. Mandy tossed the knife up and caught it, switching grip. The knife arced around with vicious speed toward Amaya's skull. Amaya exploded upward before the knife could reach her. Her palm snapped out. Mandy flew to the other end of the barn like a rag doll. She slammed into the wall and slid down it, wet-noodle-like. A horse in the stall next to her began to kick and squeal.

Amaya's strength drained. A fuzzy evil tickled her brain, trying to get in. She turned to look for Spike. Yunosho was there, both swords drawn.

What about Spike?! she thought, angry because Yunosho wasn't with him, protecting him the way he'd promised.

ॐ (Elmo)

Elmo felt a powerful urge to switch the Derringer's aim from the farmer to the back of the Duggan girl's head. It'd been that sound in her voice. He ignored it. Without her, they wouldn't be literally mere steps from their goal.

Then the Duggan girl's knife slid across the wife's neck. The whole plan blew up in Elmo's face. He had no choice. He stepped forward and fired. The farmer went down, his wife with him.

"Spidiepuses attack!" Elmo commanded. A loud chorus of clicking, whirring, and buzzing sang out from the barn's loft.

Something darted to his right—the Skopos boy sprinting

toward the Atlas girl, unaware of the blue Spidiepus dropping from the loft on course to crush him.

Perfect, Elmo thought, anticipating the boy's transformation into a lovely, bloody mess.

But someone new, a redheaded girl, appeared out of nowhere. She dove for the floor and grabbed the boy's ankles, tackling him. He sprawled forward, and the blue giant missed. A second ruined moment.

A shot cracked the air. Elmo turned to look.

Boom!

The black Spidiepus exploded. Steam spewed from it in a great cloud. Pieces of tentacle chewed into the barn walls. The remains of its disc body dropped to the floor, a tangle of bent and blackened metal. Elmo looked for the shooter, but the steam obscured his view—*a second* person Elmo hadn't anticipated.

He needed to avoid drawing attention to himself, escape the barn, and let the Spidiepuses do their job. Getting himself killed wouldn't help the mission. He could capture Amaya Atlas after the Spidiepuses took care of everyone else. Where had that dratted Duggan girl gotten to? He might still need her.

The steam cleared. Elmo spotted her, slumped against a wall at the opposite end of the barn. How on earth did she end up there?

Another crack and *boom!*

One side of the green Spidiepus blew apart, two tentacles with it. Elmo saw the shooter this time—a big man lying on the ground at the back entrance, propped on his elbows with a gun. He looked like a pro. The green Spidiepus hesitated, then scuttled toward the shooter on four of its remaining legs, waving a sword and a punching dagger with the other two. A jingle bubbled up from somewhere deep in Elmo's brain.

"Takes a licking and keeps on ticking." An absent-minded

smile spread across his face as he wended his way toward the Duggan girl. She didn't appear to be moving. At all.

शांति (Amaya)

"Duck!" Amaya cried out.

Yunosho ducked. A sword whooshed over his head. Amaya leaped to the side. Yunosho spun, blocking a thrusting dagger.

"My connection's gone." Heartbreak constricted her trachea, making it a struggle to speak. She was reeling inside, doing her best to hang on to sanity, devastated that the Peetles were gone.

"They've been programmed to leave you out of the fight." Yunosho sprang to the side, avoiding the sword slicing at his leg. He parried a dagger headed for his liver. "He's changed his mind about killing you."

"I noticed." Amaya wondered why. There had to be a reason, but they couldn't waste time trying to figure it out. "Gigi and Spike need help."

Yunosho crossed swords above his head, stopping a dagger above his skull. He sidestepped a rotary saw and chopped at the tentacle holding it to little effect. "I know. I need to get over there."

Those two were stuck in a stall on the other side of the barn. Two big robot monsters were doing their best to get at them. Amaya wanted to yell and scream at Yunosho for not staying with Spike to begin with, but that would only distract from assisting them.

"Wait here," he said.

"I will *not*." Amaya was mad with worry. "Give me a weapon."

"It's too dangerous without your power."

Why did he have to argue? She didn't want his protection. She wanted his help. Spike needed protection. She felt nauseous and wobbly. The noise was so loud her ears were ringing.

The red bot's knife came fast. Yunosho raised his sword to block it. By the time Amaya registered the hilt snapping back from the blow, it was too late. There was a hard rap to her temple. Spots danced in her head. Everything went black.

ॐ (Spike)

"Up!" Gigi wasn't messing around. "Run!"

Spike obeyed. They dove into the open stall together. Two of those machines the Victorian man called Spidiepuses scurried after them. A pop followed by a loud explosion came from the main part of the barn.

"Up against the wall!" Gigi yelled. Another explosion followed a second pop.

Spike rolled across the straw-covered floor, springing up next to Gigi. They pressed their backs against the exterior wall. Spike pushed into the boards as hard as he could, using his toes for leverage. The Spidiepuses couldn't fit through the door frame, but their tentacles could. A long, brass-handled knife danced back and forth inches from Spike's face. He kept seeing glimpses of Lord Ganesh, the elephant-headed Remover of Obstacles.

I must be delirious, he thought. The high-pitched whine of power tools buzzed in his ears. The Spidiepuses had begun to saw the support beams above him. He crossed his fingers, wishing Ganesh would remove *these* obstacles.

Yunosho flew through the air as if he'd heard Spike's prayer.

His blade fell hard, cracking one of the saws in two. He hit the ground rolling and came up behind the Spidiepuses. They turned to attack him. Spike unpeeled from the wall, gulping air, unaware he'd been holding his breath.

"Spike!" Gigi gasped. "Over there." She was bent over, her hands on her knees, catching her breath too. She shook her finger at the opposite wall. Amaya lay there, propped against the enormous tire of a tall piece of farm equipment, her head lolling on her chest. Dread coursed through Spike, the same terrible dread he'd felt when he'd seen Yunosho bent over Amaya in that field. Spike tore across the barn, Gigi abreast of him.

They reached Amaya. Gigi knelt beside her and gently lifted her head. "She's still breathing." The ground beneath Spike's feet tilted for a moment from the wave of relief that hit him. "I don't see any injuries, except for this red welt on her forehead. We could use some water."

Spike remembered a spigot with a rusty bucket beneath it. He shook off the wooziness. "Wait here," he told Gigi and ran toward the middle of the barn straight into madness.

Yunosho sailed back and forth like a circus performer, bouncing and flipping around the barn. Spidiepuses pursued him, a mish-mosh of scuttling legs and swinging tentacles. It was *loud*. Spike put his head down, urging himself forward. He kept thinking *water, water, water.*

He reached the spigot and filled the bucket. There was a sharp crack behind him as he turned to start back.

Boom!

The explosion knocked Spike sideways. The bucket flew out of his hand. Water splashed to the ground. Spike landed on his back with an oomph. He lay there wheezing, getting his breath back, when a hand reached down.

Gigi! Boy, was he glad to see her! He grabbed her hand.

She pulled him up. Her lips were moving, but all he heard was ringing. Behind her, Master Cledwyn struggled with the blue monster. He had both arms wrapped around one of its tentacles and his shoulder was dripping with blood. The tentacle kept whipping around, trying to throw him off. He looked like he needed help.

Spike's hearing began to return.

"Are you okay?!" Gigi was yelling, but she sounded muffled, like someone had stuffed bags of cotton in his ears.

"YES." His voice filled his whole head. "I'LL BE RIGHT BACK."

He snatched up the bucket, cocked his arm, and charged at the blue Spidiepus. He put his whole body into it. The white Spidiepus grabbed him by the underarm mid-swing and yanked him with tremendous force into the air.

He noticed movement above him and looked up. His stomach dropped. Yunosho was dangling upside down, the claw of a tentacle wrapped around his ankle. They were all going to die without Yunosho's help.

At least I *still have a weapon*, Spike thought. He switched the bucket to his free arm and started whacking the tentacle that held him as hard as he could, the bucket banging like a tin drum over his head. Yunosho shouted. Spike glanced up again. Yunosho looked wrong. He was glaring at Spike, furious. Spike wondered what he'd done to make Yunosho so mad. Spike wasn't sure he'd ever seen anyone *that* mad.

The veins in Yunosho's neck ballooned. His face turned as red as a fire truck. His eyes bulged. Then Yunosho disappeared, and a livid, bug-eyed monkey replaced him, sneering down at Spike with bared teeth and a face of pure malice.

I'm really losing my mind, Spike thought. He blinked hard, squeezing his eyes tight, trying with all his inner might to make the horrible monkey go away. Instead, the monkey raised its sword.

A searing pain jolted Spike's arm.

ॐ (Yunosho)

"I see an opening," Yunosho shouted to Cledwyn over the din. He pulled his body into a cannonball and sailed over the red Spidiepus, tentacles lashing out as he went.

Still four bots to go—Piercer had destroyed the black one. Cledwyn had mangled the exposed innards of the injured green one, which lay on its back now, its remaining tentacles waving helplessly, like a bug stuck upside down. They hadn't severed a single tentacle yet. But Yunosho's last strike had cut a deep gash in the plate next to the red bot's head, a weak spot discovered by Cledwyn at the cost of a punctured shoulder.

The ground approached fast. Yunosho came out of his rotation. The balls of his feet barely kissed the floor before he had to spring backward to escape the tentacles that whipped out to ensnare his leg. He flipped over the dagger the white Spidiepus sent snaking toward his heart. He slid in the straw on his knees, limbo-like, beneath the slice of the brown bot's sword, his neck dangerously exposed.

He raised his head again in time to see Cledwyn's broadsword plunge into the red bot's plate all the way to the hilt. The bot's head *popped*, rocketing straight up. Steam shot from the opening, and its body careened on two legs to the back of the barn with Cledwyn still atop, trying to free his sword.

Crack! A stall door flew backward and hit the floor, scaring up a cloud of dust. The horse had kicked the door off its hinges.

The crazed animal was tied up, kicking at nothing but air now, its desperate screams adding to the clang and bang of battle.

The white bot scurried around to confront Yunosho. He came off his knees. The other two moved into position left and right of it, hemming him in. They marched forward in tempo, their swords whipping back and forth, making a loud whoosh-whoosh as they came.

Something clanked. A horseshoe bounced off the brown bot's head. Yunosho glanced around, looking for the horseshoe's origin. He saw Cledwyn at the back of the barn *leaping* up and down like a giant leprechaun, his arms gesturing wildly. He was shouting. "Here! Over here! Come gets me, yer dumb clunker!" The brown Spidiepus pirouetted to face Cledwyn, its tentacles undulating like the arms of a dancing god. It rolled to attack, eight legs thudding against the ground, propelling it forward.

The other two bots closed ranks and charged. Yunosho dug his feet into the ground and sprinted straight at them, his arms pumping. He launched himself into the air. Tentacles stretched out: a sword, two daggers, a saw. Yunosho used them as stairs—a foot on the hilt, a step up to one dagger, a second step to the next. He kicked off the saw and somersaulted over the bots' heads, exiting his tumble on the other side of them, his feet ready to meet the ground. Cledwyn slid on his knees at the back of the barn. Yunosho's feet planted. Cledwyn's arms came up from the ground holding Piercer. The pistol cracked. The brown bot exploded with a thunderous boom. Dirt spilled from the rafters, and a mushroom cloud of steam vented toward the roof. Piercer's ammo was out.

Yunosho spun. The two remaining bots were fast, already on top of him. They attacked in tandem. One assailed him. The other pushed him back. They forced him into the corner. Twelve tentacles trapped him like prison bars. The other four rained swords and daggers, three and four hits at a time. He dropped to one knee, using the ground for leverage. Their weapons inched nearer to his flesh with every strike. His arms burned with fatigue.

A roar—something unintelligible Yunosho recognized as Welsh—punched through the clamor. Cledwyn came charging across the barn holding a long metal post above his head. He speared a blue Spidiepus tentacle with it and grabbed another with both hands. The tentacle whipsawed, trying to throw Cledwyn off. It gave Yunosho the opening he needed. He dove through the web of Spidiepus legs and almost collided with Spike, who was rushing the blue Spidiepus—with a bucket in his hand!

A bucket?! Had Spike lost his mind?

Yunosho rolled onto his feet. Spike reached the blue bot and swung. The white bot grabbed Spike under the arm and *yanked* him into the air. Yunosho's legs drove him forward, his muscles straining, stretching into powerful strides. He catapulted himself at the white bot's tentacle. He'd find the strength. He'd lop off that tentacle and get Spike down. Yunosho raised his sword.

Pluck!

Cold metal grasped his ankle, twisting it, snapping him away. Now Yunosho was stuck too, upside down above Spike. Beneath them, Cledwyn released the blue Spidiepus leg and dropped to the floor, pointing.

"Behind you!"

Yunosho twisted his torso and blocked the oncoming sword. He turned back around and saw the long blade of the blue bot's katar plunge into Cledwyn from behind, straight through the heart, the tip winking four times in and out of his chest.

"MASTER CEE!"

Cledwyn's shoulders slumped. He lifted his head and gazed up at Yunosho, smiling. He raised his arm in a lazy wave—then staggered forward and fell.

Shrapnel of pain ripped apart Yunosho's insides. A tsunami of disbelief crashed over him. He looked down at Spike. They were done for. Spike wouldn't make it. None of them were going to make it. Yunosho the Wretched, Yunosho the Useless, Yunosho the Failure, had failed them all, the same way he'd failed his mother.

He hated himself for it. The hate *boiled* into anger. The anger flooded every cell of his body, and a tremendous rage erupted like a fiery volcano behind his bloodshot eyes. He was losing control. His mind, desperate to keep it, tried to force him to remember—this had happened before. At Mr. Oniki's dojo when he was a boy.

But it was too late. Rage exploded inside his skull. A vicious, despicable monkey came screeching out of the shadows, pounding on Yunosho's brain, jumping up and down on it, paralyzing Yunosho with wave after wave of agony.

The monkey took control. Yunosho's mind screamed, *Resist!* But his muscles were no longer his to command. He raised his sword, tears spilling from his eyes, pleading with himself to stop. A blazing fury coursed through his arms—the sword fell. Spike dropped toward the ground. Gigi stood below him, her arms outstretched, her face filled with horror. Spike's body knocked her to the ground.

Shock and disgust slammed Yunosho before his sword even stopped its swing. He'd broken a sacred promise. A vile lowliness crept over him, bathing him in shame.

शांति (Amaya)

Amaya came to, groggy. She lifted her head—it weighed a hundred pounds. She looked across the barn. Spike was hanging in the air, held by one of those mechanical monstrosities. Yunosho was hanging, too, upside down right above him.

Yunosho looked wrong. He looked enraged, like he was about to murder Spike. She tried to jump up, to run, but her arms and legs had turned into rubber.

Yunosho's face transformed.

Amaya screamed, "STOP!"

But it was too late. The sword fell. Spike fell.

Amaya put her face in her hands, sobbing. All she could hear in her pain-ridden heart was, *Why?*

ॐ (Spike)

Spike opened his eyes. Gigi was kneeling beside him. He was sure glad to see *her*. But he was confused. Where were they?

"Hi, Gigi."

"Hi, Spikie." Gigi's smile made Spike giggly inside. She sounded nice. She was nice. Really nice. He liked Gigi. A lot. Then he remembered.

We're getting ice cream at the lake!

He'd wanted to bring her here for ice cream ever since they'd met. He wondered what Gigi's favorite flavor was. Probably something like peanut butter chocolate-chip salted caramel. Gigi was complicated.

She took off her vest and cut a long piece of it. Why was Gigi carrying a big knife? Why did she have blood all over her?

His face scrunched up in confusion. It was way too loud for the lake. What was all the commotion?

"This might hurt." Gigi tied the cloth on his arm, but Spike didn't feel a thing. Why was she tying a ribbon on him? Maybe they wouldn't let you order ice cream if you didn't wear a ribbon? That didn't sound right.

He turned his head to the side. An arm lay in the straw a few yards away. It looked familiar. He noticed more straw and straw bales and beams and wood. It dawned on him—they weren't at the lake at all! They were in a barn! A big, noisy barn! Then a big white metal robot crashed with a loud bang into a big blue one. The blue one fell backward onto the arm.

Gigi gasped. She grabbed Spike's chin and pulled his gaze to hers. "Keep looking at me, Spike. Don't look away."

Something terrible must've happened. Was that why the horse was screaming?

"Doesn't that horse need help?" Spike's voice sounded daydreamy and far away, like it didn't belong to him. But he was pretty sure it was his. "We better go see."

ॐ (Yunosho)

A rush of energy hit Yunosho. It was his Kamuy, his spirit animal! He could see it for the first time! It *was* a black tiger, just like in the vision his mother had told him about. The beast growled. It opened its jaws in a snarl and sprang at the demonic little monkey. But the pitiful thing jumped out of the way and scurried back into the shadows of Yunosho's brain, whimpering with its tail between its legs.

Yunosho embraced his Kamuy. Its spirit filled him. He wrested back control, breathing in the tiger's power. He swung up from the waist and hacked off the tentacle that held him with a single blow, the newfound strength surprising him. He dropped to the floor and attacked, bobbing and weaving, chopping off one Spidiepus leg, and another, and another, the blades of his weapons singing a song of revenge.

He slid under the blue bot. The white bot's plate approached from above. He dropped one of his swords—it hit the ground with a clang. He grasped the hilt of the other with both hands, calculating the speed of the white bot's roll, timing it. He closed his eyes and let the tiger inside him roar, giving voice to a flood of grief and self-loathing. He thrust upward. The blade pierced the plate and slid all the way in.

He let go of the hilt and dove out of the way.

The white bot spun in place for a moment like a top, its head vibrating madly. It bent forward, its disc body shaking. A jet of steam blew its head off, sending the body flying backward into the blue one with a crash. They tumbled together to the ground, tentacles entangled, flailing in the air. Yunosho yelled above the din to Gigi.

"Get him out!"

शांति (Elmo)

Elmo found a pulse. *Finally.*

The Duggan girl started breathing again. He'd almost given up. He'd never performed CPR on anyone, his job having been to prevent his victims from ever breathing again. So it surprised him when it worked. She wasn't conscious, but it would have to do. He lifted her onto his shoulder and turned to flee. The horse caught his eye.

He set Amanda back down. Without the faintest idea why,

he went along the half-wall to the end of the stall next to the one with the horse. The terrified creature was screaming, its face foaming with frenzy and its eyes wild with fear. Elmo reached over the wall and cut the tie with a flick of his wrist. The horse reared back, snorting loudly, shaking its head at the air. It turned and bolted out the barn's rear door.

Elmo threw Amanda back over his shoulder and followed, stopping outside to take one last look over his shoulder at his latest disaster. The Emushi boy was exiting the barn at the other end, the Atlas girl on his shoulder. The redhead was dragging the Skopos boy into the driveway. They disappeared around the corner just as the white Spidiepus exploded, taking the blue one out with it. The barn burst into flames.

CHAPTER 33

TIME OUT

(ELMO)

ELMO RACED FROM the barn. Even the weight of a solidly built girl on his shoulder couldn't slow him. He didn't want to chance an encounter with that sword-wielding Japanese boy, no matter how low the risk. He reached the vehicle he'd hidden behind the trees, strapped Amanda into the back seat, and revved off, tearing through the fields and smashing through the wooden fence at the road below.

He arrived to the suburbs of Ammoto and pulled into a strip mall. He parked around the corner at the back entrance of a hospital supply shop in a spot with no cameras. He put on his long rifle coat and black baseball cap and used the Meshter-Tek cutting tool on the shop's steel door to cut a large hole without triggering the alarm. Once inside, he grabbed ten bags of IV fluids, a few IV infusion kits, a bottle of alcohol, a bag of cotton swabs, and some extra needles. Late night had overtaken day by the time he drove through the disused gate of the abandoned Rattebane wine estate.

He carried Amanda into the cavern and laid her on the

same old rusted cot he'd tied her to when he first brought her there. He examined her but found no injuries other than bruised skin at her solar plexus. He assembled a makeshift IV unit using a wire coat hanger and the top of the door, hooked Amanda up to it, and left her. She'd either get better or die. He didn't wish her dead. Despite her massive failure back at the barn, being around her reminded Elmo of what comfortable probably used to feel like.

He went to the workshop table to review the drone footage. He'd replaced the drones' rotors with highly-responsive steam-jet propulsion, so there'd been no reason for the scout drone to miss the big man and the redhead.

He viewed the sentry drone vid, zooming to the vehicle as it pulled into the driveway leading to the farm. The Emushi boy sat at the wheel, the Atlas girl beside him. The boy Amanda called "that detestable weakling" sat in the back seat, not visible to the drone until he exited the vehicle.

Elmo examined the scout drone's footage. The drone maneuvered like it was following something in the fields behind the barn. Why couldn't Elmo see any movement?

The answer hit him. "Rats!" Someone had hijacked the drone's vid, likely that redhead. He pulled up the footage from his hat-cam and ran facial recognition. Out popped "O'Grady, Felicity, 1002 Winding River Road, #B-3003, Westwardlee, Cherokee District 67324-7562."

A real address. And an engineer to boot. He ran facial recognition on the professional. Out popped—nothing. He must have been black ops, very good, or very wealthy to have no electronic identity. *No need to worry about him, though. He's a warm pile of ashes by now.*

Elmo put all six Spidiepus vids up in a split-screen, starting with the moment they'd sprung from the loft. He wanted to see how Amanda ended up all the way across the barn. There she was, thrusting her knife at Amaya, once, twice. Amanda brought the knife overhead, and *bam!* She disappeared instantly from the camera's view. The Atlas girl had palm-punched her with incredible force!

He viewed the scene from another angle.

What have we here?

He zoomed in, shaking his head.

Oh my, that can't be good. That can't be good at all.

CHAPTER 34
DREAM ON

(Yunosho)

NIGHT HAD ALREADY cloaked the mountain when Yunosho arrived at the bat cave's entrance. He hadn't managed a wink of sleep on the train. The climb had worsened his fatigue.

The door geared open. He stepped inside. A blast of sorrow hit him and his whole body cramped. The cave reminded him of the one thing he'd tried hardest not to think about—Master Cee was *gone*.

In the time it took to hang up his jacket, open the fridge, and drink a glass of apple cider, depletion settled in. He dove into the lower bunk bed in his room—it smelled of Amaya— and fell into a deep sleep.

Yunosho returned to the Random World in his dream. It was nothing like the first time. He came out of the water onto a beach strewn with burnt rubble. The air reeked of hot soot and flames. Amaya lay on a hilltop above the valley, her eyes closed and her body jerking violently. Yunosho started to run to her but almost tumbled over himself—his feet wouldn't budge, like they'd been superglued to the ground! Gigi and Spike were shouting in the distance for him to do something, too faint to understand.

He tried yelling, "Do what?" Only rasps came out, like someone had cut out his tongue.

A rag-tag band of humans was battling an army of tall, purple-skinned aliens in the valley. Though armed only with melee weaponry, the humans fought bravely. The aliens had razor-sharp bone hands tipped with fat pointed claws that whipped around on the ends of long flexible arms, tearing the humans to pieces. The humans were losing ground—fast.

Checkerboard RiRii tried to break through the alien army's flank. Spells flew from her fingertips, mowing down aliens like pins in a bowling alley. Humans surged into the gaps she opened, giving Yunosho hope—but only for a moment. A second wave of aliens began marching up the far side of the field directly toward Amaya with no one to stop them. Yunosho needed to help her. He *had* to get free.

He yanked his feet so hard he thought his feet would rip from his ankles. Nothing happened.

An angry voice shouted in his head. "Cut them off!"

Yunosho balked. He couldn't help Amaya if he cut off his feet.

"Cut them off!" the voice commanded.

Gigi and Spike continued shouting, their voices garbled but less faint now. He could see them now too—dim outlines in the distance. They cupped their hands to their mouths like megaphones. He still couldn't understand a word.

"Do what?!" he tried shouting again, the words coming out as a pitiful croak.

All around him, the Random World crumbled. Raging fires engulfed whole sections, darkening the sky with black smoke. Checkerboard RiRii's troops, surrounded with nowhere to retreat, had lost their short-lived gains.

Panic began closing in. He *had* to act. Now!

He held the sword at his legs.

"Cut them off! Cut them off!" the voice urged. Then it snickered. "Just like Spike's arm."

Yunosho snapped. His blood boiled. That despicable monkey leaped out from the darkest corner of his mind.

"Cut them off! Cut them off!" it taunted, again and again, its voice shrill and grating. It jumped up and down on Yunosho's brain, sending bolts of agony coursing through his body. His head wanted to explode. Rage flowed like a river of bile into the pit of his stomach, sweeping away any regard for consequences. He lifted his sword and swung down hard, wanting only to stop the agony. The instant he felt the faintest kiss of cold metal on his ankle, he finally heard them.

Gigi and Spike were screaming at the top of their lungs in unison. "Stop struggling!!"

Yunosho jolted awake, his heart pounding out of his chest.

CHAPTER 35

BITTERSWEET SURPRISES

(Yunosho)

Day 10 - 5:12 a.m.

YUNOSHO STUMBLED INTO the dimly lit kitchen. The outdoor reflecting tubes provided barely enough moonlight to see where he was going. He sat for a moment in silence. Feeling Cledwyn's absence. Honoring it with his grief.

His heart weighed on him like a boulder as he spoke the unlock code he'd chosen with Cledwyn years ago.

"Alohomora."

The vidwall came to life. Cledwyn sat there, a twinkle in his eye. Yunosho cried out.

"Master!"

The vid was recent. Cledwyn must have made it while they'd all been preoccupied with training. Yunosho realized too late how much better Cledwyn had understood the measure of the danger they faced.

Cledwyn apologized for not being there any longer. But he knew as surely as anything that Yunosho was ready, ready to handle the worst and best life might throw at him. He reminded

Yunosho how much Yunosho's parents loved him. How they'd done their best to help him grow into the man he'd become—the young man both would be so proud of. How they watched out for him, even from the grave. Tears ran down Yunosho's cheeks as he listened, his heart throbbing with loss.

"Bud'll explain." Cledwyn gave the camera his trademark wink, as if letting Yunosho in on a secret.

Cledwyn's expression turned somber again. He gazed directly into the camera with his hands clasped together, resting between his knees. "Yer yer own master now." He straightened and touched three fingertips to his heart. "Remember. If yer ever needs us, it's here yer'll finds us." He tapped his fingers three times against his chest, saying, "Miaka. Evgeny. And me." The vidwall went dark.

Shame crept over Yunosho. Master Cee's words devastated him. Cledwyn would never have uttered such kind words had he known. That Yunosho had failed. That he'd lost control and hacked Spike's arm off. That Amaya hated Yunosho now.

He pushed to his feet and punched his fist into his palm.

"I'll fix this," he said to Cledwyn and his parents as though they were listening. He marched into the training cave and sat at the console.

"I'm sorry." Bud sounded truly sad. "We lost a great master."

"We sure did, Bud."

"Master Cledwyn instructed me to advise you should anything happen to him. The first thing I'm to do is give you an accounting."

"Before we do that, I'd like to find a way to retrieve Master Cledwyn's remains and his sword from the barn."

"That's already been taken care of, Master Yunosho."

"Thank you, Bud. Then I'd be honored to receive your counsel. Please proceed." Getting down to business would help focus. Maybe help break through the shame and guilt. Maybe help find a way to make amends, if that were even possible.

"The moment you unlocked Master Cledwyn's vid, several assets automatically transferred to your name. First three properties. Your mother's cottage on Soya Misaki."

"She never told me she'd kept it." The news thrilled Yunosho. He'd been born there. It represented a second tangible connection to his father—his mother had met his father on the beach not far from that cottage one night as he'd been surreptitiously stealing back into Japan. The letter his father had left him the night he died was the only other thing of his Yunosho possessed.

"She didn't. She abandoned it out of caution. Cledwyn secretly purchased it later and set it up in a numbered trust along with the other two estates. The house in Tuckwater Springs where you grew up."

"I haven't thought about that place in a long time. Probably on purpose." The image of his mother lying there came rushing back, the pang of loss cleaving his heart again. He held it in.

"Cledwyn believed your mother wanted you to remember your past, as difficult as that might be."

"That's Mom, all right." Yunosho recalled the hours she'd spent patiently teaching him her Mutsu-clan ancestry when he was little. Cledwyn was right—he needed to keep those memories alive no matter how painful. They were a part of him, a part he'd never abandon now. "She valued tradition and history."

"And then," Bud said, "you own this mountain."

"The whole mountain?" Yunosho had always understood Cledwyn to be financially comfortable, but an entire mountain?

"Yes." Bud displayed the survey. "The mountain and all that lies in a radius of approximately five miles from its center.

As for more liquid assets, my program transferred Cledwyn's general account holding over twenty million into your name."

Yunosho's eyes nearly popped out of his head. "What?!" He couldn't believe it! Cledwyn had been wealthy this whole time? They hadn't lived like it. They'd hunted and foraged most of their food. The bat cave was comfortable, not lavish.

"It pales in comparison to the rest."

"What do you mean?" Yunosho clenched his jaw. He rose from his chair, his heart racing, afraid to hear the answer.

"Cledwyn left an offshore investment account at your disposal with a value of nearly seven hundred million and a trust available to you when you attain the age of thirty holding investments with a current value of over five billion."

Yunosho's jaw dropped. His mind buzzed, unable to wrap itself around such staggering wealth. What would he even begin to do with it?

"There's more," Bud warned.

Yunosho placed both hands on the console, bracing himself, his knees going weak.

"You're now the controlling stockholder in Om-Mega Bio-Electric Industries."

Yunosho plopped down in the chair, his head spinning. OMBE was *huge*. "For Pete's sake! That's who Gigi freelances for!"

CHAPTER 36

THE SCATTERING

(SPIKE)

SPIKE AWOKE, SURPRISED to find himself in a hospital bed with Amaya, Gigi, and Tessy worrying over him. His brain was in a fog. He needed a few minutes to recall how he'd ended up there, but once he did, he was his usual self again in no time. He even held up his bandaged stub of an arm and joked about starting a new career as a slot machine.

"A one-armed bandit. Get it?"

The ladies laughed, but Amaya's heart wasn't in it.

Tessy patted Spike's hand. "You'll be up and around in no time."

"I'll be fine." Spike didn't care about himself. He was more concerned about Amaya. She looked downright morose, an expression he'd never seen her wearing before. Her lip began to quiver, her nose flared, and she broke down, tears streaming down her cheeks.

"I'm sorry," she blurted out, her voice shaking.

"For what?" Though Spike knew she was feeling guilty.

"Everything," she blubbered. "Your arm. The Peetles. Cledwyn. All my fault."

"Now, now." Tessy pulled Amaya close. She took a kerchief from her purse and made Amaya blow her nose. "You know what my dear sister would say. Past actions cloud our true nature if we act out their consequences. Blaming yourself only makes things worse."

"That's right, Minxie," Spike said. "Besides, no one blames you."

"As for Spike's arm," Gigi piped in, "I have some nifty ideas for making it even better than before."

"See?" Spike tried to console Amaya. "Even *better*. You never know what's down the road. Maybe I was supposed to lose my arm."

The encouragement didn't work. The tears stopped, but Amaya turned sullen and quiet. Spike thought she needed to be in that hospital bed more than he did. He wished he could help in some way, but once Amaya decided to blame herself, he wouldn't be able to change her mind—she'd need to work through it on her own.

Day 11

The next morning Amaya told Spike and Gigi she was going out for a walk and disappeared. They found a note under Spike's breakfast tray.

I'm sorry for everything. Please don't worry and please don't try to find me.

It didn't surprise Spike, but no matter what Amaya said, he was going to worry. On the bright side, if no one knew where

Amaya had gone, that awful little gnome wouldn't be able to find her either.

Gigi told Spike how Yunosho had slunk away to Cledwyn's cave after Amaya confronted him in the hallway. She'd told him she never wanted to see him again. Spike didn't understand why. He couldn't remember very well—everything had happened so fast. He hadn't been too lucid either. But Yunosho had saved his life. Gigi was sure he'd saved both their lives. Yunosho's rage and strange appearance had shocked her at first. But when she'd fallen halfway to the ground, the Spidiepus sword passed over Spike's face close enough to give him a shave. She said if Spike hadn't knocked her down, she would've lost her head in more ways than one. Neither Yunosho nor Amaya saw it that way. Gigi thought they didn't want to, either.

At Tessy's suggestion, Gigi called Joe over at the orphanage. Spike listened in. Joe told them about the oracle and the images it sent. He forwarded his research on the gnome's cavern to Gigi. She agreed to work with Joe on finding it after she got Spike settled. As soon as the call disconnected, she started complaining.

"It's hard enough dealing with everything. And now? An oracle? Really?"

Spike laughed. It made him want to go get that ice cream with her even more.

Gigi decided to take Spike to the lab she worked at in Ammoto as soon as the hospital discharged him. The Jove sisters gave their blessing for Spike to leave. Gigi didn't know where they'd find the money, but she assured Spike they were going to build him a new arm one way or another.

CHAPTER 37
CARRYING THAT WEIGHT

(AMAYA)

AMAYA TRUDGED WEST. She was escaping. From what? She didn't know.

She stopped when dark began its veiling approach and gathered wood, making a fire beneath a tall poplar. She unrolled her sleeping bag and sat in front of the warm blaze, trying to piece her thoughts together.

Had she killed Mandy? Amaya abhorred violence. But her heart had exulted when Mandy slammed into that barn wall and slid down it. Now she felt ashamed of her reaction. No matter what she thought of Mandy, Amaya hoped she was still alive.

Then there was Yunosho. She'd trusted him, but now she realized with horror she didn't know him at all. He'd *promised*—a *sacred* promise—instead, he'd turned into a raging mad monkey and mercilessly chopped off Spike's arm. Where had *that* come from?

Worst of all—Sam and Bob were *gone*. Forever.

The churning in her stomach told her everything *was* all

her fault. Every bit of it. Sam and Bob. Cledwyn. Even Spike's arm. Look where her desperate fixation on her parents had landed everyone. She hated herself for taking that risk. She hated herself for failing more than anything. If only she'd connected. One. Moment. Sooner.

She crawled into her sleeping bag, worn and weary from the mountain of blame she'd heaped on herself.

Amaya entered her Random World. It surprised her to come out of the ocean into a dream instead of onto the beach. Nothing like that had *ever* happened.

She walked through woods that emptied into a lush, green meadow crowded with colorful wildflowers. She crossed the meadow, breathing in bright, perfumed air.

The sun dappled a hypnotic array of shadows at the other end of the meadow. Gentle wisps of smoke curled from a branch high up in a tree. Was the tree burning? Amaya moved closer. It wasn't a branch. It was a chimney that looked like a branch and was part of a treehouse that resembled the tree itself!

A wind blew in from the meadow, rustling Amaya's clothes. The wind spoke to her with a strong female voice. It said, "Stay. Rest. Heal." A heavy weight lifted from Amaya's heart.

शांति

Day 12

Amaya awoke from her slumber, hopeful and lighthearted. Gloom snuffed it all out the moment she remembered where she was and how she'd ended up there.

She sighed, disappointed.

It was only a dream, she thought glumly.

She'd brought no food but had no appetite. So she drank some water, made sure the fire was out, and packed up to leave. Then she remembered—she'd traveled south in her dream.

She slipped the pack's straps over her shoulders and turned south. *Why not?* The direction didn't matter as long as she kept moving.

Leaving everything behind, she thought. That phrase became her mantra. She repeated it mentally every step of the way. It helped dull the raw, ugly guilt nipping at her heels.

She hiked for hours, taking a break here and there for a swig or two of water or simply to mark the passage of time. She didn't care where she was going. She didn't expect to find anything either. But the moment she spied it, she knew she'd been sent there—the meadow from her dream.

She crossed through the same wildflowers, breathing the same floral air she remembered from the dream. She stepped into the spellbinding show of shadow and light at the other end and looked up, the thrill in her heart pushing some of the sadness away.

There it was, the little treehouse. It sat high above a swift brook that slid its merry way east, the gentle bubbling and swirling of the brook's waters misting the woods with magical sounds.

Amaya cupped her hands to her mouth and called up, a sliver of hope reasserting itself inside her. "Hello?"

An echo answered.

"Is anyone there?"

Again, an echo.

A ladder woven from strong vines led up to the house. Amaya would never enter someone's home without permission. She stuffed her backpack into the space between two bare tree roots, laid her head down, and fell asleep with the water's calming music playing in her ears.

She awoke with a start into darkness held at bay by a torch in the hands of a most peculiar woman. Her frizzy, steel-colored hair fell like a giant puffball onto her shoulders. A deerskin dress draped her wiry frame down to her knees. Two luminous, black eyes gazed down at Amaya from a face that looked carved from reddish-brown clay.

"What have we here?" the woman asked.

Amaya sat up. "We have Amaya."

"A-my-ya. Are you *a* Maya, or is Amaya your name?"

"Amaya is my name."

"It's a good name. What, pray tell, are you doing in my wood?"

"I followed a dream here."

"A dream!" the woman exclaimed as if it were the rarest of things. "That's a horse of a different color. I sense hunger. Would you care for something to eat?"

The question made Amaya realize just how empty her grumbling stomach felt. "I would as a matter of fact."

"Follow me. A warm stew waits with great anticipation of being eaten."

The woman carried the torch between her teeth and climbed the ladder, humming a cheerful tune along the way. Amaya put her backpack on and followed. The pack made climbing awkward, and she dared not look down, given how dizzy she was from not eating.

The woman reached the top and pushed onto the deck with her thin, muscular arms. She placed the torch into a holder and turned back to the ladder, waiting. She offered her hand for Amaya to take when Amaya neared the top.

"Not bad for someone new to climbing." She pulled Amaya onto the deck.

"I happen to have been doing some training. How did you know?"

"By the way you climbed," the woman replied as if it were obvious. She opened the door and shooed Amaya in.

Inside, a cast-iron Dutch oven warmed on a small, clay hearth next to a rough-hewn wooden table that sat low to the floor. The smell of wild herbs, meat, and spice made Amaya's mouth water.

"Please, sit." The woman gestured at floor cushions embroidered with cornstalks that had colorful birds flitting around the ears. "My name is Ela."

"Ela," Amaya repeated as she took off her pack and laid it in the corner. She sat down on one of the cushions. "A beautiful name."

"I was named after the earth."

"I'm pleased to meet you, Ela. But I wonder why I dreamed of your treehouse."

"An interesting question." Ela lifted the cover off the Dutch oven and used a wooden ladle to fill two wooden bowls with steaming stew. "One to which I have no answer." She cast Amaya a sidelong glance. "Yet."

She placed the bowls on the table and took her place across from Amaya. She closed her eyes and raised her arms with her palms open. "We give humble thanks to our plant and rabbit friends for this feast."

Amaya pressed her palms together and bowed her head. "Thank you," she whispered.

"Please, eat. You look famished."

Amaya dug into the stew. It had a fine, wild taste, like nothing she'd ever experienced before. When she slurped the last bit of liquid from her bowl, Ela asked if she cared for more.

"The stew is delicious, but maybe I should wait. I hadn't eaten for a couple of days before this meal."

"Were you fasting?" Ela took Amaya's empty bowl and set it next to the hearth.

"No, at least not on purpose. I left in a hurry without having packed any food."

Ela raised her brow. "Did you run into trouble?"

The mention of trouble unleashed a rush of images from the barn. Grief slammed Amaya's gut. She doubled over, bursting into tears, her chest heaving with painful sobs.

Ela sprang to her side, cradled her head, and whispered, "Oh, child. Dear, dear child." But Amaya's sobs were like fierce hiccups that couldn't be stopped.

The tears pushed out so hard her eyeballs felt like they were about to burst from their sockets. Her whole body shook with tiny, violent spasms. She put her face into her hands and moaned, "No, no, no." Over and over.

CHAPTER 38

HOW DO YOU SOLVE A PROBLEM LIKE AMAYA?

(ELMO)

ELMO SAT AT his desk, about as down as a man without real feelings could feel. The interview with the Meshterek had not gone well.

You gave assurances, they'd transmitted.

My plan was perfect, Elmo told them. *Two unknowns prevented our success—the professional man and the Atlas girl's new power. If she hadn't taken Miss Duggan out of the equation, and if the professional and his armor-piercing weaponry hadn't shown up, our problem would be solved.*

Two too many ifs, Mr. Grindquist, the Meshterek chastised. *The Duggan girl is the* only *reason your plan was thwarted, professional or not. We caution you to exercise the utmost care with her in the future.*

They paused. Elmo sensed they hadn't finished.

We considered decommissioning you, but we've decided to

permit you one more attempt. For your sake, we hope three will be charming as they say in your world, Mr. Grindquist.

The transmission ended.

Elmo didn't understand why the number three should be charming. But something about threes and charms rang a bell in his Swiss-cheese memory.

What had they meant by decommissioning? He imagined something like death. He supposed the Meshterek probably had death—or something worse—in mind for him all along. He possessed but one purpose—the Atlas girl. After he fulfilled his purpose? He didn't think the Meshterek would keep anyone around longer than necessary. On the surface, Elmo didn't care. But deep down in the depths of his mostly missing memory lay a lizard-brain dread of returning to nothingness. He shuddered at the thought, then brushed it aside. He needed to focus on the new plan.

How would he finally deal the Atlas girl the defeat she so richly deserved? Each time she'd foiled him. Now he needed to account for this new and entirely unexpected addition to her gifts. Physical attacks would be much more difficult and dangerous. He needed to come at the problem from a different angle.

He leaned back in his creaky chair and gazed up at the arched ceiling. His eyes focused on a loose brick that seemed about to fall. Drops of drool ran down the corner of his mouth, while the pins of his mind tumbled and tumbled… then *snapped* into place.

A *remote* trap! The loose brick gave him the idea. It would allow him to stay out of harm's way and nab the Atlas girl at the same time. Troublesome Miss Duggan wouldn't be able to exert one whit of physical influence on the outcome.

"Roaches check in, but they don't check out," he said out

loud, the word "trap" having stirred the ashen remnants of Elmo's burned-out memory. The saying fit. Like cockroaches, the Atlas girl and her friends were proving difficult to get rid of.

He wiped the drool with his shirtsleeve along with the line of dark red blood that ran down from his nostril. He'd been right to save the Duggan girl. He still needed her. He needed to know everything she knew about Amaya Atlas to design the trap—everything.

He went to check on Amanda. She was still breathing. Her pulse was stronger. At least something was going well. He turned to leave, and her eyes fluttered open. She grabbed her chest, coughing violently. Then she bolted upright, and yelled, "Crap!"

CHAPTER 39

STRONG-ARMED

(SPIKE)

THE TREMENDOUS PLEASURE Gigi took in driving without autopilot fascinated Spike. Yunosho had left Cledwyn's vehicle for them to use. She said she'd never driven one like it—an all-wheel drive, hydrogen-powered powerhouse that handled like a sports car. Spike couldn't drive yet, so he didn't quite understand the thrill. He didn't mind. Never having been on a road trip before, he was delighted to be on one with Gigi.

The physical therapists taught Spike how to manage basic one-armed tasks before he left the hospital, like dressing and undressing himself and using his legs to hold onto things. Gigi dismissed training as unnecessary. She insisted he wouldn't need any once they installed his new arm. But Gigi had been *too* upbeat.

She'd been forcing it for his sake. "You don't need to worry about me, you know."

"I'm not worried." Gigi kept her eyes on the road.

"You might seem sunny on the outside, but on the inside?"

"You're right." Gigi nodded her head, like she'd been

expecting Spike to bring up the subject. "I should be honest. It *has* been hard. There's so much to process. I can't get the images out of my brain. But I didn't want to bother you. You have enough to deal with." Gigi pressed her lips together and glanced at Spike, her eyes worried. "One thing eats at me." Her reluctance to bring it up was palpable.

"What?" Spike *wanted* Gigi to open up.

"I feel…" She let out a breath. "Super-guilty. We didn't need the water."

"*You're* blaming yourself *too*? Don't you dare. No one's to blame. Things couldn't have turned out any differently."

"Autopilot on." Gigi turned to face Spike the moment the car confirmed. "Look… I don't know. I'd be freaking out at everyone if I were you."

"Jeej. Listen. I could blame Yunosho for chopping off my arm. I could blame Amaya for insisting on giving herself up to save the Peetles. I could blame myself for attacking the robot with a bucket." Spike punctuated the air with his remaining hand. "A *bucket*, for Pete's sake! What good does blaming do?"

"I wish Amaya was hearing this."

"Amaya needed to go off on her own. I don't think any of us can help her right now."

"I guess you're right. Poor Yunosho. He must be *really* down with *two* people blaming him."

"Amaya's angry with herself more than anything." Eventually, Amaya would recognize what she needed to do. She only needed to remove herself from the bad place she found herself in. "She'll work through it."

"They say 'time heals all wounds.' I promise, though, once we get to OMBE—*you'll* heal in no time." Gigi laughed.

"It's out of my hand." Spike wiggled his bandaged stub and

laughed too. He probably should be more upset about losing an arm, but he didn't feel any need to worry with Gigi on the case.

"Yep. For better or worse." Gigi took over driving again. "You'll see. My friends at OMBE can work miracles. What worries me is coming up with the funds."

"See? I was right." Spike tried crossing his arms over his chest, but that failed to create its intended effect. "You *are* worried. Don't be. Everything will work out in the end."

"You might be right about that too. We're going to go build you a new arm, find Victorian creep, and save the world."

All the seriousness they'd begun the conversation with dissipated, gone and forgotten. This moment in the car on the road with Gigi was perfect. Spike wouldn't mind at all if he died now. He was already in heaven.

"Boy, I can't tell you how great this car feels." Gigi gripped the wheel and stared down the road with a wide grin on her face, like a happy, mischievous, car-loving pixie.

Spike chuckled to himself. He'd thought the moment couldn't be more perfect a second ago—obviously, he'd been way wrong.

CHAPTER 40
ALL IN THE FAMILY

(Gaia)

"IT'S NOT RIGHT," Vishnu moaned.

Gaia struggled to hear above the din. She was arguing with the Lord of the Universe. The other shouting matches going on around them nearly drowned him out. It didn't surprise her that even the black hole, which should be sucking sound the same way it had sucked most of their powers, couldn't stop them from making quite the clatter all the way out here in deep space.

"What's that you say, Vish?" Poor Hanuman. The Monkey Lord apparently could barely hear over his neighbor, Cydoemus, god of noise and confusion. One of the first forgotten gods, he was already so old and feeble by Roman times they renamed him Crepitus for his constant salvo of cracks, burps, pops, and farts. How had the pitifully senile creature even managed to transport himself here?

"We shouldn't have Amaya communing with this animal-spirit woman." Vishnu spoke louder this time. "Animal spirits are too modern."

"Why don't you stay out of it!" Zeus roared.

"Who's that?" Vishnu sniffled.

"Grandfather!" Gaia chastised Zeus with the nickname she used when he acted like an ancient curmudgeon. "Show some respect!"

"That's Zeus, dear Vishnu," Indra answered. A thrill still beat in her breast every time his voice reached her ears. "We met at Gaia's splendid Hindu-Greco ball, the one you missed, my venerable old friend."

"Oh me, oh my." Vishnu fretted. "Yes, I *had* completely forgotten about that ball."

"A wonderful party!" Thinking about it made her sigh with pleasure. "Had we only known it might be our last."

"What were we saying before I was so *rudely* interrupted?" Vishnu rolled his eyes at the spot where Zeus's voice had come from. "Oh yes, the animal-spirit woman, what's-her-name."

"Ela," said Gaia. "Animal spirits aren't modern just because they come from the New World, Lord Vishnu. They're ancient, older even than we Greeks."

"You Greeks aren't all that old." Vishnu wrinkled his nose at the thought. "Certainly not as old as we Hindus."

Gaia held her tongue in check. Zeus couldn't help himself.

"How did you get on such a high horse?" he thundered. "Gaia only has the girl's best interests at heart."

"I agree with Zeus on this one, dear Vish." Hanuman's fingers tried in vain to fan away the aroma of old man and sickly-sweet rotten eggs, an odor Gaia's nose caught the occasional waft of despite her relatively safe distance.

"Our universe is at stake," Vishnu whined. "Beating the asuras in the past doesn't help now. Look at us. We're one big useless pancake. It's humiliating."

"Amaya needs to be ready for whatever comes next," Indra said. "She isn't in her current mental state."

"The girl is too young, too inexperienced," Vishnu protested. "The asuras seem different, maybe *more* powerful. And eviler. We need a good plan, one that does *not* involve a native spirit woman. We have no time for such nonsense."

"I disagree." Gaia had to be firm. Plan or not, Ela was the right approach. "Her powers will show her the way if we get her through this crisis."

"What's *your* plan?" Zeus snapped at Vishnu. Gaia could tell Zeus and Vishnu weren't going to be best friends any time soon, let alone forever. Zeus detested whining while Vishnu seemed to delight in it.

"I'm not the planner," Vishnu complained. "Indra always made the plans."

"Sadly, this is not like the last time, Lord Vishnu," Indra said.

"Maybe," Vishnu pouted. He seemed hurt by everyone's reluctance to follow his lead. "Surely, we can come up with a plan or two if we put our heads together. What if something should happen to the girl? We at least need a Plan B. She barely escaped the last mess."

"The Fates have set the stage." Indra was being theatrical. Gaia didn't think he was helping their cause. "We are mere observers."

"Indra, whenever you needed it, I always helped, didn't I?" Vishnu entreated. "Right now we need a plan."

"What kind of plan can any of us come up with stuck here?" Indra replied. "We have none of our weapons. No thunderbolts, no missiles. Not even swords."

"These demons *must* have weaknesses we can exploit even under these circumstances," Vishnu said.

"May I make a suggestion?" Praj chimed in. Gaia was glad he did, always the voice of reason. "I agree. Amaya is our best and brightest hope. Gaia's decisions are based on her good and just instincts. However, I don't see what harm there could be in the rest of us putting our experience and resources together to come up with one or two good alternatives."

"See?" Vishnu, said, vindicated. "Praj has the sense to listen to me. We only need one or two *good* plans, really. I always say it's best to plan, you know."

"I suppose you're right, Praj," Indra said. "Our last battle happened thousands of years ago. Planning could resharpen our fighting skills at the very least."

At the very least, Gaia thought, *planning might keep you from ripping out one another's jugulars.* "Who knows? We might even find our way out of here."

"At least we're somewhere." Zeus sounded wistful, a highly unusual state for him. "I should thank you Hindus for being so numerous. That black hole would have sucked all of us into it had you not plugged up the entrance."

"I can no longer recall who we lost." Vishnu sighed.

"We lost many," Praj added. "Their names no longer seem to exist."

"Erased from everything." Gaia hated the thought. It reminded her of how badly in decline the Greeks were. "Just thinking about it gives me the shivers."

Hanuman's face puckered, like the thought of being erased from time had left a sour taste in his mouth. "Let's not dwell on such things." He glared at Crepitus. "You should all be thankful you're not stuck next to Fart Man here."

"That's it!" Praj exclaimed.

"That's what?" Zeus asked.

"Trojan Plan B," Praj replied. "We wrap Fart Man here in a giant gift box and deliver him to the asuras. He'll *stink* them out of the universe!"

"What a marvelous idea!" Hanuman grinned, obviously relishing the thought of getting rid of old Crepitus.

Zeus, being Zeus, grumbled.

CHAPTER 41

THE MAN WITH THE PLAN

(AMANDA)

AMANDA COUGHED AND spluttered. "It friggin' hurts!"

Elmo poured a glass of water from the pitcher and handed it to her. She found both Elmo *and* his water disgusting. She took the glass anyway and swallowed greedily. The coughing subsided, but her lungs still burned with each breath.

"That bitch!" Amanda spat.

"It will only hurt more if you continue speaking in exclamation marks."

"At least you didn't try to undress me, you creep." Amanda crossed her arms over her chest, which helped lessen the pain. "What happened?" She glared at Elmo, blaming him.

"You were quite dead."

"Dead?" Amanda didn't believe him.

"Yes," Elmo replied. "No heartbeat. Dead. It took me a while to resuscitate you."

"I suppose you want me to thank you." Amanda was riled up. The pain from Amaya's punch felt fresh, like it'd just happened.

"No need. I only did so because I might still require your assistance."

"I suppose that means Amaya Atlas still lives?"

"She does. Thanks to you."

"Don't blame me for your catastrophe," Amanda huffed. "I'm guessing your Spidiepuses failed?"

"The Spidiepuses performed as they were meant to. Unfortunately, I hadn't factored in a skilled opponent with an armor-piercing firearm. I *certainly* couldn't have predicted your rash and impudent revenge-taking."

"It was worth it." Amanda pictured Amaya's face pulled to and fro by a mixture of emotions, the strongest of which had been horror, to Amanda's utmost satisfaction. "That look on Amaya's face was priceless. I'd do it again."

"The Atlas girl was our target. The Peetles weren't supposed to be your means for achieving revenge. Now she's still a problem, one *you* need to find a solution for."

Amanda unfolded her arms. Her chest didn't hurt quite as much now she'd calmed down. "I wanted Amaya terrified right before her death. Except the death part didn't work out."

"We didn't want her dead yet, to begin with. I have no means to check, but you might have suffered a concussion."

"I don't think so. I don't feel too bad except for the bruised chest. Right now I want to wash up, put on a fresh change of clothes, and eat. I'm so hungry I could wolf down a wolf."

Amanda bathed at the large commercial equipment sink around which she'd hung a tarp for privacy. She heard Elmo working the electric frying pan, cooking those Hillbilly Slim steaks again. She dried herself and threw on the new blue jeans and a blue-cotton pullover Elmo had picked up for her. Her mouth watered from the aroma of searing steak.

"We're always eating steak." Amanda sat down at the work desk. "Where do you get them?"

"I have a supplier."

"I'm not complaining. I love them."

"Here you go." Elmo laid the steaks on plastic plates and spooned some instant mashed next to them.

Amanda dug in. Steak was a luxury, something they'd almost never had at the orphanage. Elmo picked at his. He never seemed to have much of an appetite.

"I've had an idea about our next move." Elmo was already pestering her with his constant planning. She wanted to eat in peace. "We'll need to use a remote attack. I want to avoid any repeat of the barn fiasco. I also want to prevent any direct contact between you and the Atlas girl. You're way too volatile when she's around. I could sense you were going to do something ill-advised at the barn."

"Ha!" Amanda laughed, her mouth half-full with potatoes. She took a big swallow. "Ill-advised? I bet Amaya is licking her wounds this very moment. I did us a big favor. Though I sure didn't expect her to pack such a punch."

"That was no punch."

"What do you mean?" Amanda marveled at how *anyone* could punch so hard, let alone a wimp like Amaya.

"It's easier if I show you." Elmo instructed his AI to play the footage. Amanda watched as the sickeningly sweet Peetle woman went down, followed by her distasteful husband. The vid filled Amanda with the same thrill again. Amanda sliced, Amaya leaned back, Amanda thrust, Amaya ducked, Amanda's blade drove its way toward Amaya's skull. Amaya exploded upwards. A punch to the chest sent Amanda *flying*. Watching herself hit the wall and slide to the floor dead was eerily discomfiting.

"Pause," Elmo told the unit.

"What was I supposed to see? She punched me with some kind of super-punch she probably learned from Sword Boy."

"Watch again." Elmo pointed at the screen where he wanted to zoom. "Replay, slo-mo, zoom 300 percent."

Amanda paid attention this time. Amaya's palm never touched her. "How'd she do *that*?"

"Indeed. How *did* she do that? She's more dangerous than ever. An even more compelling reason for a remote attack."

Amanda didn't like this development at all. It would be much harder for them to destroy Amaya, and Amanda might not get to witness the end. She'd been looking forward to seeing the demise of that evil little Indian firsthand.

"You need to put all your effort into remembering every-thing about her," said Elmo.

"That won't be hard after what she did to me. Memories become so much more vivid with hate."

"That's the spirit."

CHAPTER 42

THE BEE'S KNEES

(YUNOSHO)

"OMBE CONSISTS OF three divisions."

Bud was giving Yunosho a breakdown of the company he now owned. He paid careful attention. Cledwyn had placed a lot of responsibility on his shoulders. Yunosho wasn't about to let him down again.

"BIS is the main product division." An organizational chart on the vidwall highlighted the company subdivisions as Bud spoke about them. "Brain Imaging and Sensing. The name is a little outdated. BIS expanded beyond imaging and sensing only for the brain. Remember Chakra, the sensor box that was the precursor to the advanced training suit we built to measure a person's ability to approach an enlightened state?"

"Of course. I used Chakra during my own training before you and Master Cledwyn developed the sensor suit. I'll never forget how Amaya's training with Chakra went!"

"I agree. Amaya is a unique and impressive case. But long before we adapted Chakra to assist with Amaya's training, Master Cledwyn gave OMBE the task of breaking Chakra down into its components and further developing them for both medical and nonmedical applications. Medical applications now make up the bulk of OMBE's sales with gaming components coming in a close second.

"He funneled most of the profits from the product division into two research and development divisions. The first, Robotic and Biological Combined Systems, or RoBiCS, primarily manufactures prosthetic limbs that combine advanced inorganic materials with enhanced biologicals. Your friend Gigi freelances for them."

"She and Spike are headed there right this moment." Cledwyn's vehicle had alerted Bud as soon as the power engaged. "Did you make the arrangements?"

"As instructed," Bud replied. "A guest cottage awaits them. The director of RoBiCS, Jaspar Diffenbeutel, will meet them and make sure they have everything they need."

"Gigi doesn't know yet, right?"

"No. It will be a complete surprise. They'll be arriving shortly."

"Thanks, Bud. Please, continue."

"The third division—"

"The one I understand least." Yunosho's brow knitted. "I don't get how parallel universe research relates to anything else OMBE does." Yunosho suspected it might have something to do with why Cledwyn hadn't acted the least bit incredulous about Amaya's powers.

"It was important to Master Cledwyn. The story of what inspired him to establish the Parallelities Institute might shed some light on his motivations."

"What story?"

"As you know, Master Cledwyn practiced mindfulness inside Chakra to add his own data to the research database.

Seven years ago, before you arrived, a singular blip occurred while he was meditating."

"A blip? What kind of blip?" Out-of-the-ordinary events piqued Yunosho's interest. That was why he liked Amaya so much. She gave off out-of-the-ordinary like a heady perfume.

"A kind of interference," Bud explained. "We never determined its exact nature. My best guess is that some type of gravitational waves interfered with the normal patterns of Cledwyn's brain during meditation. I'll show you." Bud brought up a split-screen with Cledwyn's brain activity imaging on one side and his brain wave patterns on the other.

"In the vid on the right, Cledwyn's brain registers activity typical of a highly effective meditator. The momentary interference is coming up... now."

The areas in Cledwyn's brain lit up by his high level of mindfulness briefly surged, resembling the Aurora Borealis. At the same time, his smooth brain wave pattern degraded into something like video signal noise. Two seconds later, everything returned to normal.

"You could definitely call that a blip," Yunosho said.

"Yes. It made quite the impression. Cledwyn went to work setting up the Parallelities Institute right after it happened. The idea had come to him the same moment the anomaly occurred."

"Still, it has nothing to do with any of the other work at OMBE." Yunosho put his hand to his chin, wondering what about that blip got Cledwyn started on parallel universes.

"Entirely unrelated," Bud agreed, "but once Cledwyn decided to pursue it, he plowed ahead. He assembled a stellar team within two years. They've been at it full steam ever since."

"I thought parallel universes were still theoretical."

"They are. Cledwyn had all the evidence he needed to start the research based on the interference. Would you care to review his five-year plan for the Institute? It will give you a good overview."

"Later." Yunosho rose from his chair, intending to head back to the training floor. He'd taken in more than enough business information for one sitting. "We need to get to work on my internal audit and find what's wrong with me."

"Understood. A high priority. But if I may delay another moment, your friends just arrived at OMBE."

Yunosho couldn't wait to see them again, but he dreaded facing Spike for the first time since the barn. They'd laid the unconscious Spike out across Amaya's lap in the back seat when they left the Peetles' farm. Yunosho had raced him to the hospital. Then Amaya sent Yunosho packing before Spike had even come out of anesthesia. He hoped Spike wouldn't shut him out the way Amaya had, that Spike would at least give Yunosho a second chance. Despite his hopes, Yunosho prepared himself for the worst. Spike had a big reason to hate him, so Yunosho expected anger and resentment. He didn't deserve anything better. "Please open the vehicle's comms." Yunosho braced himself.

"Certainly," Bud replied. The signal bell rang. Two smiling faces appeared on the vidscreen. A gust of relief lifted Yunosho's spirits—Spike appeared genuinely pleased to see him! Gigi was grinning from ear to ear!

"Hi, guys. It's me. Yunosho."

"We can see you, you dummy." Gigi giggled.

"Of course." Yunosho blushed.

"You won't believe what's happening!" Gigi bounced up and down in her seat like a kid who couldn't contain herself. "OMBE is putting us up *and* funding the entire cost of building Spike's new arm!"

"I know." Yunosho's smile held a hint of self-satisfaction.

The relief he felt continued to grow too, tempered by the fact that he'd still need to address the elephant in the room—Spike's arm—in the near future. "Bud arranged it all."

"How?" Spike asked.

"It's a long story, guys. Let's just say Uncle Cledwyn left us some clout." Yunosho laughed.

"If that isn't the bee's knees!" Gigi said.

"Bee's knees?" Spike inclined his head. "Do bees really have knees?"

"Kind of, but not really. That's a saying I learned from my Great Grams. It means the 'best.'"

"The best?" Spike paused for a second. "Then there must be more than one bee with knees around here."

"Why do you say that?" Gigi asked.

"Because you're the bee's knees too."

Gigi's cheeks turned almost as red as her hair, and she averted her eyes. Spike looked into the camera with a big smirk on his face.

Yunosho was certain of it. Something was definitely going on between those two.

CHAPTER 43

A LITTLE BIT
OF BLOODHOUND

(JOE)

THE TIME WAS nigh for Joe to do his own sleuthing. Sitting at the oracle every day had been achieving zero results. His search for the cavern had hit a dead end. He read up on basic criminal forensics and commenced his own investigation, thinking he might find missed evidence from the ghoul's break-in at the orphanage.

He wrapped his feet in cellophane, borrowed gloves from the science lab storage closet, and grabbed plastic baggies, a pair of tweezers he sterilized, and a black marker. His first stop was outside, at the basement window the ghoul used to enter the orphanage.

He didn't bother looking for shoe prints. The police and the contractor who'd repaired the window security bars had trampled the ground there. But Joe had learned from his research not to ignore anything. He scraped the top layer of soil near the window frame into a baggie marked "Soil Entry Window." Using a brand-new paintbrush borrowed from the art supply closet, he brushed dirt and debris from the outside sill into a baggie marked "Outside Window Sill Debris."

He put fresh cellophane on his feet and made his way down the basement stairway carrying the high-beam storm flashlight the sisters kept in the emergency supply closet. The police had already examined the basement in detail, and forensic bots had recorded the entire scene with super-hi-res vid and laser scans. They'd found nothing more than a couple of partial glove prints and some shoe prints in the dust—size 8, smooth-soled, unknown origin.

Things could get missed. Even forensics bots failed to find important evidence. If the bots missed something, it would most likely be in the nooks and crannies. He found an old wooden stool and commenced a painstaking examination of the wall opposite the window where the ghoul had entered. He started at the bottom and moved up the entire wall, end-to-end, in overlapping one-yard swaths, taking in every detail. He found cobwebs, a few rub marks, and some chipped paint.

He started on the wall with the window. A tiny glimmer caught his eye right away. He withstood the impulse to rush to it. Instead, he registered its exact location and patiently continued his end-to-end examination, coming upon the glimmer again when he reached the top—a single gray hair, stuck in the crack where the wall met the ceiling above the window.

Joe lifted the hair out of the crack with his tweezers, taking great care not to drop it. He placed it into an empty baggy marked "Hair at Ceiling Crack." He made two marks on the wall indicating the start and end points where he'd found the hair. He wasn't sure if the hair's location would be meaningful, but best to be safe. After that, he spent two hours combing the rest of the basement with no luck. But that hair might be a real find.

CHAPTER 44

INTRODUCTIONS ALL AROUND

(SPIKE)

JASPAR DIFFENBEUTEL LOOKED and sounded like an English professor to Spike. He spoke with a British accent and wore a brown, tweed jacket over a white, buttoned-down shirt with baggy, gray trousers.

He gestured to the door of the bubble car. "Please, hop in." Then he said, "Executive Offices," once they were all inside. The car rose to an elevated track. Diffenbeutel had explained how compressed air drove the transport system on OMBE's campus using power from a heat exchanger drilled deep into the surface. "Miss Ozzarts will meet us there. She'll be your primary point of contact."

"May is my independent work coordinator," Gigi explained to Spike. "She's one of those attractive, upper-class Boston girls, so don't get all tongue-tied when you meet her."

"I won't," Spike said. "I'm getting used to being around attractive girls lately." Gigi smiled at the veiled compliment.

Her smile gave Spike's head a sharp tingle, like someone had just clobbered him in the most pleasant of ways.

The car arrived a few minutes later at an old, restored two-story house sitting on a hillock of green grass. They climbed wide stairs, past tapered, square columns supporting a roof over the porch. The door opened. A tall, thin woman with wavy, reddish-brown hair rushed out to greet them. She looked crisp and neat in a steel-blue, bell-bottomed pants suit that matched her eye color.

"May!" Gigi hugged her.

"Darling! *Finally*, we meet in person."

Gigi had been right. May Ozzarts *was* attractive.

"Hello, Jaspar dear." May had a teasing lilt to her voice. "And you just *have* to be the famous Spike Skopos I've heard so much about," she said to Spike.

"Y-y-yes, ma'am," Spike stammered despite his promise not to let his tongue tie. Her energetic bubbliness had caught him off guard. He reached out his right hand to shake, forgetting he no longer had one. His stub jiggled at May.

Gigi nudged him. "Spike!"

"Oh, yeah. Sorry." Spike sheepishly stuck out his left hand. "I'm not used to this yet."

May took his hand in both of hers. "Don't worry your silly little head about it one little bit." She put him right at ease again. "Gigi and I shall fix you up in no time, darling."

"I'm not worried." Spike grinned. "I'm pretty sure you literally just put me in good hands."

May laughed. It was infectious. Spike couldn't help but laugh too.

"Let's go meet our CEO," said May. "Todd's office is upstairs."

"Must you call him by his first name?" Diffenbeutel sounded peeved. Spike didn't understand why he'd object, but Spike didn't understand the first thing about corporate etiquette.

"Don't be a stuffed shirt, darling." May winked at Gigi as they climbed the stairs. "If it were up to Jaspar, we'd spend so much time on formalities we'd never get *anything* done."

She ushered Spike and Gigi into a large room with a long wooden table that had swivel office chairs arranged around it. Diffenbeutel joined them.

"We're ready for our CEO," May called from the hallway. She came back into the room a few seconds later, followed by an older man with thinning blond hair in a disheveled gray suit. He resembled one of those down-and-out lawyers from the vids. "Gigi and Spike, please meet Todd Blankenship, our CEO and OMBE's walking advertisement for the utility of wrinkle-free clothing."

Todd laughed at May's joke, but Diffenbeutel frowned. Apparently, joking about the CEO also didn't fit Diffenbeutel's idea of company protocol. Spike wondered if Diffenbeutel ever laughed.

"It's quite the honor, sir." It was the first time Gigi seemed formal.

"The pleasure and honor are all ours." Blankenship shook hands with Gigi, then greeted Spike, who remembered to offer his left hand this time, impressed that Blankenship did the same.

"Please, take a seat." Blankenship gestured to the chairs and sat down beside Diffenbeutel and May. Spike took the chair next to Gigi across from them. "We've been asked to make you better than whole again, and we'll do exactly that. How are things moving along, Jaspar?"

"We're in the final production stage for the thin-metal material for the arm. But that will only temporarily solve our power problem. We can print the composite bone's base as soon as we have Mr. Skopos's stem cells for growing it. Miss O'Grady has come up with some significant improvements in the meantime."

"If Diffenbeutel's impressed"—Blankenship squeezed his hands together—"he's talking about more than minor design changes."

"The changes increase the arm's strength, which is why we need the additional power," Gigi said. "I want Spike's arm to be the strongest ever made. Right, Yu?"

Gigi must be losing her marbles. Yunosho wasn't anywhere to be seen.

The vidwall lit up with Yunosho's face. "How'd you know I was listening in?" Cledwyn's clout must reach farther than Spike had understood.

"A highly educated guess." Gigi laughed. "I do have three advanced engineering degrees, after all."

"Having none, I guess my guesses would be elementary, my dear Gigi?" Spike, who loved the Sherlock Holmes stories, cringed at Yunosho's latest addition to his string of bad jokes. "Thank you all for making this a top priority." It was strange to hear him sound like someone's boss. "Spike, I promise. We'll do our best to make you whole again."

"Thanks, Yunosho, and everyone, for doing this," Spike said. "It's pretty amazing."

"Think nothing of it." Blankenship rose, then addressed May and Diffenbeutel. "You two have your work cut out for you. Keep me apprised of your progress."

"Yessir." Spike stood and saluted.

"He doesn't mean you." Gigi nudged him.

Spike realized he'd gotten carried away again. "I don't mind," he said, "I'll do it anyway."

They all laughed. Even Diffenbeutel.

CHAPTER 45

DIGGING DEEP

(Yunosho)

YUNOSHO SAT AT the console, working on the internal audit he'd delayed while dealing with things down at OMBE. "Bud, see if you can find any irregularities in my training data since I first arrived here."

They were trying to determine what happened at the barn. Yunosho might never see Amaya again. Maybe he'd need to accept that he'd lost any chance with her. But it wouldn't stop him from fixing whatever had gone wrong. He owed it to his parents. And Master Cee.

"There are four."

"Any correlations?"

"Yes. Strong ones. All occurred during peak periods of anger and frustration."

"I can't recall any of that. During the battle with the Spidiepuses, I remembered an aggressive monkey taking control of me at Mr. Oniki's dojo when I was little. The episode must've been so terrifying that I forgot it on purpose."

It hadn't been one of Yunosho's prouder moments. He'd

been eight years old, sparring with an older boy, a hefty ten-year-old who harbored an intense dislike for Yunosho. The kid kept closing in and whispering mean things about Yunosho's mom. Racist things. Yunosho grew angrier and angrier until all he wanted was to shut the kid's mouth. When the kid came in close to whisper something again, Yunosho swept his leg. The kid fell backward. Yunosho watched the kid fall, hate blazing inside him like an inferno, growing and feeding on itself. Before the kid hit the floor, the rabid monkey darted out from the shadows. It fumed inside Yunosho's head, stomping on his brain in a crazy tantrum, screeching so loudly it drowned out any other sound.

"Kill him! Kill him! KILL HIM!"

Yunosho couldn't help himself. The agony had paralyzed him, and the monkey took control. Yunosho raised his leg high, ready to drop an axe kick and crush the boy's skull. Then Mr. Oniki appeared out of nowhere and blocked the kick.

"A monkey?" Bud sounded puzzled.

"A monkey screaming in my head. I lost more than my temper. I totally lost control."

"I'm not sure if a monkey has anything to do with these episodes during your training here, but your aura exhibited unusual activity each time one occurred. Let me show you."

Bud brought up aural imaging from one of the four training sessions. He overlaid an Emotional-Response-Gram at the bottom of the screen and the corresponding real-time vid in the upper left-hand corner. The vid showed Yunosho struggling to master a difficult combination of moves. He kept failing. Every time he failed, the training bot's sword extracted a painful punishment, and the ERG showed Yunosho's frustration level climbing. First, the aural image turned pink. Then it turned bright red as his frustration surged into the high-anger zone, and a formation, a dark shadow, appeared in his aura, bouncing hard against its edges.

The next time Yunosho failed, the bot's sword cracked his shin. Yunosho snapped. He started beating the training bot viciously without defending himself. The bot beat back at him just as hard. Bud deactivated the bot, but Yunosho didn't relent. He hacked at the deactivated bot until Cledwyn grabbed his arm and stopped him. A chilling discomfort came over Yunosho watching that vid—like Jekyll seeing Hyde for the first time.

"I can't remember it." His throat was tight. He had to swallow a couple of times to keep speaking. It was hard to see himself completely out of control, like he'd been when he lopped off Spike's arm. "My memories of these episodes got blocked or buried. Why didn't we do something to prevent it from happening again?"

"We did. Master Cledwyn halted training each time. Then the two of you would spend an hour or so meditating together. The shapeshifting in your aura was a clue, but we couldn't decipher what it meant. Master Cledwyn decided to let things take their natural course. He was certain you'd reach a point where you'd have to face whatever was inside you. And it seems he was right."

"I'm dangerous! Look what I did to Spike!" The images haunted him. Spike's severed arm falling to the ground, Spike falling on top of Gigi, his blood spurting everywhere. It racked him with anguish every time he thought about it. And he thought about it a lot. Even if Spike forgave him, Yunosho didn't think he'd get over the guilt.

"I wasn't at the barn to gather data. I assume the same anomaly occurred based on what you told me."

"There's more. My father knew something about this. He warned me in his letter."

"What letter?"

"The letter my father left for me if something ever happened to my mother. The letter that sent me here."

"What did it say?"

Yunosho had pondered the meaning of that warning ever since he'd first read it, never understanding what his father meant until the incident at the barn. "The letter said I was in danger and would need to leave. He left me the coordinates for this cave. He told me to honor the black tiger spirit inside me, and he added a warning in the form of a PS. It said, 'Watch out for that monkey.'"

"A monkey *and* a black tiger spirit. What do *you* make of it?"

"Mom told me she'd had a vision of a black tiger running across a snow-covered tundra during my birth. She and my father believed the vision was a good omen, that a black tiger spirit inhabited me. I always thought of it as metaphorical until I sensed a real black tiger spirit back at the barn. Mom never said a word about a monkey."

"It can't be a coincidence. Your parents must've known more. Your mother may have reached the same conclusion as Master Cledwyn, about letting nature take its course. I've correlated this new information with your birth date and found a fascinating fact."

"What's that?" Yunosho sat up, surprised.

"Prince Sheikh Tamim bin Bani, a wealthy collector of rare animals, killed the last black tiger on Earth outside Oymyakon in Siberia, directly north of where you were born, on the very same day around the very same time. The Sheikh's aide, Sadeep Menon, published an article about the hunt in *Saudi Life* magazine. Unfortunately or fortunately, depending on how you look at it, the Sheikh and Sadeep died in a helicopter crash illegally hunting rhinos not even six months later. Look at this excerpt from the article. Be prepared—there's a monkey in it."

We waited in the chopper. The Prince hopped in, whirling his finger.

"Let's go, Yuri," Oleg, our Russian guide, told the pilot. We lifted into the air a second later.

"We need to stay on our toes," the Prince said into his mic after putting on noise-canceling headphones. "Bransford has satellite access too. He'll be watching us and searching for the tiger at the same time."

Oleg had chosen a place beyond the first bend in the Indigirka River as the starting point for our search. But he was concerned the tiger might be moving faster than he'd calculated, so we all stayed glued to our observation nooks on the way. It was a good thing we did. The Prince spotted something on the rocks right at the riverbend.

"I see movement!" The Prince's voice betrayed his excitement.

Oleg told the pilot to drop and hold her steady.

"There!" the Prince shouted. "Portside."

The chopper's movement monitoring system beeped. The cameras confirmed a target onscreen.

"By Jove, it is *the tiger!" I could make out its black-on-black stripes even in the twilight.*

"It's almost to the water," said the Prince.

The tiger knew it was being hunted. It sprinted to the snow-bank and leaped into the air, plunging into the icy water and swimming toward the opposite shore. Oleg and I opened both the port and starboard doors and locked a rifle into each rest. The tiger had reached the cover of tall evergreens thick with snow by the time we finished.

The headphones crackled with the pilot's voice. "We've got company. Twelve clicks away and moving fast. Two-minute ETA."

"Bransford," the Prince muttered. "How long before the tiger clears the trees?"

Oleg calculated in his head. "About two minutes as well."

"Get us to the clearing," the Prince said, "Then bring the port side around. It's going to be close."

We approached the edge of the forest. Dawn had arrived, tingeing the snow, blanketing the tundra in icy blue.

"I have a visual on that chopper," the pilot shouted.

"Yes, yes, I see them!" I'd been watching out the starboard door. "Coming fast."

"Get us into position," the Prince ordered.

The pilot brought the chopper around. The Sheikh went down on one knee and put the rifle to his shoulder, not yet looking through the scope. The sun hit the tundra, turning it gleaming white.

"Don't let Bransford spook you!" the Prince yelled to the pilot. "He's going to try."

I grabbed a ceiling strap and looked out the portside door in time to see an inkblot roll out of the woods. The tiger raced across the snow-white tundra, hurtling southward, fueled by adrenaline.

The Prince put his eye to the scope, his mind automatically adjusting for wind speed and rate of drop. A loud roar cut the air, battering the chopper. Bransford had buzzed us. The Prince had anticipated it. He readjusted his aim and squeezed off the first round, the only one he'd need.

The impact knocked the tiger on its side. Red snow flowered out from under its belly. Its black tongue lolled. Bright red painted its white teeth. Up in the blue sky, Bransford backed off.

I'll never forget what I saw next. The black tiger's spirit didn't *die there on the frozen tundra. It rose out of its dead body and streaked south faster than any living creature ever could. But the strangest thing I saw that day or any day since was the mean, menacing-looking, red-eyed monkey holding onto the tiger's tail, bouncing up and down as they went.*

Yunosho stood and began pacing.

"So there *is* a connection! This Sadeep saw the tiger spirit and the monkey too!" Hope beat in Yunosho's breast for the first time since the barn. There was a reason for his failures. They could counter it somehow.

"The tiger spirit could be correlated to your talents. Master Cledwyn often remarked how you exhibit a superhuman degree of strength and prowess."

"He wouldn't be proud of me now. I let everyone down, most of all him."

"You're being too hard on yourself again."

"You're right," Yunosho said. "This is no time for a pity party. Master Cee wouldn't have put up with that one bit."

"That's the spirit—pun intended," Bud joked.

Yunosho laughed. He was glad Master Cee had programmed a sense of humor into Bud. Yunosho plopped back down and drew his fingers through his hair, growing serious again. "What does the monkey mean?"

"According to all the historical information, a monkey spirit can be mischievous, devious, and sometimes downright evil."

"That's exactly how I felt at the barn, like an evil spirit had taken control of me. If a mean monkey spirit got inside me, there's got to be a way to get it out."

"I agree."
"Do you have anything in mind?"
"Not yet. But I'm working on it."

CHAPTER 46

GOOD DAY, SUNSHINE

(AMAYA)

Day 13

AMAYA ROSE WITH the dawn to the smell of fresh-baked bread and something deliciously pungent. She stretched her arms over her head.

"Good day, Sunshine," Ela called out from the kitchen. "How are you feeling this morning?"

"Better than yesterday."

"I'm happy to hear. Come. Have some breakfast. You'll need the energy."

"Why's that?" Amaya rose from the impromptu bed Ela had prepared the night before. She stepped into the hearth room, rubbing sleep from her eyes.

"We're going on a climb."

"A climb?" Amaya didn't like the sound of this one bit. Other than getting to Cledwyn's cave, which had been more of a strenuous hike, she'd never climbed anything more difficult than stairs, this treehouse's ladder, and some hills. "But I

229

feel so drained," she complained, still sapped by the outburst of the prior evening.

"We need to fill you back up if you're empty. This soup will restore you. You'll be fine."

Amaya was far from convinced. She'd come here out of curiosity, not to face new challenges. She felt like she'd been in a horrendous car crash that stole her family and left her lying in a hospital bed, raw and bleeding inside. She didn't know what she needed, but it wasn't climbing. She decided to stay despite her reluctance. At least long enough to find out why someone had sent her to this shaman-like woman.

They ate in silence. When they'd finished, Amaya went down to the stream with a sponge and soap to bathe. By the time she returned to the treehouse, clouds of gloom had regathered around her—she already regretted her decision to stay.

"I see you don't let any happiness get in your way," said Ela.

Is that what I've done? Amaya thought. Maybe. But she had no business being happy. None at all.

"I don't have the proper footwear for climbing," Amaya fished for an excuse.

Ela went to the corner, fumbled around in a wooden box, and handed Amaya a pair of scuffed-up climbing shoes. "Here. Put these on."

Amaya looked them over. They were exactly her size, though Ela's feet were noticeably larger than Amaya's.

"I collect spares discarded by wasteful amateurs," Ela said, anticipating Amaya's question.

She would, thought Amaya ruefully. She put the shoes on, the voice in her head insisting she not, then followed Ela's instructions for gearing up. They descended the ladder and started for the mountain. Ela explained the climb on the way.

"It's an intermediate climb, but it *will* challenge you. You'll need to focus. We'll be responsible for one another's safety."

Amaya's melancholia turned into outright dread hearing that. She shuddered at the thought of being the least bit responsible for someone else's well-being again.

CHAPTER 47

THE KID WITH THE GOLDEN ARM

(SPIKE)

SPIKE SAT WITH Gigi and May in a patient room at OMBE's Healing Light Facility. They'd been prepping him for a two-day stay in a light bed. "You *printed* my new arm bones?" This was the third time he'd asked. He still couldn't get over it.

"Yep," Gigi answered, also for the third time. "We're fusing the new with the old using a special bone-joining tube. The bones will knit together using tech that accelerates the process."

"You're going to sew them?"

Gigi laughed. "Not that kind of knitting, silly. It's called knitting when the bones grow together."

"We implanted gold microtube electrode scaffolds into your stub," May added. "They'll grow into the tissue generated from your stem cells, letting your new arm communicate with your brain."

"We also created artificial joints and muscles using gold nanoparticles and cultured cells called blastogolds," Gigi explained. "Your arm's skin combines gold nanoparticles with carbon nanotubes."

"Wow!" Spike exclaimed. "I don't know what all that means, but it sounds like I'll be the kid with the golden arm."

"Sure looks like it." Gigi ruffled Spike's curls. "We can melt you down for money if anything happens to you."

"Ha, ha." Spike feigned laughter. "Gigi thinks she's funny. How will I move my muscles?" Spike wanted to know as much as he could about how his arm would work. He was a little afraid of it.

"Your new muscles use a series of tiny but powerful nano-motors connected via electro-conducting filaments that act as nerves," May explained. "Remember when you went to shake hands and automatically tried to stick out your phantom right hand?"

Spike rolled his eyes. "*That* was embarrassing."

"Well, darling, when you do that now, your new hand will automatically reach out to shake. The nerves leading from your shoulder will connect with your new arm much the same way they did before."

"Except for one thing," Gigi added.

"What?" Spike didn't care for exceptions. They made him anxious. "What's the one thing? Is it bad?"

"You'll have the most *powerful* arm in the world." Gigi smiled. "That's not bad, is it?"

"I hope not." Spike wasn't sure he wanted anything so powerful. He might fail to wield it properly when tested.

"There is a little training involved. It's important."

"Yes, Spike darling," May said. "The training will make sure you don't accidentally destroy things, like people's hands when you shake them."

Spike winced. His mind had immediately pictured a

crushed and bloodied hand in his. Gigi and May didn't seem too concerned about relieving his anxiety about the new arm. "Really?"

"You'll be fine." Gigi assured him. "We have a special training system with super-sensitive sensors and an unbreakable rubber ball for you to practice with."

The top of the light bed lifted. Gigi helped Spike inside. The bed looked like one of those tanning beds in the vids except bigger and more complicated.

May moved to the programming console. "You'll sleep two days in this unit. The light combined with the accelerants promotes growth and healing."

"Do you think Jeej can survive that long without me?" Spike grinned.

"Oh my." Gigi brushed the back of her hand across her forehead, pretending to swoon. "How could I possibly endure?"

"I've never seen you so dramatic, darling." May winked at Gigi. Spike hoped the wink meant something good.

"It's time." Gigi nodded.

"I'm as ready as I'll ever be."

"You can close your eyes if you want," Gigi said. "But you won't feel a thing with these nano-needles."

May checked the monitors. "Light Unit, commence program twelve." The top of the bed lowered over Spike. Gigi followed it down to get a last glimpse of him.

"Ciao, Spikerini," she said.

The needles entered his arm. Spike drifted off with visions of Gigi dancing in his head.

CHAPTER 48

BROKEN WINGS LEARN TO FLY

(AMAYA)

AMAYA'S EYES FOLLOWED the length of a massive slab of rock rising from the ground at a forty-five-degree angle.

Ela pointed to a rectangular hole high up in the mountain's face. "There's the cave. This slab is the first stage. It's harder than it seems." It looked difficult enough. "We'll climb a craggy wall after that, about two pitches up."

"What's a pitch?" Amaya felt exactly like the complete novice she was.

"It's a length of one of these." Ela patted one of the ropes attached to her climbing pack. "You'll see."

Amaya didn't want to see. How could Ela possibly think a miserable failure like Amaya could even attempt this climb?

Ela turned her attention from the rope she was loosening to Amaya. She closed one eye and raised the other's brow. Then she cocked her head and jabbed a finger into Amaya's stomach. "It grumbles and bumbles in there, does it?"

Amaya drew back a step, startled by the sudden gruffness. "What does?"

"Don't listen," Ela chastised, her tone curt.

Apparently, Ela could read minds. Amaya *had* bumbled—a completely inept, bumbling disaster. She had a terrible foreboding that this climb, and likely the rest of her life, wouldn't turn out any differently.

"I'll go first, free solo, letting rope out behind me." Ela acted as if her gruff behavior never happened. "I'll belay you after that, taking up slack as you climb. Get your harness on. And the chalk bag. The holds on the slab are small. Your hands will need help. Take your time and keep maximum shoe rubber on the rock. You'll be fine."

Amaya didn't think she'd be fine. She didn't *want* to be fine. She didn't deserve to be.

Ela adjusted Amaya's harness, then scampered up the slab, adding to Amaya's feeling of inadequacy. Ela set a nut at the top and clipped the rope into it.

"Come on up." She gestured with her arm, her words echoing off the cliff walls. "There's nothing to be afraid of." She pointed at the rope. "I've got you."

Amaya began the climb. It felt far steeper than it looked. She moved slowly and methodically, choosing what she could only guess would be the best bumps and indentations for holds. When she finally joined Ela, she looked up, hoping to be nearer their goal—but the cave didn't appear any closer *or* easier to get to.

Doubt tickled the back of Amaya's neck like a bad omen telling her to leave. "I'm pretty sure I can't do this." The resistance at the beginning of this trip had only grown stronger. She resented being here. She wanted to go back to the treehouse, lie beside that magical brook, and fall asleep, enveloped in the gentle music of the woods—hopefully forever.

"Too heavy, is it?" Ela snorted, aggravated again.

"What is?" Amaya didn't understand. Her pack was light, not heavy.

"Your *obstacle*." Ela gave her a look of exasperation, as if it should be obvious what she'd meant.

"What *obstacle*?" Amaya pleaded. Ela ignored her and turned away. Amaya felt like an unjustly berated child. She'd begun this trek all mixed up, thinking Ela might make things better. Ela seemed intent on making them worse.

She pointed up the steep wall. "I'll place plenty of protection on the way up," she said, again, as if nothing strange had just happened. "Go at your own pace. You'll be fine."

Amaya bristled at the word "fine." She *wasn't* fine. It irked her to be told she would be. Amaya grew more agitated when Ela showed her how to work the ropes and go from locked to unlocked position with the belay device. Amaya didn't *want* to be responsible for Ela's safety. For anyone's safety. Not even her own.

Ela made sure Amaya clipped in. "Ready?"

Amaya had never been less ready in her life.

"I'll climb to a small ledge above us," Ela said. "I'll let out rope as I go. If I should fall, which I won't, hit the brake and use the wall as leverage to stop me. Pay attention to how I place nuts. You'll be doing the same on the next leg. You'll have to choose the right-sized nut and give it a tug. The rock needs to be solid, not crumbly."

"Are you *sure* you want to trust me?" Amaya squeaked. She was responsible for getting the Peetles and Cledwyn killed. Maybe Mandy too. It wouldn't surprise her at all if Ela ended up falling off the face of the cliff to a gory, bone-smashing death because Amaya Atlas messed up again.

"Of course," Ela responded and was off.

Amaya did as instructed. Ela moved fast, so Amaya had to pay attention. Her hands trembled every time she adjusted the rope. Ten minutes later, Ela pulled herself onto the ledge, still in one piece.

"It's beautiful up here!" she yelled down. "Your turn."

Amaya swallowed hard, trying to push down the fear that had climbed up to grip her throat. She began her ascent.

"Take it slowly," Ela said. "Try to feel stuck to the rock. Like you're a part of it."

Amaya knew what it meant to be one with things, but being one with a rock sounded like a dumb idea right now. She also hadn't exactly achieved anything good trying to be one with things lately.

She climbed the crag with purpose, her legs and arms burning from the effort. Her hands hurt because she dug tightly into the holds, afraid she might fall and pull Ela off the mountain with her. Focusing helped. Before she knew it, she stepped tip-pytoed onto a ledge that barely had enough room for the two of them. Amaya gazed out at a breathtaking view.

The blue sky was clear and vibrant. The air smelled brisk and cool, a light breeze blowing from the north. A turkey buzzard sailed lazily on the upper currents. She heard the young eagle's shrill whistle before she saw it swoop down into the woods, harassed by a pair of territorial crows.

"We'll approach the cave from a wider ledge above us," Ela said, gazing up. "It's basically the same exercise with you leading."

Amaya turned sideways and glanced up. The closer they got, the more difficult the climb appeared. With her confidence at an all-time low, her anxiety swelled again. She looked down. Nausea and dizziness swept over her. And she nearly stumbled.

"Down is a long way." Ela warned.

"I see that." Amaya took a breath to calm herself.

Ela snapped. "Not hiding behind that wall, you don't!"

What *wall*? What did Ela mean now? Amaya didn't bother to ask this time. Maybe Ela's mood swings were the result of some kind of bipolar disorder. Leave it to *Amaya the Fool* to end up standing on a narrow ledge on a cliff next to a crazy woman. Ela probably brought her here to push her off for fun. Amaya pictured herself falling from the cliff, her arms waving madly for purchase, Ela's demented cackling ringing in her ears.

"Don't worry," Ela said, her voice kind again, her personality shifts starting to frustrate *and* infuriate Amaya. "You'll be fine."

That did it. Amaya balled her hands into fists, her resentment boiling over. She *wouldn't* be fine. She *never* wanted to be fine again.

She started up the wall, trying to focus on one hold at a time, her face twisted by the anger permeating her mood. She couldn't focus. She couldn't stop hating herself for agreeing to come along on this stupid climb. She fumed instead of paying attention. She went to place her first nut but had nowhere to put it. She had to backtrack—a direction at least ten times scarier than up.

"That's right," Ela called up. "Try a different route if you're stuck. You're doing great."

Amaya was pretty sure she wasn't doing great. Her next step proved it. Her foot grabbed empty space instead of the rock she was sure had been there. She lost her balance.

And fell.

Her feet pedaled the air as she passed Ela on the way down.

Ela was bracing herself with that brake thing in her hands. And she was grinning! Hadn't Ela noticed the look of *terror* on Amaya's face?

Snap!

The harness bit into her. She hit the wall, gasping and wheezing, struggling to get back the breath the collision had knocked out of her.

"Take a minute," Ela called down, not showing the least bit of concern. That angered Amaya even more—because it hurt. She could *feel* parts of her body turning black and blue. Didn't Ela care? "Let me know when you're ready."

Amaya hung there for a minute, breathing through her teeth, angrier at herself for falling than anything else. She steadied herself, then struggled back to the ledge. Ela grabbed her arm and helped her up. Of all things! Ela had a smirk on her face!

"Good!" Ela gave her a stern nod as if scolding a child. "You *needed* to let go."

Amaya recoiled, stunned. How could *anyone* think falling off a cliff was a good thing? She regretted following that dream—she'd been much better off marching through the woods on her own. Lonely misery had to be preferable to the insufferable company of the mentally disordered. When Ela had said this climb would fill her up, Amaya hadn't imagined she'd meant with nonsense.

"You have to try again." The patient and genial part of Ela's split personality reappeared. "Set your first nut earlier this time."

Amaya was disgusted with herself and tired of Ela's obscure riddles. Her body ached. She *really* didn't want to start over again. But she gritted her teeth and resigned herself to getting this whole ordeal over with. Fifty minutes later, she dragged herself up to the next ledge, spent. She gave her quivering muscles a rest while she took stock of the situation. Her surroundings didn't look promising. The ledge, about three feet wide and fifteen long, dropped into a deep chasm. The cave across the chasm sat lower than the ledge, but the gap still looked way too far for jumping.

"Great job, Amaya!" Ela called up. "I'm on my way. Are you ready?"

Amaya reluctantly pushed to her feet, set a nut, and clipped the rope in. Her resentment was giving way to exhaustion, and the exhaustion was fraying her ability to keep her guilt at bay. Her thoughts returned to the tree next to the brook again. She desperately wanted to go lie down beneath it and forget everything. For years and years. They'd call her Rip van Atlas—except she'd never wake up.

"I guess so," she muttered, barely loud enough for Ela to hear. Amaya handled the rope even better this time despite her misgivings. Ela made the ledge with no trouble at all.

"You're doing well," Ela said as she stowed one rope and prepared the other. "The next part is the last difficult thing we do today but also the hardest." She pointed at a lip of stone directly above the cave's entrance. "You'll have to run down this ledge, jump, and grab that lip to slow your momentum so you can swing into the cave without crashing. It's dangerous if you don't slow yourself."

The distance from the ledge to the cave had to be almost twenty feet. Amaya had never been a good jumper. She was tired and sore, and her muscles twitched.

"Give me your pack," Ela said.

Amaya obeyed. She handed her pack to Ela, who launched it across the chasm with a full twist of her body. The pack sailed into the cave's entrance, slid along the floor, and stopped, perfectly nestled against the cave's wall. Was there anything Ela *wasn't* good at?

"When you jump, you need to let go," Ela said. "I want you to roar. As loud as you can. It'll help drown out your doubts. I'll go first so you can see how it's done. You'll be tied into my rope when you go, but you'll still hit the wall if you miss. So don't."

Amaya's muscles cramped—the idea of slamming into another wall filled her with dread, an experience she'd had more than enough of the past couple of days.

Ela gave Amaya a crazy madwoman grin, confirming Amaya's diagnosis of mental illness, and sprinted toward the chasm. She hurled her sinewy body into wide-open space and roared like a lioness, sailing in a perfect arc toward the cave. She grabbed the lip, slowed herself, and dropped to the cave's smooth floor with her knees bent, using one hand to stop her travel. Amaya's mouth gaped in awe.

Ela set her pack next to Amaya's, placed a nut, and clipped the rope in. The prospect of trying to recreate what she'd just witnessed numbed Amaya. She clipped in her end of the rope, her hands shaking worse than before.

"Your turn." Ela stood at the cave's entrance, holding the rope. "Don't forget to roar!"

Amaya would feel foolish roaring. Roar or not, the jump was unlikely to be successful. She had no choice. Going back down alone wasn't an option given her last backtracking disaster. She'd just have to give in to the madness.

She set her sights on the cave. She ran full-speed at the chasm, not leaving a second to talk herself out of it. She let out a wobbly Tarzan-like yell as she pushed off the ledge, surprised by the sudden, deep emptiness beneath her feet.

Her heart pounded. The wind rushed through her hair, its hiss in her ears. The cave rushed toward her.

The lip! She thought. *Grab the lip!* The lip was there, right at her fingertips!

She grabbed on as tightly as she could. *Got it!*

Too tightly. And too long. Her legs rolled upward, the force tearing her fingers from their grasp. She hurtled toward the rock floor, headfirst, spinning out of control.

Strong hands dug into her shoulders. Ela slid beneath Amaya and pulled her to her chest, breaking the fall. They tumbled into the cave together, a tangle of arms and legs, and slid to a stop. Ela rolled onto her back. They lay there, side-by-side, gazing up at the ceiling.

Ela let out the big breath she must have been holding. "*That* was close."

Amaya barely heard her. She was too preoccupied fighting back tears. She'd failed again. And she hated herself for failing.

She'd done the hard part; she'd reached the lip. Why hadn't she let go one second sooner? Too late—the story of her life. Too late to save the Peetles. Too late to save Spike's arm. The epitaph on her tombstone after she botched the rest of her life would read—*R.I.P. Amaya Atlas: She Was Always Too Late*. She wrapped her arms around herself—not for comfort but because she thought she might be able to crush herself to death. At least dying would rid her of the hateful loathing eating her insides.

I could have trained harder. She squeezed her chest, her face warped by sorrow and regret. *I could have saved the Peetles. I could have saved Cledwyn. I could have saved Spike's arm. I could have stopped Mandy.* The sorrow intensified, turning into quicksand. Amaya sank deeper and deeper into it.

She looked over at Ela for sympathy, for help. But Ela had begun to laugh, tears running from her crinkled eyes down the sides of her reddish-brown face.

It made Amaya furious! Laughing Ela! Uncaring Ela!

Madwoman Ela! Silly-riddle Ela! Walls, obstacles, falling down, letting go? Didn't Ela see? Amaya couldn't let go, not with the blood of three, maybe *four*, people on her hands! She should have ignored that dark disturbance. She should *never* have gone looking for her parents.

Guilt coursed like poison through her veins. Shame burned beneath her skin. Ugly thoughts swept over her in waves, pushing her to the edge, telling her over and over, *It's all your fault.*

She dug her nails into her palms and squeezed her eyes shut. She wished the thoughts away. But they kept coming, flying at her in a frenzy, like thousands of swallows pecking at millions of strands of memory, hoping to find a shred of meaning in everything that had happened. Why? Why had she ended up here, in *this* now, the one with all this death and despair in it?

She covered her eyes with her hands. Wetness leaked from the spaces between her fingers. Her breath came in tiny gasps. Her senses deserted her. She was being been torn apart. Falling to pieces.

A howl rang out. It was Ela, laughing even harder. Amaya tried to be angry, but she no longer had it in her. Her wall of anger collapsed, letting Ela's laughter reach inside her, letting her see that Ela hadn't been laughing *at* her. She'd been laughing at life itself, crazily, bravely, in the face of death. The laughter became a lifeline—Amaya grabbed it, the same way she'd grabbed Ela's hand at the treehouse. The mad laughter filled her ears and pulled her up, out of darkness and despair.

Her senses returned. The rock floor's steadfastness pushed against her spine again. The cave's cool, damp air kissed her skin, calming her. Her mind emptied. She lay there thoroughly drained, thankful to think of nothing, when a shocking flash of understanding struck her, opening her eyes with heart-aching clarity to the secret she'd hidden all these years. The lost little girl, sickened by the fear that her parents didn't love her and didn't want her. The fortress she'd built against the fear. The story she'd told herself over and over until it became her truth. That her parents had only gotten lost. That Amaya would find them and *prove* they hadn't abandoned her, *prove* they'd loved her all along. She'd clung to that story like a toddler to a security blanket, clutching it tightly, too tightly—the same way she'd held too tightly to the rock. And the rope. And the lip.

Her mouth filled with the bitterness of lost illusion—how blind she'd been to believe her worth lay outside her. The log fell from her eye. The fortress crumbled. Her heart gave way, grief rushing into it like a torrent from a broken dam, washing away every remnant of guilt and shame. She welcomed the grief this time. It felt awful. And it felt good.

She breathed… she sighed.

Her tears slowed… then stopped.

She looked over once more at the laughing, fuzzy-headed woman lying next to her and knew what to do. She let go— and laughed too. Right alongside Ela. Two girls lying on their backs, laughing in a cave.

This was turning out to be a good day after all.

CHAPTER 49
FINDING ELMO

(JOE)

Day 14

GIGI'S CALL SURPRISED Joe. He hadn't expected her to follow up. He'd thought she was just being polite.

"That's pretty good sleuthing, Mr. Trubly." Joe appreciated Gigi's compliment. "Can you send the hair and soil samples down to me?"

"A drone's picking them up any second."

"Any more luck with the oracle?"

"Not yet. The first message might have been its last gasp." Joe had been at it the same time each day. He didn't think more would come of it. But the oracle was too important to give up on. What if a message came through that saved someone's life?

"I'm having a hard time with this oracle thing, to be honest."

"You'd be a lot less doubtful if you'd been there with me." Joe laughed to himself, remembering how the oracle had blown him off the bench onto his butt.

"I guess. I've seen Amaya harnessing wavicles, after all. An encounter with a living, breathing oracle shouldn't be much more difficult to swallow."

"You can take comfort that you're not the only one having a hard time. What's our next step?" Joe wanted to contribute more. With his sleuthing done, sitting at the oracle every day wouldn't be enough. He itched to get more involved.

"Find this kidnapper weirdo. The best labs in the world are right here at our disposal. They gave me carte blanche."

"White card? What does that mean?" Joe understood the words separately but not what the phrase meant.

"It means our check, our ticket, is blank. We can write what we want on it."

"Write your own ticket. Must be nice. I wish I could be there with you."

"You know what they say," Gigi warned.

"What's that?"

"Be careful what you wish for."

CHAPTER 50

CRACK IN THE WALL

(AMANDA)

Day 15

AMANDA LAY ON her cot in the office playing vidgames while Elmo worked on his plan at his desk in the cavern. The games helped her think. Elmo thought they were a complete waste of time.

"Are you working on our problem?" Elmo yelled.

"Yes!" Amanda lied. "Stop bugging me!"

Elmo had already decided on the location of the next attack—here in his headquarters. He said he could set up everything the way he wanted, yet watch and control it all remotely. He would lure Amaya's friends to the cave and put them in danger. Danger was the "Atlas Mouseketeer's cheese." According to Elmo, Amaya couldn't resist it. He'd implode the whole cave on top of them with demolition explosives once they were all together. The plan was good, except it would deny Amanda the ultimate satisfaction of seeing Amaya crushed to death firsthand.

Elmo had one problem. He needed to make sure the little

Indian she-devil wouldn't use her new abilities to counter the blast. She'd need to be completely preoccupied with something. Amanda's job was to find that something.

She did a long jump with a triple flip and bopped the growling bear on the nose, grabbing three bananas from the gorilla at once. It unlocked a secret door. She stepped through into the next level—and remembered.

She ran into the cave, excited.

"Got it!"

Elmo looked up from his drawings. "Got what? Got milk?"

Amanda glared at him. "Why do you keep saying that stupid crap? It's getting really annoying."

"I don't know, but I do enjoy when it happens." Amanda sat on the edge of the other work table. Elmo spun his chair around to face her. "I'm much more interested in what you have."

"I remembered something about Amaya."

"Let's hear it."

"When we were little, I overheard Amaya telling Spike a secret in the rec room. Everyone else had gone down for lunch. I was in the bathroom, so they didn't know I was still upstairs. I came out and heard Amaya's weaselly voice through the doorway. I snuck up and listened in." Amanda's face puckered. Her eyes squinted. Just thinking about Amaya pissed her off. "I spied on the little witch every chance I got."

"Yes, yes." Elmo sounded impatient. "What were they talking about?"

"She told that runt Spike how she found this place she called her random world one night at bedtime."

"A random world?"

"She thought this world was a gift from the gods. A whisperer guided her to it."

"Gods! And whispering!" Elmo seemed upset by the news.

"Who could've been whispering? There shouldn't be anyone left to do any whispering or give any gifts."

"Look, Grindquist." Amanda didn't understand why Elmo was getting so worked up. "Don't get all huffy and puffy."

"Huffy and puffy are not in my repertoire." He sat up. "But I'm troubled."

"What? By the gods part? Those idiotic Jove sisters believe their gods are real."

"Of course they're real."

Amanda recoiled in shock. She couldn't believe her ears. First, powerful beings called Meshterek had come along and upended her world. Now Elmo had confirmed what those batty old Jove sisters had been saying all along.

"Are you *sure*?"

"I am. Except they're supposed to be gone. I'll explain later. Can we please return to what you've got? That's far more important."

"You're going to explain later, right?" She wanted to understand the forces at work behind the scenes. She might be able to parlay this whole Amaya Atlas escapade into something bigger and better for herself once they succeeded in establishing an Amaya-less Earth.

"Yes, yes. Whatever." Elmo's promise didn't sound very convincing. Amanda would make sure he didn't forget.

"Amaya said they gave her this random world. It's like a totally different universe she goes into it every night right before she goes to sleep."

"I don't see how that might be useful. You're supposed to find me a hole in her powers. This is a tiny crack in the wall, at most."

"Think, dummy." Amanda reached over and rapped Elmo's greasy forehead with her knuckles. "When Amaya's in this

Random-World different-universe thingy, she's vulnerable, right?"

A lightbulb must have switched on in Elmo's ugly head. His eyes rolled up, and that hideous smile spread across his face. Amanda still couldn't help being creeped out by that smile, except now she knew it meant he had an idea.

"What?" Amada asked.

"You said this Random World was like being in a different universe?" The point seemed important to Elmo. Amanda didn't understand why.

"Yes. Her exact words. I remember because it sounded like heaven, being able to step out of this crappy world into an entirely new universe."

"Or hell, depending on your perspective and which universe you step into."

"I was just a kid. I wasn't thinking deeply."

"I suppose not." Elmo nodded. "It doesn't matter. This *might* be our plan for dealing with the Atlas girl. The Meshterek could be quite pleased with this news."

"What kind of plan?" Amanda sincerely hoped they could get rid of Amaya soon. The world was going to be so much cheerier with Amaya erased from it.

"I need to confirm my idea will work."

"I told you I'd come up with something."

"That you did."

"Newsflash!" Amanda batted her eyelashes. "Amanda Duggan delivers the goods!"

"That remains to be seen."

"Oh, I'm pretty sure." She slid off the table, grinning. "I have a good feeling about this."

"I do too, though it's unusual."

"What, me being right again?"

"No. That I would feel anything at all."

Amanda snorted. "Like I say, you're a true weirdo, Grindquist."

252

CHAPTER 51

APOLLO'S GOOD DEED

(Gaia)

GAIA GAVE UP, frustrated.

"The connection's broken." She'd been trying to open a line of communication with the oracle to send another message to young Trubly, even if only part of the first message had gotten through.

"What should we do?" Indra lamented.

"Amaya may have to face the asuras without our help." It pained Gaia to say it. She'd insisted on helping all along. Now she felt utterly useless.

"I know," Indra said, deflated. "Though if we'd lost our powers without being stuck here, we might interfere more and in a much less helpful way."

"And muck it up most likely. We might get a message to Trubly another way."

"What have you in mind?"

"Maybe I can't get that oracle to work, but Apollo might. After all, he was master of the oracle in his day."

"What's that?" A thin, effeminate voice peeped from some-where in deep, dark space. "Did I hear my name?"

"Be patient," Gaia whispered. "Apollo's not nearly what he used to be. He's pretty much the poster child for all the senile Greek gods and goddesses under my care, you know, the Dearly Nearly Departed."

"I heard that," Apollo complained. "What's this Hear-Ye-Hear-Ye-Refarted of which you speak?"

As if on cue, Crepitus let out a loud one.

"See what I mean?" Gaia whispered to Indra. "Apollo's mind *and* hearing are going."

"Are you sure about this?" Indra asked.

"No," Gaia said, "but it's worth a shot."

"Apollo, dear." Gaia spoke as clearly as she could, her voice dripping with sugar. "By any chance, might you still be able to speak through oracles?"

"What's that you say?" Apollo asked, confounded. "Icicles?"

"No, no, Apollo." Gaia spoke louder. "I said oracles. Can you still speak through oracles?"

"Oracles?"

"Yes. Oracles. Can. You. Still. Speak. Through. Oracles?"

"Why, I don't know," he replied. "It's been a while. Per-haps Delphi a thousand or so years ago, or maybe Didyma, or it could have been Dodona. I can't remember very well these days."

"He's more than rusty," Indra whispered to Gaia, "but keep going."

"Well, it's Dodona we're interested in," she said

"Ramona?" Apollo asked, perplexed. "Who's she?"

"No, no." Gaia spoke even louder. "Dodona. We want you to send a message through Dodona."

"Well, I might still manage. Who knows…" Apollo trailed

off. Gaia thought he might be falling asleep. Then he yelled, "Oh my!"

"What's wrong?" Gaia hoped he hadn't fallen into the black hole somehow.

"Oh, dear. I killed your son Python, and I can't remember why." Apollo seemed about to cry, whether from regret or because his memory was going, Gaia couldn't tell.

"That was a long, long time ago, Apollo." Gaia didn't want to rehash the past. Hers wasn't exactly pristine. "Please focus. We're talking about getting a message through Dodona."

"Why do you keep talking about this Ramona?" Apollo sounded peeved now. "Who *is* she?"

"I said—Dodona!" Gaia shouted.

"Oh, that! What do you want with Dodona?"

"For you to send a message through Dodona!" Gaia was reaching the end of her rope.

"All right, all right!" Apollo complained loudly. "You don't have to get snappy. What's the message?"

"It's 'Keep – Your – Eyes – Peeled.'" Gaia pronounced each word slowly and separately, keeping the message as simple as possible so Apollo couldn't screw it up.

"Got it. Keep ice peeled."

"No. NO! KEEP. YOUR. EYES. PEELED." Gaia shouted.

"Eyes peeled?" Apollo asked tentatively.

"YES!" Gaia yelled at the top of her lungs, exasperated.

"All righty! You don't have to shout, you know. I'll do it."

Apollo grumbled to himself for a few seconds, then confirmed he'd sent the message.

CHAPTER 52

FINDING ELMO TOO

(JOE)

GIGI CALLED JOE. She'd found a match for the hair sample. "Elmo Grindquist. He's dead."

"Dead?" The dead part surprised Joe, but surprise was a good thing—he'd begun to worry nothing could surprise him any longer.

"He died five years ago."

"How's that possible?" The idea of a dead guy trying to kill Amaya felt pretty creepy.

"Your guess is as good as mine," Gigi replied. "I couldn't find evidence of record tampering, so no one faked his death. I also couldn't find any pics. Someone erased them, which makes the whole thing way more suspicious. The descriptions I found match the Victorian weirdo at the Peetles to a tee, even down to the facial scar, which was fresh when he died. Now we have a dead guy hell-bent on killing an uptight Hindu girl who can harness the power of wavicles and doesn't know where she came from." Joe hadn't been in the lab when they'd tested Amaya. But

Gigi had told him about the special imaging, and how it had shown Amaya used wavicles to power her mind melding thing.

"Has anyone figured out where she went?" Joe didn't like the idea of Amaya wandering around on her own. Especially not with a dead guy after her.

She'd never done *anything* irresponsible before running away with Spike. Now this, the most irresponsible thing of all—heading out in the face of all this danger without anyone to help. The Jove sisters would give her a good talking to when she returned.

"Not yet. I haven't been looking, to be honest. Too busy pulling data together from what you sent me *and* getting Spike's arm in shape."

"How's that going?"

"Great! He just needs to build confidence so he can use his arm without injuring anyone."

"It's that powerful?"

"It sure is. Advanced prosthetic technology is becoming mainstream. Yakuza in Japan have been replacing perfectly good arms with cyber-arms. Look."

Gigi flashed a news page with a pic of a headless Yakuza lying on the ground. The caption said they'd executed him for disloyalty. The bloody headless part was nauseating, but the metallic arm looked really cool with elaborate full-color tattoos etched into it and retractable knives sticking from its fingers. "Way more primitive than what we've developed for Spike but still powerful. And no fingerprints."

"Crazy. Did you get anything from the dirt?"

"I did," Gigi replied. "Another good find. The soil contains a unique mix of high-magnesium chalk and high-iron clay, a combination only found in a few areas around the country. One of them is about a third of the entire state around Ammoto, so we'll need to narrow it down."

"Anything else I can do?" Joe was fishing for a new assignment. He wanted to get more involved, though he didn't exactly relish the idea of an encounter with a dead, murderous ghoul.

"You can keep trying with the oracle. Try to think of other ways we might figure out where our dead man is hiding too."

"Speaking of oracles, time for me to go practice my daily meditation there."

"Time for me to go too. I need to get Spike through his training."

"Talk to you soon." Joe waved.

"Okay, Detective Trubly. Over and out." Gigi waved. The vid cut off.

Joe smiled to himself. He loved that Gigi called him a detective. He'd been thinking about becoming one.

He left the office and headed upstairs to the twins' sitting room. He grabbed the medusa hook, pulled down the rickety accordion stairs, and climbed them, then took his usual spot on the white marble bench to wait.

He no longer expected results, so his mind wandered. He thought about what the team's next steps might be. If Gigi could locate this Grindquist gnome, they'd surely head there to confront him. But where was Amaya? They needed to find her. They needed to warn her about Grindquist being dead; maybe warn Amanda too. Joe hadn't come up with a reason why a dead man would want to kill Amaya. There had to be one. Maybe he and Gigi could discover the reason together.

Joe snapped to attention. He thought he'd heard something. He listened for a full minute. Nothing else happened, so he decided he'd only imagined it.

Sessy was almost back to her old self. Tessy's worried looks were increasingly rare. Maybe after Sessy fully healed, Joe would ask the Jove sisters how they acquired this oracle for their attic. *That* was a mystery he wanted to solve.

A tinkle, unmistakably from the oracle this time. Joe's heart rate ticked up a few notches—the oracle *was* trying to communicate again. His subconscious prepared him for the storm of noise like the last time, but the oracle seemed to be struggling. He closed his eyes and focused, thinking that might help…

One pianissimo chord—all the chimes sounded together, filling Joe's mind with a stark image—a large block of ice beside a bright yellow banana peel against a pure white background.

The attic went dead silent.

What kind of message was that?! Joe thought, flabbergasted. *Block of ice with a banana peel?* It looked more like a modern still-life than a message.

He waited another fifteen minutes, sure there had to be more to it. He went downstairs to the office to report the news to Tessy and Sessy when nothing else happened.

"A block of ice and a banana peel," Tessy repeated. She and Sessy sat behind their desks next to one another, reminding Joe of the way they interviewed children who'd gotten into trouble. They made a formidable impression side-by-side like that, one younger Joe had been subjected to more than once. "How could they be related?"

"I don't know." Joe plopped down into the seat across from Tessy, feeling stymied. "But that's the message."

"To be sure." Sessy tapped her index finger on the desk, looking puzzled, "Oracles aren't usually quite *that* obscure. Let's think."

Joe knew the message didn't mean something dumb, like Amaya was cold and hungry. It must be more urgent than that. He decided to use the technique for puzzle solving he'd read about in a detective novel. He closed his eyes and pictured a picnic blanket in a field. He arranged all the known pieces of the puzzle on the blanket—the ice block, the banana peel, the white background, Amaya, Amanda, the dead ghoul as Joe imagined him, and the oracle. He examined them, one by one, emptying his mind, trying to let the answer come of its own accord rather than searching for it. Supposedly, the answer wouldn't run away from you if you didn't search for it. He felt a jolt of recognition before a minute had passed.

"Charades!" he cried out, excited to have discovered the message's format.

"Are you sure?" Sessy didn't sound convinced. "Seems an odd way to send a message, especially for an ancient Greek oracle."

"I think Joe's right, Sis," Tessy said.

"It's definitely a word message in pictures." Joe stood and began to pace. "I don't think they meant banana peel. Just peel. Peel and ice."

He went back and forth, spouting off whatever came to his mind, so focused on solving the charade he forgot Tessy and Sessy were in the room. "Peel ice. Pee lice. Lice pee. Pelice. Plice. Ice peel. I spiel. Eyes peel."

"Wait!" The answer came to Joe. "It's not peel. The banana is peeled. That's it!" Joe was sure now. "They're telling me to keep my eyes peeled. But for what?!"

"I'm not sure, Joseph, but I'm certain you solved it. It has something to do with Amaya." Sessy sounded convinced now.

"Everything points to Ammoto," Tessy said.

"Funny." Joe thought back to his conversation with Gigi. "I told Gigi less than an hour ago I wanted to be down there with them. You'll never guess what she said."

"What was it?" Tessy and Sessy asked in unison, the way twins sometimes do.

"She told me to be careful what I wish for."

"You better go pack," Tessy instructed with a foreboding solemnity.

CHAPTER 53

HAND JIVE

(SPIKE)

"RATS!"

Spike had virtually crushed someone's hand again. He was sitting at a training machine in the large, open warehouse space that housed OMBE's prosthetics division labs.

"Better than the last try, darling," May encouraged.

"Practice makes perfect." Gigi playfully poked Spike in his real arm with her finger. She was standing beside him so she could observe the cyber-arm's motor functions for variances that might need adjustment. "You've got this."

"What if my arm goes seriously haywire and I hurt someone?" The arm seemed too powerful. Spike would have to be super-vigilant if he didn't want to accidentally maim or even kill someone.

"The arm has ten layers of redundancy, all with intertwining crosschecks." Diffenbeutel was standing beside May, observing Spike's practice from the other side of the machine. "The likelihood of you hurting someone due to technological failure is infinitesimally small. Smaller than the probability that someone might blow one of us to smithereens in the next sixty seconds."

"Really?" Spike glanced over at Diffenbeutel, hopeful.

"Really, darling," May confirmed. "Don't bother your sweet little head about it one bit."

"Spike…" Gigi put her hand on his shoulder. He tingled all over again. He might even feel tingling in his new cyber-arm. "The main issue you'll have is mechanical breakdowns, especially when you push its limits."

"Why would I do that?" He couldn't imagine why he'd want to. He was uncomfortable with its power to begin with.

"Human nature," May said.

"May's right," Diffenbeutel added. "Power demands to be wielded."

"Goodness gracious." May fanned her cheek with her fingers and dropped her jaw in surprise. "Jasper just gave me a compliment." Diffenbeutel shrugged his shoulders, blushing.

"I did it!" Spike beamed. It had taken mental effort, but he'd squeezed the flex-ball without crushing the virtual hand, though the handshake had still registered as painful.

"See?" Gigi said. "All in one twenty-minute session."

"Amazing!" Spike tried again. No pain registered this time.

"Perfect, darling." May smiled at him. "We told you there was nothing to worry about. Let's start on the finer motor skills, like picking up a paper clip."

Diffenbeutel gasped, like someone had punched the air out of him. Spike looked up from the machine. A young man with a buzzcut pulled a knife out of Diffenbeutel's back, twisting it as he did. Diffenbeutel fell to the floor, his face frozen in a puzzled expression. The man turned toward Gigi, the knife in front of him.

Gigi picked up a lab tray and swung at the knife. She

missed. The man was too fast. Spike pushed up from his chair, kicking it out of the way. May wrapped her arms around the man's neck from behind, pulling him backward. He grabbed her and tossed her over his head like a rag doll. He moved toward Gigi again.

Spike moved faster. He took two quick steps around the machine, grabbed the shoulder of the arm holding the knife, and squeezed. Bones crunched. Blood seeped out of the man's shoulder like juice from an orange. He didn't scream. And he wouldn't let go of the knife.

He looked Spike in the eye. Their faces were close, close enough for Spike to recognize something familiar.

The man switched the knife to his other hand. Gigi slammed his knife arm with the lab tray. The man still didn't let go. He tried to stab Gigi, but Spike held fast. The man tried sticking Spike in the side, instead.

Spike grasped the man's knife hand at the wrist. He let go of his shoulder, stared into his face, and punched it. The man *flew* across the room, the amount of force surprising Spike. He bounced across three desks as he went, sending papers and desk trays spraying into the air. Then he smashed into the glass wall of a lab cleanroom with a pop. Glass shattered everywhere. He lay in the broken shards, his forearms flopping like two fish suffocating on dry land.

"Are you okay?" The man hadn't touched Gigi, but Spike wanted to be sure. Other than her wide eyes and short breaths, she appeared to be holding it together.

"Yes. You?"

"I'm fine," Spike said. "Gigi, you amaze me." Gigi's bravery had astonished him for the second time since meeting her.

"Did the arm do that or you?" She was asking whether

he'd meant to hit the guy that hard. He worried about what she might think of him, but no way was he going to lie to her.

"Not the arm."

Gigi gave him a sharp nod—he'd done the right thing; maybe he and Gigi had just discovered another thing in common.

They checked on May. She was sprawled out on the floor but conscious.

"I'm okay." She sounded groggy. "I think my shoulder separated." Spike helped her sit up and lean against a desk. She gasped from the pain. "What about Jaspar?" she asked through clenched teeth.

A group had gathered around Diffenbeutel. A woman in a lab coat who'd been kneeling beside him got to her feet.

"I'm sorry," she said, her eyes cast down. "He didn't make it." She looked at Gigi, tears in her eyes. It was obvious she'd known Diffenbeutel. "The knife tore through his heart."

May fell to pieces, sobbing. Gigi put her hand on May's good shoulder.

"Listen, May." Gigi's voice was firm and supportive. "We need to leave you here for a minute, but we'll be right back. We need to get all the information we can out of the attacker." May nodded through the tears.

Another good sign. Gigi and Spike felt the same way about dealing with the assailant. "Let's go," Spike said.

They pushed through the crowd. Some looked aghast. Some held their hands over their mouths or shielded their eyes. Spike saw why when they reached him. The punch had pushed the man's entire face into the cavity of his skull. Somehow, he was still alive.

Spike knelt next to him beside Gigi.

"Who are you?" Gigi glared at the man. Spike had never seen her so angry.

The man didn't answer. Gigi hauled back and backhanded his face, or the little left of it, surprising Spike. He wouldn't have thought her capable of it, though seconds ago, he wouldn't have thought himself capable of punching a guy like that either.

"Who are you?" She added more force to her voice, staring at eyes only partially sitting in their caved-in sockets.

"You'll never find Grindquist." The words sounded more like gurgles burbling up from a pile of oozing animal innards. A short "pfft" issued from the hole where his mouth used to be. He stopped moving at all.

CHAPTER 54
ALL SET TO EXPLODE

(AMANDA)

AMANDA WAITED FOR Elmo to come out of his communion with the Meshterek. She enjoyed watching his sessions with them now. It was the strangest thing. His eyeballs rolled around under closed eyelids. His tongue spasmed, pushing against his ugly lips in random places while each lip pursed and un-pursed separately. And the weird blotchiness his skin took on was disgusting but also kind of fascinating.

Occasionally a word or two would escape. This time he'd said "gravity" and "black hole." She had no clue how those things related to their plans for Amaya. All the same, Amanda had shoplifted a little black notebook when they'd gone out. She'd begun to keep notes on the Meshterek, writing down her observations and the words she heard.

He opened his eyes. "We're all set." A line of dark red blood ran down the side of his nose from one of his tear ducts.

"What do you mean?"

"The plan has been greenlighted. The Meshterek are pleased

about this Random World, though they weren't happy to hear of its origins."

"The gift from the gods part?" Amanda wanted to understand the Meshterek. The more she knew about them, the more valuable she could make herself—or escape. Her notes could end up being important.

"There's nothing we can do about it. We focus on the Atlas girl for now."

"Why don't these Meshterek kill her themselves if they're so all-powerful?"

"The Meshterek have limited ability to operate in this particular physical world."

"Hardly seems all-powerful." It seemed like a major weakness, in fact. Like the kind that always proves fatal in the vids. She needed to pay even more attention. She needed to be prepared for both outcomes.

"Don't worry your pretty little head about it, Ms. Duggan. I'll deal with the Meshterek. You and I need to execute our plan."

Amanda kicked back in her chair and propped her feet on the table. "I did my part. Didn't I just save your butt from the Meshterek again?"

"Perhaps. Don't forget—you're also the reason Miss Atlas still lives."

The immense joy of seeing Amaya's terror at the barn hadn't lessened Amanda's tremendous displeasure over Amaya escaping with her life. "We'll get her this time," she said under her breath. "You'll see."

"High motivation," Elmo observed. "I like that." He turned his attention to the vidscreen on his work table, which glowed with some kind of construction diagram. "They'll investigate once I message the O'Grady girl the coordinates for our humble abode. Our primary rat, Miss Atlas, will walk right into the trap if her friends are in danger. Knowing it's a trap won't stop her."

"I still don't get how she does it. I mean, how'd she know the Peetles were in danger?"

"She sensed it. My first attack proved that."

"That's why I never could hurt her? She can sense the attacks coming?"

"Precisely. That and the new power that nearly brought about your death are what concern the Meshterek."

This new information gave Amanda more confidence, though she was feeling pretty confident these days anyway. It had been stupid to blame herself for her failures when obviously it was the little witch's fault.

"If she can sense the danger, isn't she going to know the cave is set to explode?"

"The Meshterek assured me they can prevent that," Elmo replied.

"How?"

"They didn't explain. I'm guessing by keeping her occupied the way we'd planned. They'll signal us when the time is right."

"A signal? For what?"

"To blow this cave to smithereens, my dear. We'll wipe out her *and* her pestilent friends."

"Where will we be? Didn't you say you wanted this to be a remote attack?" She hoped they'd be able to watch. Amanda wanted proof of death, not to mention the sheer pleasure of witnessing the event she'd worked so hard to bring about.

"Don't worry, my dear." Elmo laughed his death-rattle laugh. "I found the perfect little hiding place."

CHAPTER 55

INTO THE STORM

(Yunosho)

"GOTTAMINT!"

Yunosho remembered when he'd first heard that, walking with his mother. A man had been coming from the opposite direction, talking to someone on his phone. He ran head-first into a streetlamp.

"Mama, why did that man say 'gottamint' when he hit the pole?" Yunosho was curious. He loved mints. Especially chocolate ones.

His mother laughed. Yunosho loved her laugh. It wafted like a light, cheery breeze across his face, never failing to make him look up at her and smile. They'd stopped in the middle of the sidewalk. His mother crouched down to his level, took both of his hands in hers, and looked him in the eye.

"That's something people say when they're frustrated or angry with themselves, sweetie."

To a little chocolate-mint lover like Yunosho, there couldn't have been a more perfect thing to do when having a bad day— picture chocolate mints in your head. It worked. Chocolate mints always took his mind off his troubles. Right now he needed to take his mind off the pain one of the training bots had just inflicted.

"Gottamint!" Yunosho cried out.

Bud chuckled. "Haven't heard you say that in a while."

Bud was running RibbonMaker, the sword training program Cledwyn had developed for his state-of-the-art training floor. It controlled six virtually indestructible rubber-coated bot attackers wirelessly via powerful electromagnetic currents beneath the floor and in the ceiling. Yunosho was training again to stay focused. He'd taken on all six bots at once. One had just given his kidney a painful jab.

"Only because I haven't trained this hard in a while." Yunosho blocked two bot swords coming from his right, then slid under a third bot whose leg he virtually sliced open where the femoral artery would be. He came off the ground and spun around to defend again when the program froze.

"There's a call coming in from OMBE marked urgent," said Bud.

"Put it onscreen." Yunosho laid his training swords on the equipment table and sat down at the console. Gigi and Spike appeared on the vidwall.

"Yu, we've been attacked!" Gigi looked distraught, but Spike was smiling—that kid's ability to stay positive was impressive. Yunosho's first reaction when Gigi described what happened was pride—his friends had handled themselves well. But he felt terrible about Diffenbeutel. He'd make sure OMBE took care of his family. He was glad to have the resources for it, though it was intimidating to be responsible for so many people's livelihoods and the well-being of their families. "I figure the guy was a plant. He must've been watching internal data traffic at OMBE and came for me because I was digging up info on Grindquist."

Gigi had forwarded the information about Grindquist's status as a dead man to Yunosho. He and Bud had already sorted through the implications, confirming what Gigi said from the outset—they were dealing with more technologically advanced aliens or alternate universes.

"He was a dead guy too." Spike was nodding. "Same as Grindquist. I knew it the moment I looked into his eyes."

"We don't know that for sure," Gigi corrected. "He was a data processor who'd been working at OMBE for over two years. I found no record of him dying, but given the amount of damage he suffered before he died, maybe for the second time, the likelihood of Spike being right is high."

"This scheme is more involved than we thought. I mean, if they have plants at OMBE—"

"There's more," Gigi interrupted. "I received a message via my Webineers page."

"What's Webineers?"

"Only *the* site for engineers." Gigi seemed to think it should be obvious. "Any engineer worth their salt keeps a Webineers page. It's a cooperative problem-solving site, but it's also a social forum for geeks. We have this cool logo too. A black silhouette of a round robot head that looks like the Mickey Mouse silhouette? But instead of mouse ears, the robot has radio telescope ears."

Yunosho laughed. Gigi had gone into full geek mode. "Sorry, Jeej. Only engineers would find that cool."

Spike poked Gigi's arm as if to say, *See?*

"The message contained those coordinates and nothing else?" Yunosho asked.

"Affirmative." Gigi nudged Spike away with her elbow. "I

couldn't trace its origins. Whoever sent the message used a dead guy's account to access the system."

"The Grindquist gnome's?" Yunosho asked.

"Nope, he's not an engineer. Some other dead guy. A real AI engineer named Robert Lille. They stole his access keys. Webineers is super-secure. Every user needs to be triple validated, and it uses three-factor authentication. I don't believe they could've hacked in. I can't rule it out either since other-worldly technology might be involved."

Something didn't add up. "Why would they send someone to kill you if they wanted you to receive the coordinates?"

"Either a lack of communication, or the attacker was on autopilot. Probably the latter. Seemed to me he was carrying out predetermined instructions. I mean, the guy never said a word until the end. Then all he told us was we'd never find Grindquist."

"He's laying a trap for Amaya. We need to check out those coordinates. Even if it's a trap. Grindquist probably sent the coordinates to lure you."

"The coordinates point to an old, abandoned vineyard called *Rattebane* on the other side of the city," said Gigi. "Its soil profile matches the sample Joe Trubly sent. I think Grindquist has been operating out of there. It creeps me out to know we're dealing with dead guys."

"You and me both."

"Count me in," Spike added, cheerfully waving his hand in the air. "I'm creeped out too."

Yunosho was glad Spike hadn't lost any of his goofiness. "You think Amaya's going to show up there?"

"Almost 100 percent certain," Spike answered.

"She might be headed there now?" Yunosho surmised.

"Exactly," Gigi said. "That's why Spike and I need to get over there right away."

"I don't like it, Jeej." Yunosho felt helpless sitting in the bat cave with no one else but Bud. "You and Spike aren't equipped to deal with Grindquist on your own. He's going to try to kidnap you the same way he kidnapped the Peetles—or worse." Worse was more likely. Grindquist didn't seem like the type who would try a failed stunt two times in a row. Those Samurai Spidiepuses were a big improvement over robot dragonflies.

"We can't let Amaya show up by herself," Gigi worried.

"You're right. We can't." Spike's expression turned grave. "And we won't. We need to warn Amaya as soon as she arrives. She'll need help. I'm going no matter what."

"Okay, you've convinced me." There was nothing more to discuss. Someone needed to be there. It would take Yunosho too much time to get there. "I'll have Blankenship provide security bots for you. They can be lookouts while you're checking the place out. But I don't want OMBE to know what we're up to yet. The attack at the lab tells me we can't trust anyone. Bud, the private jet?"

"Already in process."

"It'll take a few hours before I can join you. I need to get to the airport first."

"Soooo…" Gigi raised an inquisitive brow. "Do you *run* OMBE? I knew you had pull, but seems like way more than that."

"Sort of." Yunosho didn't want to freak anyone out yet with how terrifyingly wealthy he'd become. It still scared him to death, though he was doing his best not to show it. "I'll fill you in later. No one's heard from Amaya, right?"

"Not a peep," Gigi said. "I know you're worried, but she went totally off-grid."

"I think she's wandering the woods trying to sort things out," Spike said.

A faint hope burned in Yunosho that sorting things out might include, through some small miracle, forgiving him, even a little—not that he deserved it.

"Yeah. She could show up at *Rattebane* any moment," Gigi said. "Luckily, it's only thirty minutes away."

"Gigi, do you know how to use a sidearm?" Yunosho asked.

A smile spread across Gigi's face. "Funny you should ask. My dad's military. He taught me how to shoot."

"That might come in handy," Yunosho said. "We can't send in armed bots. It's illegal. Besides, they're programmed to do no harm."

"Just so you know, "Gigi warned, "I never shot anything other than inanimate targets. I hope to keep it that way."

"The weapon is only for backup. I'll rest easier if you're armed. There'll be a sidearm waiting for you in the transport vehicle."

Spike's head bobbed. "I'll rest easier too after seeing what dead people can do."

The time seemed right. Yunosho had fretted and fretted about apologizing for Spike's arm. But he had to do it. "Spike, I understand your arm is fully operational."

"Yep." Spike held his new arm up for Yunosho to see. "I'm still nervous about it, but I think I have pretty good control."

"For sure," Gigi said. "He did a bang-up job on our attacker, literally."

"Spike, I can't tell you how sorry I am about your arm." Yunosho wanted to make sure Spike understood how heavily his lapse at the barn weighed on him.

"Stop." Spike stuck out his cyber-hand like a traffic cop.

"You did the right thing, Yu," Gigi said.

"We don't know that. It would've been for the wrong reason even if I had. It would help a lot if you two could forgive me."

"Gigi's right." Spike seemed dead serious. "There's nothing to forgive. You and Master Cledwyn saved us all."

Yunosho flinched at the mention of Master Cee. That pain wouldn't disappear anytime soon. "What I did was wrong." Yunosho was adamant. "I'm asking for your forgiveness."

"If that's all you need, it's yours," Spike said.

"Mine too," Gigi added.

"On one condition," Spike added, gazing directly at the camera, his expression unusually grave.

"What's that?"

"Never raise this issue again." Yunosho had never seen Spike more in earnest. "You're forgiven. That means it's over and done."

Just like that—every bit of Yunosho's guilt about cutting off Spike's arm washed away, cleansed by the purest water on Earth—complete, sincere forgiveness. Yunosho actually *felt* like he weighed less. "Thank you, Spike." His voice cracked. He put his palms together and bowed his head toward the camera, immensely humbled.

"You both forget there's someone who *really* needs to forgive Yunosho," Gigi reminded them.

The sudden, empty pang of something irretrievably lost squeezed Yunosho's heart. He almost gasped from the spasm. "I can't imagine asking her."

"We'll help," Spike said. "We're all in this together."

"You betcha." Gigi pumped her fist. "We won't let you down."

"I'll understand and accept it if she never forgives me."

"You'll see," Spike said. "Everything's going to be all right."

Yunosho loved Spike for his never-fading optimism, but he didn't think it would help in this case.

"It will. Right now we need to move it," Gigi said.

"Right." Yunosho forced himself to get back to business. "The bot transport will be ready shortly. Gather whatever equipment you need. I'll see you soon."

"Roger that." Gigi saluted.

Spike saluted too. Yunosho almost couldn't tell the new arm wasn't the original.

CHAPTER 56

ARRIVEDERCI ELA

(AMAYA)

SPIKE AND GIGI *are in danger!*

The unexpected connection hit Amaya hard, halfway up the ladder at Ela's treehouse. Amaya had to wrap her arm around a rung to keep herself from falling. She told Ela she had to go—*right away.* They packed Amaya's things. Then Ela hastened her through the woods to the Yellowbird train station, where Amaya would catch the train to Ammoto.

Dusk hurried its way west as they climbed the steps to the raised platform. They'd arrived at the southbound track with barely a minute or two to spare. Neatly ordered rows of orange puffballs dotted the sky, reflecting the light from the setting sun. The air smelled cool, though there was no chill to it.

"You will face grave danger." Ela's face was somber. "My heart worries for you."

"I'm unafraid." Amaya felt strong standing next to Ela, ready for whatever might come. She'd made a decision and committed to it. "But I fear for my friends."

"You will be tested."

"My whole life has led me here. I see that now. I accept it too—not as my fate but as my duty."

The rumble of the approaching train reached Amaya's ears.

Ela smiled. "Remember, you carry a piece of me in your heart. Call upon it anytime you're in need."

Amaya worried her lip to keep it from trembling. She held the tears back, wanting to remain stalwart. She gazed at Ela's weathered face and into her shiny eyes.

"To whoever sent me your way, I give my utmost thanks." Amaya took a step back and bowed.

She came erect again. A teary-eyed Ela stepped forward and embraced her, whispering into her ear. "I *will* see you again, my little one."

The train came to a stop. Amaya looked into Ela's eyes one last time.

"Until then."

"Until then," Ela echoed.

Amaya had to exert great discipline to pull herself away and board the train. Ela followed along the platform until Amaya found a window seat and settled in. The train clanked, jerking forward. Ela stood there waving as it left the platform. Amaya looked out the window with sad puppy-dog eyes, her palm flat on the window, her heartstrings tugging. A part of her, the little girl inside, suddenly alone and afraid, wanted desperately to stay.

CHAPTER 57
TREE PEOPLE

(SPIKE)

SPIKE CLIMBED INTO the back of the black transport van at OMBE with Gigi. She accepted the sidearm one of the guard bots handed her, checked the safety, then put on the paddle holster and holstered it. Spike kept sneaking glances at her. She had no clue how attractive and formidable she came off in her sensor suit with the sidearm on her thigh. She'd retrofitted the suit with a lot of micro-tools. It could sniff bombs, analyze chemicals, detect movement, scramble signals, and look inside things. She'd also added a gravity-field sensor on a hunch that gravitational forces might be at work. Her fashionably red goggs not only relayed her suit's data, they could also zoom and light up the night in color as if it were daytime.

The Jove sisters had rung Gigi as soon as she and Spike had hung up with Yunosho, anxious to explain the latest oracle incident and how they'd taken Joe straight to the train station after.

"Joe's on his way too?" Spike asked. The van moved silently through the evening dusk.

"Yep. His train left Redbird over an hour ago according to

the schedule. I can't get over that message, though. Ice peel. An oracle that plays charades."

Spike laughed. "Never a dull moment at Just-So."

The transport turned off the secondary road onto a disused gravel driveway at an aging wooden sign with faded green grapes carved into it. The sign read *Rattebane Vineyards*. The van turned again onto what was more like a trail and stopped about a minute later at the trail's end in front of a tall hill. The three guard bots disembarked. Spike and Gigi followed.

"Bots," Gigi commanded. "Set up a triangle perimeter forty feet apart. Keep your sensors wide open."

"Confirmed. Forty-foot triangle perimeter." The bots took up position.

Gigi and Spike examined the hillside in the dying light. The overgrowth was thick. They pushed aside vines and brush and found the entrance to the cavern.

"This must be the place," Spike said.

"Right where the coordinates land. Must be a wine cave built into this hillside. I guess Grindquist wants us in there."

Spike closed his eyes and folded his arms in front of him like a djinni. "The cave speaks to me."

Gigi laughed. "Spike, you crack me up. Aren't you afraid?"

"Not really."

"Tell me what the cave says."

"It says, 'Proceed with caution.'"

"Very funny. But true. Let's do our perimeter check before we see what's inside. My goggs confirm Grindquist has been using this space."

"To trap us?"

"For more than that. The trail's been in use for a while. Let's finish the check before anyone else gets here."

They walked the trail, away from the hillside, stopping

every twenty feet so Gigi could scope out the area without the added noise of their movement. Nothing looked or sounded out of the ordinary. None of her sensors gave off any alarms. A hundred feet down the trail, they stopped again. The night was almost black, the moon a sliver.

"I'm not picking up anything unusual," said Gigi.

"I guess there's no trap out here."

"Can't say that with certainty. We don't have a clue what this Grindquist jerk might be planning. All I can say for sure is that I'm getting nothing."

"Time to check out the cave?" Spike gestured back down the trail.

"Great minds think alike."

शांति (Amanda)

Amanda let out a mental "whew" when Spike and Gigi turned back toward the cave. She was sitting with Elmo inside the trunk of a massive oak about fifty feet into the woods from where Spike and Gigi had just stopped to chat.

"I told you I had the best spot for our remote operation," Elmo whispered.

"How'd you find this thing?" Amanda asked.

"I researched the history of the property. An old newspaper article about one of the former owners described how a lightning strike blew this tree's trunk open more than a century ago. The tree survived, and the hollowed-out trunk grew into a small room the owner's children used to play in."

"Lucky this thing shields sound as well as movement," Amanda said.

Elmo had stuffed the entry hole, about the height of a

six-year-old, with a large piece of heavily insulated ply-wood. "I suspected our little engineer would outfit herself with electronics."

"What do we do now?"

"We wait." A smile twisted Elmo's lip. "It's all coming together. Soon the Atlas girl will arrive. Once Amaya enters her Random World, it won't matter whether the Emushi boy makes it or not. It won't matter at all."

CHAPTER 58

SERENDIPITOUSLY COINCIDENTAL

(JOE)

JOE TOOK HIS assignment seriously on the train to Ammoto, his forehead wrinkled in thought much of the way.

Why had the oracle commanded him to keep his eyes peeled? Peeled for what? He couldn't think of anything specific. He wondered if the oracle's message came down to details. He had a knack for those. He remembered that saying, "the devil's in the details." Grindquist was a kind of devil, so maybe that was the key. Joe would literally have to keep his eyes peeled for every detail. Each one could be important.

Joe hadn't packed much: a change of clothes, a ham-and-cream-cheese sandwich he ate halfway through the trip, two bottles of water, a bunch of fruit and nut bars the sisters gave him "in case anyone gets hungry." No one knew what to expect. Gigi had been right about wishing. As exciting as it might be to be involved in this adventure, he felt nervous. Knowing what happened to the Peetles and Master Cee sure didn't help.

"Last stop, Sedan Station, Ammoto!" a canned female voice boomed over the loudspeaker. "All passengers must disembark."

Joe rose with the others as the train pulled into the station. He exited the car and turned left with the herd. Most of the passengers looked tired and worn, a small sea of unsmiling, grayish faces. He reached the main hall of the station. Homeless people had camped out in the corners using makeshift tents and large boxes for privacy amid boarded up shops. The city looked dingy and lifeless from here, like it was falling apart.

He needed to find the Pickup Street exit. He heard a familiar voice behind him as he looked around for a sign.

"Joe! Joseph Trubly! What in the name of the gods are you doing here?"

Amaya! She ran up and gave him a big hug, He felt the blood rush to his face. He'd never seen Amaya hug anyone other than the Peetles. Not even Spike. Something was different about her.

"I'm so glad to see a familiar face," Amaya said as if she'd been away for ages.

"Where were you?"

"We can talk about that later. Where are you headed?"

"A little east of here," Joe replied. "Here." He pulled the map up on the phone the Jove sisters had given him for the trip.

"I'm headed there as well."

"Another one of your spells?" Amaya's ability to sense things was just one more piece of the big-picture puzzle—who was Amaya Atlas, where had she come from, who wanted her dead, and why?

"Yes. Everyone is in danger."

"I know."

"How?"

"I'll tell you on the way," Joe said. "It's kind of a funny story."

"How are you getting there?"

"Transport. Gigi arranged for it. This way." Joe pointed toward the Pickup Street exit after locating it while they'd been talking. "Follow me." They started toward the exit.

"Is Spike with her? Where are they?"

"They're both waiting for us. We didn't want you to show up alone." Joe picked his way through the crowd. Amaya stuck right with him. She seemed more agile, too—he didn't have to slow his normally fast pace for her to keep up. "We also found out who the Victorian guy is."

"Who?"

"I'll let Gigi fill you in. She has all the details. She's sure we're walking into his trap." They exited down the stairs where the transport awaited.

"Let's hope so," Amaya said as she climbed in.

It alarmed Joe how Amaya was determined to walk into a trap.

CHAPTER 59

PORTRAIT OF THE ARTISTE AS A DEAD MAN

(AMANDA)

AMANDA SAT ON a folding chair at a makeshift desk Elmo had constructed using plastic grape-harvesting cartons.

He'd insisted they dress in funereal black. They were attending one, in his opinion. He wore a black version of his bowler hat, black wool pants with brass buttons down the fly, and a brass-buttoned black vest over a white shirt with ruffled sleeves. Amanda had found her perfect little black dress, a formfitting, mid-thigh Lycra one with a skin-revealing lattice down both sides.

"We'll show her this time," Amanda growled. She only needed to think about that spiteful sorceress and hatred careered through her veins. "Amaya Atlas isn't so special."

The vidscreen showed the main room of the cavern as well as the outside entrance all the way down the trail. Elmo had hidden a nanocam in the cavern's vaulted ceiling and one in the tree at the cavern's entrance so they could watch the action unfold. He'd hardwired and shielded them to avoid detection. The redheaded geek hadn't been able to find them despite all her fancy equipment, though Elmo had warned she might jam the devices themselves.

"I have to hand it to you, Grindquist. You're quite the artist. This little treehouse is terrific. And the plan we came up with is genius. *If* you're certain about the Meshterek keeping that witch's powers in check."

"You've hit the nail on the head. The parts of the plan for which we are responsible are falling into place. The Meshterek need to keep the Atlas girl occupied in her little world and signal us at the right time to trigger the explosives."

"Assuming they can." The Meshterek seemed to be the weakest link. Amanda didn't trust they'd be able to keep Amaya occupied. Amanda didn't trust they even existed. Sometimes she wondered if Elmo might be a lunatic who'd made the whole thing up.

"This is why our plan is so excellent." Elmo put his hands together and leaned back, rubbing his palms.

"What do you mean?"

"Deniability. The plan relies on the Meshterek preventing the Atlas girl from sensing what's coming. All I need to do is set off the explosives on signal. We won't be at fault if anything goes wrong."

It bothered Amanda that Elmo felt the need to stay blameless. She wondered what power the Meshterek had over him, given how they apparently had trouble operating in this world. "What happened to capturing Amaya instead of killing her?"

"This plan will get the Meshterek what they need. Then— kaboom! No arrivederci for you, Amaya Atlas."

"I'm still curious about what's in store after we succeed." Amanda suspected Grindquist wouldn't hesitate to get rid of her once she no longer served his purpose. She'd hidden a pocket knife she'd found at the cave in her bra just in case.

"We'll cross that bridge when we come to it," Elmo replied. His eyes rolled back into his head, and Amanda knew what was coming. "How do *you* spell relief?"

"Not again, Grindquist. Don't you think these advert episodes of yours are getting more frequent?"

"You would know better than I."

"I don't keep a running count, but sure seems it."

Elmo straightened up. "Ho, ho!"

"What?" Amanda asked.

"Activity! It's the Atlas girl. Who's with her?"

A transport had pulled up. Amaya exited with a tall, gangly person whom Amanda recognized from his hat before she'd even seen his face. "What's Joe Trubly doing here?"

"Who's Joe Trubly?" Elmo bristled with irritation.

"One of the older boys at the orphanage. Another one I love to hate." Spike ran up to Amaya and hugged her. Amanda recoiled at the thought of intimate physical contact with a creature as vile as Amaya.

"Any reason you can think of why he's here?"

"Maybe the Jove sisters sent him?"

"How'd he find Amaya?"

"Your guess is as good as mine. He's not important. One more despicable do-gooder, always helping the Jove sisters." Joe Trubly was a nobody. Amanda didn't understand Elmo's concern.

"I don't like it," Elmo fretted. "It's another unknown. The last time we faced unknowns, it didn't turn out so well."

"He's not a fighter. He doesn't have a weapon. He's just a dumb kid." Amanda wasn't concerned about Joe Trubly showing up. He deserved what he'd stumbled into. It'd be one extra spoonful of joy when the cave blew up with him inside.

"I still don't like it. At least our primary target is entering the trap. We'll need to keep our eyes peeled for anything that might upset our plan."

"I can help. I have pretty good eyes."

Elmo turned a derisive gaze on her. "Let's hope so."

CHAPTER 60

READY TO GO

(SPIKE)

THE TRANSPORT PULLED up where Spike and Gigi waited. "Minxie!" Spike ran to Amaya and hugged her. "I was so worried!"

Amaya took a step back to look at him. "Heavens to Lakshmi, Spike. Did you grow a new arm?"

"Yeah. Jeej fixed me up pretty good. With a lot of help from Yunosho." Spike mentioned Yunosho on purpose to gauge Amaya's reaction. His statement met with silence and her face clouded over. He'd have to wait for a better opportunity to broach the subject again, hoping he could help resolve matters between those two. "This thing is strong," he said after an awkward pause.

"It *looks* real. Do you have full functionality?"

"More than full. It feels too." Spike rubbed his forearm to demonstrate. "Different from my normal arm but close. It can do all these other cool things my regular arm couldn't."

"I'm so relieved. Spike. I should never have left you. I was such a jumble inside and—"

"—you don't have to explain." Spike patted Amaya's shoulder with his cyber-hand.

Gigi joined them. "Spike was a super-trooper. He never complained."

"Thank you for taking care of him, Gigi." Amaya put her arm around Gigi and squeezed. Something had changed in Amaya.

"See?" Spike said. "Everything worked out like we said it would."

Gigi offered her hand to Joe. They shook. "Nice to meet you in person, Mr. Trubly. We're sure Grindquist has set some kind of trap here. We should get away from here now that Amaya's arrived."

"Who's Grindquist?" Amaya asked.

"Only the dead guy who's been trying to kill you," Spike said.

"Dead guy?" Amaya eyes widened.

"The Victorian man," Joe explained.

"The man who teamed up with your arch enemy Mandy is a dead guy. Detective Trubly here"—Gigi wriggled her index finger at Joe—"found a hair in the orphanage basement the police missed. I ran the DNA into the database, and out popped 'Grindquist, Elmo: Deceased.' He died five years ago in prison. Mysteriously."

Amaya's face screwed up. "That sure qualifies as creepy."

"We all had pretty much the same reaction." Spike was getting used to the idea of things being creepy after encountering poison robot dragonflies, crazy robot Samurais, and two dead killers walking around.

"That's not all," Gigi added. "He was a specialty contract assassin—untraceable poisons, mechanical failures, remote robotic attacks, things like that. One of the best."

ॐ (Amanda)

Amanda drew back in surprise. She couldn't believe her ears! She looked at Elmo with renewed disgust. "You're dead?"

"Do I look dead?"

"Yeah, kind of." Amanda thought it was suddenly obvious: the gray skin pallor, the deadened eyes, the gelatinous blood, the missing memories.

"Let's just say I'm dead, but I don't act it."

"*Ewww*, now you're creeping *me* out." Amanda slid her chair away from him, wondering if her knife would even be of use.

ॐ (Amaya)

"Gigi's right," Spike said. "We have no reason to stay here."

"It's too dangerous," Gigi added.

"The danger here is fuzzy." It was a little less fuzzy now at the wine cave. Maybe they were getting closer. "That same fuzziness led me to the dragonflies in the first place. This time I need to face it." The nature of the fight had changed. Amaya didn't know how, but she was in the middle of it. "But I must face it alone. I can't allow you to place yourselves in peril again. I insist that you all leave."

Spike snorted. "Funny, Amaya. As if."

"Yeah." Gigi smiled. "We're not going anywhere, kiddo."

"I'm in, too," Joe said. "I'm scared, but I'm not leaving. The oracle gave me a mission. I'm seeing it through."

They stood in front of Amaya like an immovable wall, shoulder-to-shoulder, arms crossed. The black night suddenly turned sinister. A slight wind prickled Amaya's skin, making her jumpy.

I'm going to get my friends killed. The thought came unbidden, and with it all the guilt and self-doubt rushed back into her like a violent squall into a door someone had forgotten to close, rattling her conviction and throwing her confidence to the wind. How could she even *think* about putting her friends in danger again? She should leave with them, forget her parents, forget her purpose, spare them all. Her chest constricted, squeezing her breath. She closed her eyes, trying to push back the anguish. Before any tears could fall, she found herself wrapped in a six-armed hug.

"We've got your back," Gigi whispered in her ear.

"We'll find the trap," Joe said.

"We're *not* leaving," Spike said.

Her friends' resolve flowed into her, buoying her up again. She remembered her decision back on the mountain and the strength that came with it, the same strength her friends were giving her now. There'd be no convincing them to leave—not true friends like these. "I certainly do not like it." The momentary weakness had passed. "But I can tell that changing your minds would be like trying to change you into mules."

Spike grinned. "She means we're as stubborn as mules."

Amaya grew defensive. "I do *not* require a translator."

"I'm not so sure about that," Spike said. They all laughed. Spike's goofiness always put her more at ease.

"All right, then." Gigi gestured toward the cave's doorway. "Allow me to introduce you to our new abode, aka… *The Trap.*"

शांति (Yunosho)

Yunosho spent his time on the flight to Ammoto pondering options. They didn't know what *kind* of trap Grindquist had set. Surely, this one would be more dangerous than the last. He hoped Amaya would leave with Gigi and Spike once she showed up at the coordinates, but they probably had only one choice given Amaya's stubborn nature: Let the trap reveal itself and be faster and smarter than the enemy. One thing was certain—he wouldn't let Amaya send him away this time, no matter what. Not now, not under these circumstances.

His phone buzzed. The message was from Gigi.

Amaya's here. She's not leaving. There's a wine cave built into the hillside. We'll be inside. Not a good time yet.

Yunosho didn't like the part about staying in the cave at all.

ॐ (Amaya)

Amaya and Spike began clearing mechanical parts from the large work table. They both reached for the same part at the same time.

Spike shivered—Spidiepus parts. "He's definitely been using this place for his operations."

"Do you want me to finish?" Amaya hoped the memories weren't too painful for Spike. It ate at her. Every time the subject came up, she saw that awful vision again: A mad-looking monkey-like Yunosho slicing through Spike's arm, his red eyes ablaze with insane purpose.

"No, Minxie. It just took me by surprise. I'm fine."

"Let's start in that office over there," Gigi said to Joe.

Those two were conducting a thorough examination of the cave. Amaya hoped they'd find something useful. The Band of Murugan needed all the help it could get.

ॐ (Amanda)

"Crap!" The redhead and Joe Trubly entered the office to search it. Amanda remembered her little black notebook. Her mind frantically searched her memory, trying to make sure there was nothing in the notebook that could tip off Little Miss Viper and her brood of snakes. Especially that Trubly. He was nosy.

"What's the matter?" Elmo asked.

"I started keeping notes. I left them in my drawer."

"Notes? Notes on what?" The news irritated him. Elmo hated unknowns.

"Fortunately, nothing about our plans for today."

"What then?"

"Kind of general random stuff, like listing Amaya's potential weaknesses."

"I'm glad you were doing more than playing vidgames. But leaving notes behind was careless. Are you sure there's nothing in them we need to worry about?"

"No, nothing." Amanda had been unable to recall anything problematic. "I don't mention the Random World. I do mention the Meshterek, but I don't say who they are. Not that *I* would know."

"We should be fine, then. The Mouseketeers will all be dead before they have a chance to figure anything out. The pieces are falling into place. Remember. Everything boils down to the Meshterek."

Elmo's eyes rolled up into his head. Spittle bubbled around the edges of his hideous smile. Another advert was on its way. These episodes were happening more frequently, maybe even with more severity.

"*The antidote for civilization,*" Elmo sang, though coming from him, the tune sounded more like mildly musical scratching.

"Not again, Grindquist." Amanda had never heard that one before. It bothered her. She didn't like a lot of things about the world. But she didn't think it needed an antidote either.

शांति (Joe)

As Gigi rifled through the drawers of the little side table, trying to find anything of importance, Joe thought about how odd it felt to be inside the cave the oracle showed him in its first message. To him, it meant the second message must be even more important. Gigi pulled out a tiny notebook hidden beneath some clothes.

"What's that?" Joe peered over Gigi's shoulder as she paged through the book. "It's Mandy's." He recognized the handwriting.

Only a few pages had writing on them, one with the heading "Weaknesses," followed by a list:

1. Peetles (RIP)

2. Big professional man (RIP)

3. Jove sisters

4. Spike

5. Cute Japanese boy

6. Other orphans

7.???

"She didn't get far with the list. That might be good news." Gigi continued flipping through the notebook.

"What's that say?" Joe pointed to another page with writing.

Gigi read out loud. "'Keep an eye on the Meshterek.' Who or what are Meshterek?"

"Never heard of them. Maybe some kind of cult?"

"I don't think so. I'm sure they have something to do with why Grindquist is after Amaya. Let's keep looking." Gigi shut the drawer and pocketed the notebook. "We need to make sure we're safe. We'll save these Meshterek for later."

Joe liked that idea. He was happy yet another mystery would be waiting to be solved.

If they made it out alive.

ॐ (Spike)

"Where'd you go after you left the hospital?" Spike asked.

They'd almost finished transforming the work table into beds for the girls. Amaya seemed different. She'd always been brave, but he detected a quiet, deeper confidence in her now.

"Into the woods. I needed to get away."

"I was scared for you. I never saw you so upset before." Spike didn't know how to broach Amaya's personal feelings. He knew how awkward she felt discussing them. But there was no better time to stop worrying about uncomfortable conversations, given they could all be dead soon. "So… what happened? *Something* did." They arranged the sleeping bags side-by-side on the table.

"The first night, I dreamed about a treehouse. The next morning, I hiked in the direction the dream pointed me and found the exact same treehouse."

"Somebody sent you there?"

"Ela said I'd been sent."

"Who's Ela?"

"The woman in the treehouse." A momentary wistfulness clouded Amaya's eyes like a passing fog. "She brought me back."

ॐ (Amanda)

Elmo snickered. "Ha! I was right. The Meshterek *do* need to be concerned."

"What do you mean?" Amanda still didn't understand how a piece of trash like Amaya Atlas could be so important to the Meshterek.

"Didn't you hear?"

"Hear what?"

"The part about being sent."

"Are you back on that god stuff again? I'm not sure I believe it even if it does explain a few things." She wanted to know how the Meshterek and the gods were related. She needed to get all her questions answered if she was going to claim her place in the new world order. As soon as that pestilence named Amaya Atlas no longer darkened the Earth, Amanda would sit Elmo down and make him explain everything. Every bit of it. He'd been holding back too long.

"Your beliefs are immaterial. Even more reason to pay attention to that Trubly boy."

"He's a nobody." Amanda wished Elmo would quit harping about Joe Trubly. He didn't matter at all.

शांति (Yunosho)

Yunosho disembarked at the Ammoto private jet terminal. The terminal building was deserted except for the clerk at the desk, who had his head buried in a magazine. A driverless transport waited for Yunosho just outside the security gate, which for some strange reason was unmanned. A group of people stood in front of the transport, blocking it from entering the tarmac.

He might have mistaken them for homeless, except they had cars—not luxury vehicles but not junky ones either. They'd parked them in a circle facing one another in the lot next to the security booth with the headlights on, like they were preparing for a nighttime show of some kind.

Something was amiss. Yunosho walked toward the gate anyway, whistling an aimless tune as if nothing were wrong, telling himself he was being paranoid.

An unpleasant muttering rippled through the crowd as he neared it. Someone cried out.

"Get him!"

He froze. Were they talking about him?

"Yeah, get him!" another voice joined in.

"Kill him!" someone screeched.

The whole crowd turned to face him, their shoulders hunched and angry, their eyes burning with hatred. A few pounded their fists. Some waved baseball bats in the air. The clerk inside the terminal moved to the window, peering out with an anxious look on his face. The mob charged Yunosho, cheering all at once. The clerk ran to the doors and locked them, trapping Yunosho outside.

There were twenty-two of them. They seemed to be under the influence of something. Drugs maybe. Yunosho decided to leave his swords where they were—packed in his duffel. He didn't know who these people were or why they might want to murder him. But he was sure of one thing—they didn't deserve to die.

The fastest had a bat—a plastic whiffle ball bat. Yunosho would've laughed if the scene weren't so surreal. The man swung at the side of Yunosho's head with a lot of misplaced conviction. Yunosho dropped into a squat and grabbed the man's wrist and ankle. He pushed up from his knees and lofted the man forward, knocking down the next closest three.

A snarling woman in a neon-green "I'm with Penniless →" t-shirt sprang over her fallen comrades, waving a curling iron in her hand. Behind her, a middle-aged Humpty-Dumpty in cutoff jeans shorts with a half-naked beer belly skirted the puddle of bodies, moving like a teetering mountain of gelatin. He cocked a full-sized umbrella behind his shoulder and swung, putting his entire weight into it. Penniless swiped her curling-iron cutlass. Yunosho leaned back, hard. The umbrella missed Yunosho but smacked Penniless in the head with enough force to snap the stem in two. She fell to her knees, screaming in agony. Beer Belly couldn't stop his forward momentum. He tripped over his own feet and hit the ground face-first, the sound of scraping skin coming off the tarmac as he slid.

Yunosho kicked into a flip from his lean. He stuck his landing and reached up to grab the fat end of a real baseball bat with a skinny shaved-head guy attached to it, trying to wrest the bat free. Yunosho twisted sideways without letting go and ducked the oversized red plastic purse an elderly woman with lilac-colored hair aimed at his chin. She spun, losing her balance, and collapsed to the ground in a heap. A steak fell from the sky and landed with a plop on Yunosho's chest.

Steak? Senior citizens? Are they trying to bewilder me to death?! Things had gone too far.

Yunosho wrenched the bat from the skinny guy, then bopped him and two others on the head. They went down.

Four more bops. Another four hit the ground. Yunosho had room to grab his duffle and run. He sprinted to the van, knocking down two more along the way. He opened the door and threw himself into the passenger seat along with his duffle.

"Lock the doors and drive. Now!" he ordered the transport as he slammed the door.

The locks clicked. Someone started banging on the rear doors of the van. He looked back. A girl with dirty-blonde hair was trying to get in. She grabbed the door handles as the van made a U-turn and accelerated away from the rest of the mob. She ran along, bouncing up and down in the air when her feet couldn't keep up any longer, screaming, "Um gonna keel yew. Um gonna keel yew, Ninja Boy."

Yunosho counted to seven before she lost her grip. She dropped to the ground and tumbled through the gravel, screaming even louder from the painful fall. He faced forward again and saw a label stuck to the windshield. It said, "Hillbilly Slim's Perfect Aged Beef Sirloin."

Something was happening with the world. And it wasn't good.

ॐ (Amanda)

"That's a bunch of crap!" Amanda complained bitterly. "Those two never cared about me."

She and Elmo were watching the vid from the camera hidden in the cave. Gigi and Joe had finished checking the place. The whole group sat in a circle on the floor of the cave, like at a campfire without the fire, telling stories about the orphanage. Spike had just finished saying how sorry they felt for Mandy after overhearing the Jove sisters speak to Chief Raynor on the porch about Mandy's mother being in prison and why.

"That's enough. What's taking so long?" Amanda had grown tired of holing up in a half-dead tree with a whole-dead Elmo, listening to stories about a place she hated.

"I, too, am experiencing what I faintly remember as impatience. Where's that Emushi boy? It wouldn't do to still have him around after all this is over. He'd never relent."

"*I* wouldn't mind keeping him around for a while."

Elmo frowned. "Don't get any ideas."

ॐ (Yunosho)

The transport arrived at the wine cave. Yunosho stepped out. Everything was quiet. He checked with the sentry bots. They reported nothing abnormal. He found the cave's entrance. Gigi had told him to wait. He unrolled his sleeping bag, crawled in, and lay next to the doorway, the thought of facing Amaya in the morning more terrifying than any potential encounter with the bad guys.

शांति (Amaya)

Day 16

"Guys, I need some shut-eye," Joe said.

"Me too," Spike agreed. "It's been a long day."

"We girls need our beauty sleep." Gigi gave Amaya a wink.

Amaya was glad Gigi was there. Spike and Joe too. She was glad they all stayed. She wouldn't have to face this alone. She only hoped she could keep everyone safe.

Joe and Spike headed over to their makeshift beds. Gigi and Amaya climbed into their sleeping bags on the large work table.

"Good night, all," Joe said.

"Shoot," Gigi said.

"What's wrong?" asked Spike.

"I forgot to turn on my jammer. Can't be too careful." She fumbled around for a second. Amaya heard a faint click. "Night, everyone."

"Good night," Amaya said.

Spike turned out the lights. "Nighty night, girls."

ॐ (Amanda)

Noise replaced the vid and audio.

"What happened?" Amanda asked.

"We've actually been lucky," Elmo said. "I thought for sure she'd jam us earlier."

"I wouldn't necessarily agree with the lucky part. Listening to those dummies was unbearable."

What Spike and Amaya had said had been unexpected. Did they honestly care? She thought about it for all of one second because it didn't matter. They wouldn't be around to care about anything in just a little while. That was fine and dandy with her.

ॐ (Amaya)

Amaya stared up into the darkness.

No matter what, I am with friends, she thought.

She closed her eyes.

And dove into the water.

CHAPTER 61

AND IN THE END

(SPIKE)

"AMAYA!" GIGI SOUNDED like she was shouting underwater. "Amaya!"

Spike heard it again—louder and clearer this time. He dragged himself awake. "What's going on?"

"I don't know," Gigi said. "Get the lights."

Spike jumped up and hit the switch. The lights came on. Joe was already up, standing beside his sleeping bag.

Spike joined Gigi at the table. She was gazing down at Amaya, a helpless look on her face. "It's Amaya. I don't know what to do."

Something was definitely wrong. Amaya had her eyes closed, but they were rolling around under her eyelids. She'd clenched her jaws tight as a vice, and she was waving her arms like a demonic orchestra conductor.

"She's having a bad dream." Spike shook her. "Minxie! Wake up!"

Gigi and Spike both shook her. Hard. She wouldn't wake up.

"I think it's starting." Spike's voice went deep from the tension. "Get Yunosho."

शांति (Joe)

This is the moment.

Joe wandered off to the middle of the cavern as soon as he saw Amaya like that. He and Gigi had checked everything except the arched ceiling.

He began at the corner to his left in front of him, mentally dividing the ceiling into a grid, canvassing each section of the grid, one at a time.

Time to do my job, he thought, determined to follow the oracle's instruction. *Time to keep my eyes peeled.*

ॐ (Yunosho)

Adrenaline had pumped Yunosho alert in the few seconds it took him to arrive. "What's wrong?"

"Amaya hit me in the face as I was drifting off," Gigi answered. "She kept flailing around and wouldn't wake up. Spike turned on the lights, and this is how we found her, stuck in some kind of nightmare."

"It's not a nightmare," Yunosho said. "It's her Random World."

"What's *that*?" Gigi grabbed her backpack from the table and pulled out a black case. She took three tiny electronic devices from it.

"A kind of parallel reality she visits."

"Yeah." Spike nodded. "The gods gave it to her as a gift."

Gigi frowned, shaking her head. "Silly me. Here I was thinking things couldn't get any weirder." She plugged the devices into her goggs, put the goggs on, and began scanning the area around Amaya.

"I've been there." Yunosho hoped he wasn't betraying Amaya's confidence by telling them. He was on bad enough terms with her, though this wasn't the time to worry about it.

"I didn't know anyone else could get in," Spike said. Yunosho thought he could detect a slight hurt in Spike's voice. Maybe he only imagined it.

"Amaya didn't know either, but the thought occurred to her, so we tried. It worked."

Amaya's thrashing worsened. Spike's real arm was fighting to keep her still. "She's in trouble. It has something to do with the trap."

Gigi swept her goggs along length of the table. "I'm getting a strange reading. There's a disturbance in the gravity field around Amaya."

"She's *definitely* in trouble," Spike said. "Yunosho, you need to get in there. Get her out before something bad happens."

"Exactly." Yunosho crawled onto the table into lotus position next to Amaya. "Here goes nothing." He closed his eyes. Exactly nothing happened. He tried again and again. He opened his eyes, frowning with frustration. "I'm blocked!" His frustration began quickening into panic.

"What do you mean?" Spike asked.

"I synchronized with Amaya and reached the water, but I can't dive in."

Gigi threw her hands up. "What *water*?" She pulled off her goggs, exasperated.

"A deep pool of ocean water," said Yunosho. "You dive in. Then you come up onto a beach in the Random World."

Gigi rolled her eyes, shaking her head.

"Try again!" Spike implored.

Amaya grimaced. Her jaws clenched and unclenched, her facial muscles contorting in twisting spasms. Yunosho took a few deep breaths, trying to calm himself. He closed his eyes and tried again.

There was the water. He was definitely at the entrance. But he couldn't move. He tried diving in, but his feet were stuck, an all too familiar experience.

"I can't!" Yunosho opened his eyes again, the panic returning worse than before. "It's the same as the nightmare."

"What happened in the nightmare?" Gigi asked.

"I was stuck in the dream too. You and Spike kept shouting at me to do something. I couldn't hear what you were saying. A voice told me to cut off my feet."

"Cut off your *feet*?" Spike asked as if Yunosho had said something totally nuts.

"It was only virtual reality. I wouldn't actually cut off my own feet. So I decided to do it. But—"

"But *what*?" Spike and Gigi yelled in unison, obviously panicked too.

"My sword swung down to lop my feet from my ankles. Then I heard you. You were screaming, 'Stop struggling!'"

"Can you do that?" Spike's voice sounded like it was struggling against its own tightness. "Stop struggling?"

"Spike's right," Gigi said. "Strange as it may seem, that's the answer. But you need to hurry."

"Okay." Yunosho couldn't help thinking how hurrying to calm down sounded completely oxymoronic. "I'll have to clear myself. That won't be easy under the circumstances."

Yunosho knew what he needed to do. He'd trained for it all his life. He closed his eyes again. He gazed out at the ocean and imagined taking his desperation and compressing it into an unbreakable transparent ball. His panic stormed in protest. It crackled with lightning and bounced hard against every inch of the ball's insides, trying to break free. He let the ball float in front of him. It banged back and forth mid-air, like a tightly anchored tetherball.

The panic in the ball screamed at him. "Hurry up, you dummy! Get in there! She'll die!"

He ignored it, concentrating on his breathing instead. He paid attention. He listened to the rise and fall of his lungs and diaphragm. Slower. Deeper. Using every bit of each breath to blow the ball farther and farther into the horizon until…

…the ball became a speck…

…his mind detached…

…he was in.

He came out of the water onto the beach. This was bad. The wondrous Random World was gone, reduced to a jumbled, flaming confusion. Fires dotted the landscape, illuminating its charcoal blackness. Curls of dark gray smoke licked the air, the wondrous sky replaced by a suffocating, orange-tinged presence overhead.

He walked past the Peetle chairs. Burnt. A pile of ash lay on the ground where the green-grass table had been. A battle raged in the valley, much bigger than the one in his dream. Amaya lay face-up on the hilltop, her body jerking back and forth like a deranged puppet master had taken control of it—no wonder Spike was having such a hard time holding her down.

He needed to cross the valley to reach Amaya. A lot of obstacles stood in his way. He needed a plan. Some help would be nice too.

ॐ (Amaya)

Amaya rose out of the water. She paused on the beach. She could feel it—the fuzzy disturbance wasn't fuzzy any more.

They were creatures. She could sense them somewhere across the valley. She called Checkerboard RiRii and Warrior Gigi to her side and set off to find the creatures, determined to destroy them. She didn't know how, or even why she should.

They reached the valley's entrance. The creatures unleashed legions to stop them. Aliens of all different shapes and sizes, many of them terrifying to look at, marched up from the beach and from the other side of the valley, forming a pincer. They came in unrelenting waves, slashing and burning everything in their path.

Amaya retreated to a hill. She assembled her own army, any kind of army as fast as she could. She appointed Warrior Gigi and Checkerboard RiRii as her captains and put them in charge of her meager troops. Her captains led the troops into the valley to thwart the enemy's progress.

Before she could muster more, the creatures launched a barrage. Missiles rained down from the dark sky, long tails of orange flame trailing them. They exploded all at once. The blast blew Amaya backward onto the ground where slithery black tentacles broke through the earth and wrapped around her. Then they dragged her down, like heavy clothes drenched in icy water, pulling her into the inky deep of a lonely, desolate river. The missiles had been armed with misery. *Lots of it.*

She couldn't breathe.

I'm dying.

शांति (Yunosho)

The Random World was like Yunosho's nightmare, except the purple-skinned aliens weren't the only bad guys here. There were plenty more, and they liked making noise. A cacophony of cries, screams, roars, chirps, tweets, and other unrecognizable sounds punctuated the general roar blanketing the battlefield.

Checkerboard RiRii spun and rolled to his right, dodging rapid-fire volleys from a platoon of tall obsidian stalagmite-monsters shooting black glass daggers at her. She feinted and countered, hurling spells from her fingertips. One by one, the monsters disintegrated into sparkling clouds of dust that wafted to the ground.

A crop of red hair bobbed up and down not far from RiRii. It was Gigi! Or rather a Random-World Viking-warrior version of Gigi. It surprised Yunosho to see her there. He hadn't thought Amaya cared that much for Gigi.

Fat, yellow, thorn-shaped insects had Warrior Gigi surrounded, skittering along on knobby, stick-like legs. Their sharp, red beaks snapped at her, trying to tear off her flesh. But Warrior Gigi spun like a whirlwind. Her body crouched and rose and crouched and rose, her broadsword's powerful strokes smashing the thorn bugs to pieces.

The rest of Amaya's army—a bunch of humans she'd only managed to arm with melee weaponry—was getting clobbered. Vines whipped out from hissing green mounds, encircling their victims in a mesh that pulled tighter and tighter until gore-covered cubes of human flesh dropped to the ground in a heap. A rainstorm of blood, brain, and bone trailed a line of huge, hairless long-toothed rabbits as they marched forward, biting heads off, chewing them up, and spitting the mess into the air.

The situation seemed hopeless. Amaya's army had been split up, separated into pockets. They were engulfed, surrounded, and outnumbered. At least Yunosho had found some help. He had a plan now too.

ॐ (Amaya)

A filthy hunger licked Amaya. The creatures were examining her, prying at every neuron, looking for weaknesses. Every one of their loathsome mental touches made her retch.

A name came to her like a whispered threat.

Meshterek.

The name they called themselves. Their thoughts had begun to leak through. She grasped why they'd been fuzzy before.

They come from a different universe.

That's why they'd chosen the Random World. It was an in-between place—a place they could enter and hold sway. Amaya had been right to be concerned during her visit here with Yunosho.

She struggled to lift her head. She saw them on the hill opposite hers across the battlefield—a massive mound of rotten, gelatinous flesh, polka-dotted with pulsating orange and green pustules. She'd never truly hated anyone before, not even Mandy. Yet she couldn't find a single redeemable shred of anything in the odious evil skulking around inside her. She hated these Meshterek with every ounce of her being.

She had to resist. She had to stay alive.

She ignored the agony and forced another breath.

ॐ (Yunosho)

Yunosho gazed out from the edge of the battlefield, seeking the best path forward. He had good material to work with—Amaya's army might be getting clobbered, but they fought bravely.

Two muscular black females in leather body armor hacked off the razor-sharp hands of a purple alien while their male companion drove a lance through its chest. A rabbit creature bent down to bite off the shaved head of a human giantess. She cracked its teeth with a mace and split open one of its pink eyes with a chain.

Yunosho needed to fight his way to the middle of the field so he could combine forces with Warrior Gigi and Checkerboard RiRii. Then they could consolidate the scattered human army and expand out from the center, clearing the way to Amaya.

Not a complicated plan at all, he thought, *except for these ugly, ten-foot-tall, crab-looking things blocking my way.*

The creatures' black lips smiled with hunger. Thick drool dribbled down the sides of their mouths. They sidled toward him on six legs. He moved forward to meet them, and they attacked. Saw-toothed pincers stabbed from above. He feinted. The pincers missed, snapping sharply as they hit the ground.

Yunosho barreled ahead. He swung his swords left and right, hacking his way through. Shells cracked. Pieces of meat flew into the air. Whitish liquid sprayed everywhere. Amputee crabs fell on their sides. Others dropped to the ground dead, a vile-smelling yellow fluid leaking from the gashes he'd cut along their abdomens.

He hadn't reached Gigi and RiRii yet, but he was within earshot.

"The army's too scattered!" he cried above the din. "We've got to rally the troops. Let's move out from here. We can pick up survivors along the way."

"Gotcha!" Warrior Gigi yelled.

"Bet on it!" Checkerboard RiRii pumped her fist into the air, then flicked her fingertips at a stalagmite monster. It collapsed into a pile of shards, dead.

शांति (Amaya)

Yunosho!

Amaya could breathe again! His arrival had forced the Meshterek to shift focus, changing the battlefield's dynamics. The Random World suddenly seemed a little brighter. The respite from the onslaught was brief, but it was all she needed. She pushed herself onto her feet and amassed enough wavicles to form an energy grid, throwing up a kind of Faraday cage to block the overwhelming deluge of misery and suffering the Meshterek continued to bombard her with.

The grid worked, but it leaked. The leaks were potent. Grisly images violated her—

A wretch cowers in the corner of an empty construction lot, an angry crowd at the gate cutting off his escape. They lift the stone bricks piled next to the entrance and let them fly. He raises his arms, blocking the first barrage. The next snaps his forearms in two. A brick tears his lower jaw loose. Another cracks open his skull, spraying blood and brain into the air. The Meshterek exult.

A fire burns at a camp in the jungle night. A woman screams. Two elephant-skinned soldiers pin her by the shoulders. Two more sever her legs. They lift the bloody limbs to the sky like an offering to their gods, their faces shiny with mad euphoria. They gnaw hungrily on her still-bleeding flesh. She watches, dying, her eyes filled with terror, her screams diminishing into senseless whimpers. The Meshterek shiver with bliss.

The Meshterek were demons. Hellish demons. They conjured misery and suffering to feast on. How many other worlds had suffered this fate? Amaya's stomach churned—they meant hers to be next.

But Yunosho had given her an idea—she could stop them. *If* she could keep them occupied.

ॐ (Yunosho)

Yunosho directed the troops, molding and shaping the battlefront into a circle. They divvied the circle into three arcs, Yunosho, Gigi and RiRii, each taking lead of one. They began expanding, Yunosho's arc fighting its way toward Amaya. The plan was working. They picked up pockets of surviving humans along the way.

The nearer Yunosho got to Amaya, the worse she looked. Her eyes had sunk deep into their sockets. She was leaning forward, like she'd just left the ramp of a ski jump. Her arms hung at her sides, her hands balled into fists. Sweat dripped from her face, her soaking wet dress plastered to skin and bones.

ॐ   (Amaya)

Amaya began building an absolute void behind her wall. She drew more and more energy into herself from the space around her. She channeled every bit of power into her protective grid, making it more and more difficult for the Meshterek to break through. As she'd hoped, they met every bit of her power with theirs.

Her whole body shook, every muscle vibrating with effort. She lifted off the ground, hovering above it, energy streaming through her into the grid. The grid grew, glowing brighter and brighter. The Meshterek pushed back harder and harder—and harder, still.

How desperately they wanted to get to her. How focused they were on getting through, wholly unaware she was going to let them.

शांति (Yunosho)

Yunosho wished he had a few tons of salt.

Salt might kill these giant, green slug things he and his troops had run up against. His swords couldn't penetrate deep enough.

The slugs slimed their way forward on heavy foot muscles that rippled beneath them. Thick necks pressed fat heads to the ground, where bloated, pink lips skimmed the surface, vacuuming up humans so forcefully some were gone before the screams forming on their faces could be heard. Yunosho needed to get that head off the ground if he wanted to inflict real damage.

He charged the line of slugs and dove into the air, somersaulting over them. He landed behind their line and slid into a spin, reversing direction. He ran up the tail of the nearest one and pushed off its head into a twisting forward flip, then stuck a sword deep into the slug's eye on his way back to the ground. Using his weight, he let the sword slice all the way to the bottom as he dropped, cleaving the eye in two. He rolled when he hit the ground to stay clear of the lips and came up again, his swords at the ready.

The slug stopped sucking. Red gelatin oozed from the cut eye. It lifted its lumbering head off the ground and shook it, spraying milky green phlegm everywhere. Yunosho wiped his forearm across his face, gagging from the stench. He stepped in before the slug had a chance to recover and sliced off a big chunk of its puffy lip, disabling its vacuum.

Then angelfish attacked. At least they looked like angelfish. Big, silver, *flying* angelfish.

ॐ (Amaya)

The fish creatures swooped down like Harpies. Yunosho disappeared into a cloud of them. He was going to die unless Amaya helped.

She panicked. She wanted to help. More than anything. The second Yunosho stepped back into the Random World, she'd recognized her true feelings for him. She just didn't know what they meant. Maybe this moment was why she couldn't *let* them mean anything.

Her trap of traps was ready to spring. She'd lose more than she'd lost at the barn if she failed this time. She'd lose the fight. She'd lose Spike. And Gigi. And Joe. Maybe everyone.

She thought about her last time in the Random World with Yunosho. She regretted not having touched his face. She wished she'd been more open with him. She wished she'd given him a chance to explain—there had to be a reason behind what he'd done. But no amount of wishing would help here. She stood at a crossroads, but she couldn't bear to make the choice. There *had* to be a universe where Yunosho lived *and* she defeated the Meshterek. Why should *she* have to make an impossible choice?

Tears mixed with the hot sweat dripping from her face. A gruesome resolve stiffened her spine. Every neuron in her body screamed against it.

But she did it.

She turned her back on him.

It crushed her heart.

ॐ (Yunosho)

Swords weren't cutting it.

These fish fins were tough. And razor-sharp. They'd already nicked Yunosho a few times, and the fight had only just begun.

A fin lashed out at his leg. He sprang over it. Two more followed right behind. He rolled over mid-air and hit the ground flat on his back. Fish swarmed over him like frenzied sharks. He blocked one fin, then another, and another, his feet pushing him backward along the ground. They kept coming. A fin stabbed his arm, pinning him to the ground.

He pulled to free himself, but the fish weighed too much and pulling only made the cut deeper. *This is it.* He didn't have a chance. Not with one arm, one sword. Not against these things.

He'd done his best. He couldn't get frustrated—he didn't want to give that monkey an opportunity. Instead, he bought himself enough time to take one last precious glance at Amaya up on the hill. She was going to win. She looked like a frightful, determined demon in her own right. Maybe you needed to become a little evil to vanquish evil. He only wished for one last chance to tell her how he felt.

He said it in his mind and imagined kissing her forehead, the only kiss he'd ever get.

The fish closed in tighter. Fins cut his pinned arm—once, twice. Another stabbed his shoulder.

Metal flashed.

शांति (Spike)

What was Yunosho *doing* in the Random World? Amaya looked worse, not better. She'd wasted away on the table right before Spike's eyes.

A hole appeared in Yunosho's arm, then two cuts. Then another hole near his shoulder with blood squirting from it. Gigi, the tourniquet expert, made one using Yunosho's sleeve, stopping the worst of the flow.

She finished tying it and glanced at Spike, her eyes wide. "I'm *really* worried."

Spike felt the same way but didn't say so. He wanted to be a rock. He looked her straight in the eye. "Jeej. Everything's going to be all right."

ॐ (Yunosho)

A blade!

The tip traveled diagonally across the fish. Its two halves fell to the ground. Warrior Gigi stood behind it, her broadsword in both hands. She cleaved another fish in two, and another, then the one pinning Yunosho. He pulled the severed fin from his arm.

"Here." She grabbed his hand and helped him up. Her troops rushed in, their battle cries resounding across the field. "You handle the slugs. I'll take care of the fish."

She decimated the fish. Yunosho and his troops took the slugs out of commission, the whole line of them wandering disoriented in circles, their lips bloodied and their mouths disabled. Amaya's army had turned the tide.

Warrior Gigi waved at Yunosho from the middle of the field. "Victory!" she cried, pumping her sword in the air.

A cloud of red dust swirled up from the ground, sweeping

into her nose and mouth. Her face turned purple. Her sword rattled to the ground. She fell to her knees, clawing at her neck. She'd dropped on her side by the time Yunosho reached her. He hacked and hacked at the cloud until the dust dropped to the ground and seeped into it. But Warrior Gigi wasn't breathing.

ॐ (Spike)

Gigi slumped to the floor. Spike dropped to his knees and cradled her head. "Gigi! What's wrong?!"

He lifted her onto the table next to Amaya. Her breathing was steady, but when he shook her, she wouldn't respond. Two people Spike loved were in serious trouble. He needed help.

Where was Joe?!

Spike looked around. Joe was at the back of the cavern, gazing up at the ceiling. He appeared to be counting things.

"Joe, help!" Spike shouted, wondering what in the name of Zeus he was doing.

शांति (Amaya)

Amaya amassed the last of the energy and completed the void. The Meshterek's desire was white-hot—a shrill, all-consuming need to destroy her. They threw everything they had at the grid. But it wasn't too much for Amaya to bear.

A monstrous creaking arose, like two hulking battleships colliding full-speed at sea. It was time—time to drop the wall.

ॐ (Yunosho)

Yunosho dropped both swords and rolled Warrior Gigi onto her back. He hoped with all his heart that Gigi in the real world was unharmed.

The air hummed and buzzed as he worked, compressing Gigi's chest. The noise swelled above him, its volume rising louder and louder, becoming a horrific metallic scraping. Yunosho glanced up. Amaya's hilltop exploded with a deafening boom. A mass of blazingly brilliant blue-white particles shot from the hill and filled the Random World, illuminating it. Then everything froze—except the mysterious wooden door. The silver fist at the end of the key hammered down where the five thunderbolts joined. The door blew open, spinning rapidly in mid-air, releasing a flipbook of images—a handsome god in colorful silks; an alluring blonde goddess in a sultry, green gown; a waltz at a Hindu-Greco ball; their first delicious kiss; demons setting a trap at a black hole; god and goddess meld minds; a thunderbolt cracks in a cornfield where a naked little girl, little Amaya, appears out of thin air.

Time unfroze. The door shattered into splinters. The Random World ripped apart, shredding into itself, disintegrating and disappearing. Yunosho flew off the table at the wine cave and fell to the floor, the breath knocked out of him. He gasped for air and looked up.

Thank goodness! Gigi was sitting on the edge of the table, dazed but unharmed. Spike was there, too, worrying over Amaya.

Yunosho heaved as he picked himself off the ground. "It's over," he gasped.

ॐ (Elmo)

Amanda's pestering annoyed Elmo.

"Where is it? Where's the signal?" It was her third time asking. She was certain something had gone wrong. Elmo worried too. As soon as the vid had jammed, seconds had begun to feel like minutes. They'd been waiting for what seemed like forever. What was happening in that cave?

"Not yet." Elmo hissed. He had his eyes closed, his mind focusing, waiting for the signal.

"When?" Amanda whined. "It's taking too long."

"It's coming. I'm sure of it." He wasn't sure. And he didn't want to be the one to pay for it if the Meshterek screwed up. They'd still find a way to blame *him* if they sent the signal too late. Maybe he could pawn the blame off on Amanda. They hadn't been too happy with her so far.

His eyes popped open. The signal came through. "Now!" He flipped the switch. The corner of his mouth lifted into its hideous smile.

शांति (Spike)

"Gigi! Up there!"

Joe was yelling, pointing like a madman at something in the ceiling. Spike couldn't see anything but bricks.

"BOMB!" Gigi cried out. "EVERYBODY OUT! NOW!"

Spike helped Gigi off the table toward the exit. Joe followed behind her. Yunosho lifted Amaya over his shoulder and ran for the doorway with Spike behind him.

Spike reached the column that held the entryway arch and stopped.

"Spike!" Gigi stopped too, almost to the door. "Come on!"

she screamed, her eyes desperate, her arm pleading, waving and waving him toward her.

Spike gave her a look he hoped said that he loved her. He was pretty sure he was messing it up. He pushed his cyber-arm against the column to support it. A tremendous explosion boomed. The cave imploded, the shock wave knocking everyone to the ground. Except Spike. He held his ground. The column held too.

ॐ (Amanda)

Amanda ripped back the soundproofing and ducked out of the tree. She rushed into the trail with Elmo following. Clouds of rock dust hung over a giant pile of rubble that had tumbled down over the cave's entrance at the end of the trail. Amanda had never been more ecstatic in her life. She bounced up and down, clapping her hands, screaming with glee.

"We did it, Elmo, you turd! We did it!"

But pieces of stone and brick started rolling down the mound as she celebrated one of the happiest moments of her life. Two fingers poked out of it. Then a hand.

"What's that?" Elmo asked, pointing.

Amanda stopped celebrating. She peered down the trail at the pile. The hand grew into a forearm. The arm carved out a hole. Spike crawled out looking ghostly, covered in white powder. A girl followed—the redhead. The Japanese boy came next. Amanda's heart sank when he and Joe Trubly pulled Amaya from the rubble.

Amanda had never been more disappointed in her life. Her lower lip began to tremble. She was about to cry. She *never* cried. Then Japanese boy looked up the trail and saw them.

"Time to go," Elmo said. They turned and ran. She heard footfalls gaining behind them. Elmo reached up and touched the brim of his bowler hat.

She couldn't believe how much smoke came out of that thing. Heavy white smoke blew everywhere in great, billowing clouds. And how much noise it made too. Elmo pulled her to the left. They ran for a while. He dropped the hat and pulled her to the right. They topped a hill when they finally came out of the smoke. The footfalls were gone.

ॐ (Gaia)

Gaia felt giddy. "She did it!" She was smiling, her eyes tearing up from the joy brimming over in her heart.

"Yes, she did, my love." Indra loved Amaya too; Gaia had sensed it when they'd mind-birthed her together.

"She knows!" Gaia's breast was bursting with happiness. Amaya finally knew—after eleven years.

"Yes, my love."

"She doesn't yet know how *much* we love her," Gaia pouted. Her pent-up maternal feelings wanted out. She wanted to hold Amaya in her arms, to be a real mother, not some ephemeral wisp of one. She wanted Amaya to see with her own eyes how proud they were of her. How much love they held for her in their hearts.

"Yes, my love. We will find a way, just as we've always found the means to help her."

"You're right, my love." Gaia's voice had grown tender.

She thought about the kiss she'd shared with Indra that night on the terrace before they'd all been trapped. She wished she could kiss him again. She would give him a hundred such kisses if she could, each day for the next hundreds or even hundreds of thousands of days.

She hadn't wanted to fall in love. He'd clung to his bachelor's life. But love had prevailed despite themselves. Thank goodness it had. They wouldn't have their brave Amaya out there saving the day otherwise.

"Indra, my love, I just had a peculiar thought."

"What's that, my love?"

"If I should ever regret falling in love, know this: I'll never, ever regret it being with you."

"I, neither, my love. Never."

CHAPTER 62
SWISS HITS AND MISSES

(YUNOSHO)

THE SMOKE HAD begun to clear by the time Yunosho came back out of it. Spike was there, waiting. "Lost them?"

"Yeah." Yunosho shook his head, disappointed.

"That's okay." Spike clapped his real hand on Yunosho's good shoulder. Spike's cyber-arm looked like it'd been in a fight with a metal shredder. "We need to go. Amaya's in bad shape."

"Your arm's not looking too good either."

"I'll be fine. Your arm's not looking too good either."

Yunosho laughed. Spike had a knack for choosing the right time to be funny. "I'll be fine. Thanks for saving us, Spike."

"That wasn't me. It was my arm. Pretty cool, huh? Think about it. We'd all be dead or dying in that cave if it hadn't been for you." Spike meant well, but a deep pang of guilt hit Yunosho all the same.

They jogged back to the destroyed cave entrance. Yunosho introduced himself to Joe, who helped lift Amaya into the transport. Her breathing seemed normal, but she weighed so little and looked so ashen. Yunosho hurried everyone else into the van as soon as they strapped her in. He turned off the auto-pilot and drove as fast as he could for the hospital. He called Blankenship on the way to make sure Amaya would receive the best care and attention the moment they arrived.

Blankenship didn't disappoint. The hospital skipped its standard intake procedure. A crew of nurses and doctors whisked Amaya into the ICU, where they began running a battery of tests.

"Everything came back negative," the Head of Emergency Medicine told them an hour later. "We found no sign of injury, no infections, and no other markers of illness. She may be suffering from an exhaustion-induced coma or some kind of mental breakdown. What was she doing before this happened?"

"She'd been training intensively," Yunosho half lied. Gigi and Spike nodded their approval.

"That could be causal," the doctor surmised. "She may have pushed herself too hard without paying enough attention to nutrition and hydration, though her condition is too drastic for only that. We've got her on an IV, and we're monitoring her vitals. We'd be happy to keep her here, but I understand she's a ward of the Just-So Orphanage in Redbird?"

"She is," Spike said. "I already contacted the Jove sisters."

"Have them provide instructions to the head administrator if they want to move her. Your friend will need intensive care and observation wherever she goes. In the meantime"—the doctor pointed at Yunosho's arm—"let's take care of those wounds. What happened?"

Yunosho fabricated a whole lie this time. "I fell climbing up a steep hill and got impaled by some branches." He figured they'd send *him* to be shrunken if he dared tell the truth.

He refused to let them sedate him. He wanted to remain

alert, so he and Gigi could situate Amaya as quickly as possible. The medical crew cleaned his wounds and sewed them up.

They rolled Yunosho into the recovery room. Gigi was waiting. "Jeej, did you find the best coma treatment facility in the world?"

Gigi glanced up from her screen. "The consensus seems to be *Das Alpentraum -Therapiezentrum am Obersee im Nicht-So-Hohen Turm mit Rotem Kreuz.*"

"That's a mouthful!" He laughed at the name but also at Gigi's pronunciation. It sounded genuine, though Yunosho didn't know German at all. The nurse locked the bed into place. Yunosho sat up on the edge. His shoulder ached, but the pain was bearable. He'd been through worse in training.

"I can tell you're dying to know," Gigi winked at him. "It means the Alpine Dream Therapy Center on the Upper Lake in the Not-So-Tall Tower with the Red Cross. That name isn't descriptive enough, though. They need to add '*with Beds and Things,*' so we know what's *in* the tower."

Yunosho chuckled. "*Beds and Things* it is, then. I'll settle Amaya there while you take Spike back to OMBE and repair his arm."

"That won't take long. We grew three spare exoskeletons."

"Has Joe gotten the Jove sisters up to speed? Do we have their authorization to take Amaya wherever we want?" Yunosho would disappear again once he got Amaya under proper care. He didn't want his presence upsetting her when she came out of her coma. That should take at least a week, given how terrible she looked. He'd have flown Gigi and Spike over to keep watch by then, though they didn't know that was his plan yet.

"Done and done."

"Where is *Beds and Things*, by the way?" They walked side-by-side out of the recovery room, Yunosho's left arm in a sling.

"Arosa, Switzerland. Apparently, a stunning little alpine village."

शांति (Spike)

Spike wanted to stay with Amaya. "I wish we were going too." He wanted to make sure she'd get better. He didn't know how to do that other than by sitting at her bedside the whole time.

"We're going to get your arm fixed, Mister," Gigi said. "That's where *we're* going." Spike would do what Gigi said because it sure sounded like "no" for an answer was out of the question. Besides, his arm did look pathetic.

The hospital prepped Amaya on the air-travel stretcher. Yunosho arranged for the head nurse to accompany him on the flight to Switzerland. Joe was headed back to the orphanage. They needed his help because Brea was out with exhaustion—the strain caused by Sessy's stabbing had proven too much for her fragile nervous system.

They gathered at the hospital's emergency entrance. The black transport waited there to take Joe to the train station. The door of the transport opened for Joe to board. Yunosho put his hand on Joe's shoulder to stop him.

"Joe." He shook Joe's hand. "Thanks."

"Yeah." Spike offered his left hand to Joe. They shook. "Thanks."

"Really." Gigi gave Joe a hug, standing on her tiptoes because of how tall he was. Her eyes were shiny with tears when she stepped back. "Thanks. You're a true detective, Trubly."

Joe put his hands in his pockets and lifted his shoulders, looking awkward about saying goodbye. "You sure know how to embarrass a guy. I'll miss the sleuthing, though I seem to remember a few mysteries still need solving. Take good care of Amaya."

"Will do, Joe," Yunosho said.

Joe slid into the back of the vehicle. The door shut behind him. The transport started down the road with Joe waving out the rear window. Spike waved back, sad to see him go. Spike didn't like it—the Band of Murugan going their separate ways. He'd gone through his share of mayhem in the past few days. Being together with his new band of friends had made up for a lot of it.

"Let's get to it," Yunosho said.

"Sure thing." Gigi wiped away a tear with the back of her hand.

They exited the back of the ambulance at the airport. Yunosho stood there holding his duffle, saying his goodbyes while the crew and the nurse secured Amaya in the passenger compartment. "Every time I look at her, it kills me. It's hard to imagine she'll recover."

"Amaya's super-strong," Gigi said. "She'll pull through. Don't forget. You both need to heal."

"I *know* she'll be okay," Spike said. "She's in the best hands in the universe. By that, I mean you, not those Swiss guys, though I bet they're pretty good too."

Yunosho gave Gigi a hug and Spike's mangled hand a gentle squeeze. He climbed the airstairs, stepped through the cabin door, and turned around with a big grin on his face, waving at them with his good arm like a maniac. "See you in a couple of days!" he yelled down before disappearing into the plane.

Spike laughed, shaking his head. "See, Gigi? Wishes *do* come true."

"Maybe." She was laughing along with him, her smiling

eyes serving up more delicious goosebumps. "But it sure helps to have a Yunosho."

ॐ (Yunosho)

Day 17

The plane landed at the Zurich private airport under a dark sky. The chopper waited where they disembarked. It touched down forty minutes later at the *Beds and Things* heliport. A line of four crisp white uniforms greeted them. The crew unloaded the stretcher. The nurses ran forward, pressing against the chopper's wind, taking their places at the corners of the stretcher. They rolled Amaya to a tall arch-shaped glass and wood-beam entrance, through imposing wooden doors.

True to its name, *Beds and Things* was a squat, two-floor tower with a red neon cross. Yunosho followed the stretcher to the entryway where a thin, short, petite woman with silver-blonde hair who had *Doktor Segenfrieden* embroidered on her green doctor's jacket met him.

She gave Yunosho a pleasant smile and offered her bony hand with a sharp flick of the wrist. "Doktor Segenfrieden. Pleased to meet you."

"Likewise." Yunosho took her hand. She had a strong grip and radiated competence and efficiency. "Is everything ready?"

"*Ja, ja.*"

"The room has a cot for me as well?"

"*Nein, nein.*" The doctor shook her head disapprovingly, the corners of her mouth dropping into a frown. "Much better zan a kott for Herr Emushi. A *real* bett. Zere's *plenty* of space."

The "room" was indeed more than spacious—a two-bedroom

suite with a state-of-the-art hospital bed that would monitor vital signs, conduct tests, and gently exercise Amaya's body at optimal intervals. The nurses situated her. The doctor gave Yunosho a mini-orientation on the facilities. The exhaustion Yunosho had been holding at bay hit him as soon as everyone finished their jobs and left the room. He hadn't even managed a nap on the flight over, replaying the battle of the Random World in his head, trying to figure out what everything meant, especially those images that appeared when the mysterious door exploded. He understood by now. And the answer was stranger than anything.

He hadn't mentioned the door and what it had revealed to Spike or Gigi. He could scarcely believe it himself. Amaya, a goddess? She was just a girl to him until that moment. Well, okay, an extraordinarily courageous girl who faced an evil menace on her own.

He discarded his sling—he didn't need it any longer—and went to unpack the little he'd brought. He put his duffel on the luggage rack and noticed the bowl of mint chocolates sitting on the dresser. They were dark chocolate. His favorite. He unwrapped one and put it in his mouth.

The chocolate liquified on his tongue. He stood there, letting it, reminiscing about "gottamint" and his mother. About how much he loved her. And how terribly he missed her. About how happy it made him that Amaya had survived. And how miserable that she hated him. His chest heaved a sigh—and he thought about how life, just like the chocolate, could be so heart-achingly bittersweet.

He glanced over at Amaya. She was tiny in that huge hospital bed. The nurses had sponge-bathed her and washed and dried her hair. None of it helped her pallor. She still looked gray. He moved the plush armchair next to her and sat down in it. He leaned forward and took her hand in both of his, gazing into her closed, sunken eyes.

"Amaya, please come back." He squeezed her hand, anguish squeezing his heart. "Even if you never forgive me. Even if you never speak to me again, come back. Please. I'll do anything. I'll disappear off the face of the earth if you want. I'm so sorry, sorry for everything."

Day 18

Yunosho awoke in the chair, not sure what the time was. He could see through the window night had turned to day. But the expression on Amaya's face confused him more than anything. She was sitting on the bed in lotus position… and smiling at him!

He stammered. "Amaya, I…"

"Where are we?" She was *still* smiling. Surely, she could see him sitting there. He was pretty certain she'd heard him speak too. Yet she appeared *glad* to see him. Temporary brain damage. That must be it.

"We're, uh, in Switzerland." She looked completely recuperated, like nothing had ever happened.

"Switzerland. How wonderful! I've never been to Europe. I've never even been out of the country. How long was I out?"

"Going on two days. Listen, Amaya. I didn't mean to be here when you woke up. We didn't think you would for a while. You looked so awful yesterday, but—"

Amaya held her palm out, interrupting him. "Stop, Yunosho. It's fine." Her voice was tender, giving Yunosho hope. "I forgave you the moment you stepped into the Random World."

"You did? Why?" Yunosho couldn't believe his ears. Or his ecstatic heart.

"Maybe because the world was at stake. Maybe because I almost died in there."

"Is that even possible? You saw it, right? The wooden door. The images. The god and goddess."

"Yes. Everything came together, didn't it? Those are my parents, Indra and Gaia. I finally know what happened. They *didn't* abandon me. And I don't think they're dead." Her voice trembled. "Those demons were the very same asuras my father defeated ages ago, only from a different universe. Please don't tell anyone. It has to remain our secret, okay?"

"Whatever you want, Amaya. I was prepared to disappear off the face of the earth if you asked me."

"I heard that. I heard everything you said. I'm glad I heard it."

Yunosho's whole world had turned topsy-turvy. He'd fallen asleep thinking he might never speak to Amaya again. Then he died and awoke in heaven. He was so giddy he wanted to blurt out then and there how he truly felt.

A knock at the door interrupted him.

A deep, muffled female voice came from behind the door, like a dorm matron checking curfew. "What's going on in there?" the voice said. The door opened. Gigi and Spike bustled into the room together, giggling like little children.

"Spike!" Amaya's face lit up. "And Gigi! Thank goodness you're both all right."

"Thank goodness *you're* all right!" They ran over and wrapped their arms around Amaya, all three of them laughing together.

"I only needed a couple of hours to replace Spike's arm," Gigi said.

"We caught the very next flight over," Spike said. "What a surprise! How'd you manage to look so much better so soon?"

"You're the second person to mention how terrible I looked." Amaya gave Yunosho the evil eye, tempered with a wry smile. "Was it that bad?"

"Yes!" they all said in unison.

ॐ (Amaya)

Amaya scooted the boys out the door and told them to go for a walk along the lake. She wanted to talk to Gigi alone.

"You changed," Gigi said. They sat facing one another on the bed. It reminded Amaya of their wonderful girl-to-girl chat, Amaya's first, in Yunosho's room what already seemed like ages ago. "I noticed right away."

"Do I *look* different?"

"No,"—Gigi waved the idea away—"of course not. It's your demeanor. You're way more relaxed… and confident."

Amaya laughed. "Gigi, the scientist, observes everything. I hadn't noticed. It's probably because of how I feel about time now." A wistful breeze blew through Amaya. Her breath caught for a moment. She let out a small, involuntary sigh. It was nice to be all together again without danger breathing down their necks. But she'd lost a lot. They would all need a while to fully recover.

Gigi gazed at her, curious. "What do you mean?"

"I suppose I've been ignoring things or… maybe I'm naïve. That's why I wanted to speak to you alone. I have something important to say. I want to tell you this—you must grab the bullhorns."

"Um… I think you mean take the bull *by* the horns?"

They both giggled at Amaya's mistake. "Of course I meant that," Amaya said once the giggling subsided. "You know who I'm talking about," she said, serious again. "I see how much Spike likes you. He needs a push."

"Are you saying I need to be more forward with Spike?"

"I'm telling you not to waste precious time. For both your sakes. You need to go ahead." Amaya grinned and pounded her fist in her palm. "Just *do* it."

"What about you and Yunosho?"

Amaya sighed. "*That's* a tad more complicated." Gigi had taken Amaya aside earlier and explained how he'd saved her and Spike's lives back at the barn. Amaya had more or less figured that out on her own. She'd reconciled her feelings for Yunosho. The problem was what to do with them.

"Is it?" Gigi asked, concerned.

"More than you could know."

शांति (Spike)

Doctor Segenfrieden certified Amaya recovered enough to go out for the evening. Spike loved the doctor's German accent. Amaya needed to take things easy, but she'd be permitted to attend dinner "on ze lake." The speed of Amaya's recovery had been nothing short of miraculous, even by the Swiss doc's standards.

Yunosho made reservations at a fancy restaurant built out over the lake. Their table had a view of the Alps through a long wall of floor-to-ceiling windows, the majestic peak of the Weisshorn rising magically from the water. Spike had never seen anything so spectacular—except for Gigi. She looked stunning. Yunosho had sent her and Amaya out to buy whatever they wanted. Gigi had chosen a curve-accentuating, just-below-the-knee, white gown with a thin, blue-suede belt, pearl earrings, and a pearl necklace. Fortunately, she refused to wear dress heels—Spike adored those motorcycle boots.

"Let's make a toast." Yunosho grabbed his glass by the stem and raised it.

"Are you sure?" Spike didn't want any Swiss police dressed like the ones in pictures of the Vatican jumping out and arresting him. "I mean, we're not old enough to drink."

"I checked it out before we came." Gigi had an impish grin on her face. "The drinking age is sixteen in Switzerland. No one in Arosa's going to care if you have a glass too."

"In that case"—Spike raised his glass—"here's to Amaya and Gigi. Life *and* world savers!"

Yunosho muttered under his breath. "If you'll just give me a second…" He cleared his throat looking sheepish, then thrust his glass into the air again with a flourish, crying out, "Then by Jove sisters, I'll *second* that!"

"The bad puns keep coming," Amaya deadpanned.

They all laughed, touching glasses, drinking champagne for the first time in their lives, the bubbles tickling Spike's nose. He wanted to talk about a lot of things. How Yunosho suddenly had so much money to throw around. Whether they should worry about more dead people showing up. How, despite the terrible things Mandy had done, he felt even more concern for her. He was glad Amaya reacted with real relief to the news that Mandy wasn't dead. He thought he may have noticed a new, hardened edge to Amaya. It was good to see she hadn't changed too much. He also knew they all wanted to forget the serious stuff and have a good time. He didn't mind. He could save the questions for later. Everyone, himself included, badly needed a break.

The meal was the most sophisticated Spike had ever eaten. He loved the pasta in cream sauce with shaved white mushrooms that tasted like delicious dirt. He got a little tipsy on his second glass of champagne. They regaled one another with their versions of what had happened during the now-and-forever-to-be-famous battle of the Random World. Spike said when the hole appeared in Yunosho's arm, he glanced over at Gigi, and she had "the face of a baby who'd just pooped itself."

Gigi tapped her index finger to her cheek. "At least Spike got the babyface part right."

Gigi reminded them that Joe should be there too. So they gleefully toasted him, not once but three times, with lively "Hip-Hip-Hoorahs."

Gigi opted for the chocolate mousse cookie with salted caramel ice cream when they ordered dessert. She nudged Spike and asked if he wanted to go check out the view from the terrace while they waited for dessert to arrive. There was nothing he wanted more in the world, though his nerves trembled at the prospect of being in such a romantic setting with Gigi alone.

They reached the railing and stood there, their shoulders touching, gazing down at the lake. Star shimmer reflected off its black water.

"Are you hoping something more develops between Yunosho and Amaya as well?" Butterflies flitted in Spike's stomach just from standing close to Gigi.

"I am, but Amaya said some things that make me wonder if that's ever going to happen."

"That's Amaya. It's hard to know what's she's thinking. Look how she forgave Yunosho all of a sudden. Not that I'm complaining."

Gigi sighed. "I'm just glad everything worked out in the end."

Spike felt Gigi's fingers slip into his. His pulse quickened. He panicked. Was Gigi giving him a sign? Should he say something? What if that ruined the moment? He definitely didn't want her to take her hand away.

Her other hand touched his cheek. She pulled his face toward hers. Though he'd thought about it a thousand times, he still couldn't believe it was happening. She kissed him!

Spike's brain went all fuzzy. His toes tingled like mad. It crossed his mind that this must be swooning. He would've bet his life that the illustration in the dictionary of swooning was a picture of Gigi kissing him like this. This Gigi, this geek girl, this wonderful person he'd loved the moment he first laid eyes on her, had stolen his heart all over again.

ॐ (Amaya)

One thing still troubled Amaya. A better time wouldn't come.

"Yunosho"—she lowered her eyes—"I'm sorry I didn't save you."

"You mean when those lovely-looking angelfish things were about to kill me?"

"Yes." She looked up again, hopeful.

"I didn't suppose you'd save me. I didn't even know you could. You had way more important things to deal with. Besides, Warrior Gigi saved me. She was part of you."

"I didn't have any control over Warrior Gigi at the time. I had a choice. I chose." Amaya thought about the things she'd done she could never have imagined needing to do. Almost murder someone. Choose to let a person die. Vanquishing evil seemed to come with a high inner cost.

"You made the right choice. There's nothing more to say."

"There is." Amaya took another sip of champagne. "This is delicious, by the way. I might never have tasted it if it weren't for you."

"Don't change the subject." He gazed at her, expectant.

"I'm sorry. I didn't mean to." She looked away for a moment, embarrassed. She *had* been stalling. Why was opening up so difficult for her? She wanted to let him know. She *had* to. She bit down on her lip, forcing herself to speak. "What I want to say is this—I didn't want to make that choice." Tears gathered behind her eyes. "It was the most difficult choice of my life."

Yunosho took a deep breath. "That's more than I could have hoped to hear." He fell silent, staring at his glass, waiting for her to say more. But the momentousness of telling him in her own peculiar way that she loved him had left her foggy and unable to think.

Uneasy seconds ticked by. Yunosho finally broke the silence.

"Now?" He sounded a little lost.

She didn't have a clue. She thought about it. A smile lit her face as the answer suddenly came to her.

"What is it?" he asked, returning the smile.

"We need to make another toast." She raised her chin and her glass. "To us." She gave her head a little toss, proud of how far they'd all come.

"To us." Yunosho touched his glass to Amaya's. The glasses clinked.

She gazed into his eyes, her heart swelling with happiness. She didn't know where they were headed. It didn't matter in the grand scheme of things. It mattered only that they were on a journey and that they were on it together right now. "Wherever that may lead."

THE END

ॐ शांति ॐ

ACKNOWLEDGEMENTS

Dear Readers: This book wouldn't have been written (and some of you might think it never should have been!) without the assistance and encouragement of a lot of folks. Bill Reeder, retired Dean at George Mason University's College of Visual and Performing Arts, got DJ back into meditation, making Bill directly responsible for the premise of the book: a teen girl with the superpower of enhanced enlightenment. When DJ and LA decided they wouldn't continue writing if the first fifty pages showed no promise, Paul Mahon read the pages and bade the two novice authors continue, even making available the services of his sister, Martha Bullen, book whisperer extraordinaire, who ended up shepherding the story to the finish line with Paul's never-wavering support.

Heartfelt thanks are due to Cori McCarthy, who had the unpleasant task of editing the completed first draft, a bloated mess she helped turn into less of one, and Peter Ford, author, news correspondent, and inventor of the NeuroNode® (a technological boon to people suffering from ALS), for pushing us forward every step of the way.

We'd like to thank our beta readers: Rick Davis from GMU, Rachel Cieplak, Erika Wright, Yu Oniki (whose mom, Kumi, helped develop Yunosho's made-up Japanese name and whose family name became the name of Yunosho's sensei), Kinga

Kiraly, Jean Steiner, Karl Herold, and Nicole Njmatwijiw. We'd also like to thank Charles Dickens, whose works inspired the development of the main characters, and LA's late grandparents, a factory worker/opera singer and a nurse/artist who encouraged all of their kids and grandkids to create.

And finally, we'd like to gratefully acknowledge LA's mother, Gabriella Kardos, who patiently read endless drafts and sat through endless plot and character development sessions, and who contributed not only pieces of the story, but a giant dollop of her ever-magnanimous love.

To all of you, thanks!